CORALENA

Michael Mail was born in Glasgow in 1959. He studied law at Strathclyde University, followed by further academic study in Jerusalem and Boston before settling in London. In 1999 he won the Macallan *Scotland on Sunday* short story competition, Britain's premier award for short story writing. *Coralena* is his first novel.

CORALENA

Michael Mail

Scribner

First published in Great Britain by Scribner, 2002
This edition published by Scribner, 2003
An imprint of Simon & Schuster UK Ltd
A Viacom Company

1 3 5 7 9 10 8 6 4 2

Simon & Schuster UK Ltd
Africa House
64–78 Kingsway
London WC2B 6AH

Simon & Schuster Australia
Sydney

A CIP catalogue record for this book is available
from the British Library

ISBN 0–7432–2062–5

Typeset in Fournier by M Rules
Printed and bound in Great Britain by
Cox & Wyman Ltd, Reading, Berkshire

To
Zelda & Ronnie

Acknowledgements

Much thanks to Elise Bittenbinder, Sallyann Brown, Paul Chambers, Michael Lawton, Elisabeth Pivcevic, Katy Rae, Udo Rauchmaul and Lloyd Salmon.

Special thanks to Giles Gordon and Tim Binding for their belief and support.

PART 1

SUMMER 1971

1

The day began in brightness confounding the fierce rainstorm in the night, its legacy quickly evaporating in the early sunshine. Night workers heading homeward shared the quiet of the city with early risers and runners splashing eccentric colours across suburban streets.

In the stillness of the early morning, Kussel could almost be imagined as the village it once was, situated at one of the earliest crossing points of the mighty River Rhine, gateway to the Germanic lands. It was the river that had given Kussel its life, ensuring its transformation into a great city of Germany – built, destroyed and rebuilt throughout its menaced history.

The river itself was already bustling with traffic – great pencil barges heading downstream as far as Rotterdam, upstream to Koblenz, Mainz, all the way to Basel; the first passenger ferries berthing from Düsseldorf and Bonn; the graceful cranes of the Sterzenbach Container Depot bobbing their heads, stocking the city for a new day.

The explosion happened around 6.45 a.m. inside the Central Courthouse on Blumenstrasse. The newspapers would later describe it as a powerful incendiary device, confirmed by the scale of damage caused. The devastation made its own spontaneous broadcast to the city through a twisting stream of angry black smoke that spewed skyward. No one was in the Courthouse at the time. Several passers-by suffered injury, one was in a critical condition. A battalion of police and local militia promptly descended, sealing off the area except for emergency service vehicles screeching to and fro. Firemen engaged with the blaze across the day.

Sophia heard about the bomb when her mother burst into her bedroom just as she was wrestling on shoes. She seemed almost hysterical but all Sophia could think about was disruption to the trams and the implications for her journey to work.

Her mother was of course shocked that she was still planning to see through her daily commute. 'Shocking mother' had long been their own special game, largely devoid of substance, certainly as far as Sophia was concerned. And time was finally, finally running out for the two of them. Her mother now knew that.

'Shouldn't you wait and telephone first?' 'The store surely wouldn't open today.' 'The city's not safe!'

Sophia wasn't going to allow herself to become bothered. The previous night she'd announced to her parents her intention to move out. Her mother had greeted the news with a predictable hostility, her father made unconvincing conscript to the apparent bafflement.

'I'm only thinking about you!' She repeated her sentiment from the night before.

It was such an unlikely statement, Sophia couldn't think her mother honestly believed that.

Sophia had made this promise to herself so long ago she couldn't remember when. Her plan was finally declared, and she was feeling that she *would* see this through. That was why she was so pleased with herself. It would be a good day, whatever. She finished brushing her hair and left.

2

Sophia took her boss's understanding as a positive sign. Having got out of work early, she now faced the novel task of finding tram number 23 which the old lady on the telephone had told her she must catch from Königstrasse. She would get off at Domplatz from where she had a walk of a few streets. The woman had also told her not to be late. It was said in a manner that surprised Sophia, so definitive as to be familiar, as if she had been late before.

The Altstadt district of Kussel had held a special allure for Sophia ever since she first visited it as a child. She loved the old world atmosphere of the neighbourhood which was one of the few largely to survive the war bombing. Her father would regularly take her and her brother to the opening of Carnival held in Marienplatz, the largest square in the Altstadt. She would marvel at the outrageous mock uniforms, colourful brass bands, teetering street performers and the beery cheer of the people. It felt as if the Altstadt contained a reimagined Kussel where, under the guise of history and tradition, the rules that restrained the rest of the city could be gaily broken.

When Sophia started skimming the papers for rooms, she resolved to focus exclusively on the Altstadt. It required more resolution than she had originally supposed as she came to realize how few there actually were. One property agent enthusiastically explained that she was looking in the wrong area. The Alstadt contained long-term residents – settled families, the elderly. She should consider areas like the Hofgarten, renowned and notorious for its student colony. Sophia was not keen on reacquiring a status of which she had so recently, and gratifyingly, divested herself. As the quest grew to a challenge, it drew out of Sophia an uncharacteristic determination that surprised even her. Sophia's loyalty remained steadfast and she scoured the papers, bombarded local agents, chased up every lead with any hint of potential. Having finally, reluctantly broadened her sphere of operations, she was thrilled to come across this latest advertisement with its position at the Altstadt's heart. It was more than she had wanted to pay but not by too much. And Sophia was being offered more than a room. It was described as a small studio apartment. She was excited, intrigued.

Sophia deliberately positioned her wait at the tram stop by an advertising hoarding that demanded 'Make It Today!' Two number 23 trams arrived at the same time, which Sophia took as another good omen. She decided to hang back and take the second, enabling her to choose her seat close to the driver with its panoramic view of the city streets. She immediately lit up a Claremont cigarette, her favourite ever since she read it was Warren Beatty's, and, in regal pose, began her progress down Königstrasse.

Shoppers were clearly out in force, encouraged by the late afternoon sunshine and the promise of summer sales, busying in and out of boutiques with fashions that Sophia longed to afford. She quietly cursed the crowds outside Store Lorenz on Friedrichstrasse, her own company's main rival, staring hard at the opulent window displays in search of clues that would confirm their obvious inferiority.

The tram soon passed into Neumarkt with its parade of shiny geometric glass and concrete office buildings – banks, insurance, corporations – competing for dominance yet forming a collective, all products of the 1950s economic boom that had resurrected the city. Sophia regularly saw fancied images of New York in their emphatic modernity, the brashness.

The increased profile on the streets of the *Polizei* green was much in evidence, explained by the stop on Blumenstrasse. The tram transformed to a gallery with all eyes on the Central Courthouse on the junction's other side. There was a cordon around the site. The building itself was draped in loose plastic sheeting behind which the blackened ruin was clearly visible. Sophia heard a voice behind exclaim that it looked like a scene from the war.

Nearby, a small group had formed in some kind of protest, handing out leaflets that Sophia assumed were connected with the trial. Judge Eggert had acquitted the war criminal Krombach of the murder of 90,000 Jews in a Russian forest. The wrecked building was the Red Revolutionary Front's response to 'bourgeois justice', delivered in characteristic and infamous fashion.

The passage across the city went swiftly, eased by lighter

summer traffic. The grand steeples of the Cathedral were now assertively visible, fixing, like pins on a great map, the Altstadt's location. Not having previously approached the district via this particular route, Sophia was eagerly anticipating the border crossing – the point at which the city centre met the first buildings of the Altstadt. In the end, it involved simply trundling across a nondescript back street yet its effect was no less dramatic. There was an immediate sense of having passed to another place markedly out of sync with what had gone before. Sophia was fascinated by the garish pinks and yellows of the narrow triangle-topped tenements that escorted the tram on either side down Ulrichgasse. The heavy wooden shop façades, the angular cobbled roadways, even the distinctive squat onion-headed street lights – everything seemed on a different scale from the rest of the city that had so profoundly left this world, its past, behind.

As the tram ventured through the neighbourhood, Sophia tried to eliminate from her mind the blight of patrolling tourists by imagining the area as its striking physicality evoked. She now saw the streets in sepia browns, horse-drawn carriages clopping along, elegant store fronts, men swinging canes in top hats and morning coats, women in summer gowns and feather-filled hats, clothing she had once studied as an art college project, the one winning her most acclaim. She even put herself in the scene, parading down the street in a flowing frilly dress, accepting the flirtatious bows of gentlemen, breathing in the air and feeling alive.

She knew she was nearing her destination from the looming

pre-eminence of the Cathedral, its soaring blackened red towers now dominating the view, symbol of the city's continuity and most Catholic pride. She was approaching the Cathedral from the very angle known to every citizen of Kussel. The one immortalized in the famous war photograph, standing solid and immutable amidst a world in flame.

Her stop left a final journey of a few streets. Following the instructions, she was glad to step into side turnings that took her away from the crowds besieging the Cathedral, into the tight alleyways that characterized her romance with the Altstadt. Soon she was in the Rheingasse, soon she had found the Coralena.

3

The building was situated at 33 Rheingasse although no such indication was actually proffered. Instead, its name 'Coralena' was carved on the two tree-trunk pillars flanking the elaborately panelled doorway. To announce such a building through mere numbering would clearly have been an act of gross discourtesy. Sophia stood back to pursue her admiring scrutiny.

The Coralena was one of the smaller of the terraced buildings in the Rheingasse although what it lost in bulk it made up for in appearance, displaying an impressive neo-classical façade of rich grey sandstone made courageous by the many pockmarks and gouges. The windows, which ran in twin sets down the building, were ornately framed and deep-set like sockets. Under one window, there was a stream of discoloration to the ground as if tears had once poured from a wounded eye. The imposing pillars by the entrance were half sunk into the wall and above the doorway Sophia made out the decorous shape of a face, young and girlish, framed in curls.

As Sophia absorbed the building's look, she felt a strange stunning elation well up inside her. It was perfect, too perfect.

The doorbells were distinguished by number only, which presented Sophia with a conundrum. She only had a name. She resolved to press the bottom bell, but then changed her mind and pressed the top one. As she waited, she reciprocated the stare from the nymph above. Her gaze conveyed an intimation of empathy. Sophia was sure this first introduction was going well. She pressed the bell again, this time with greater firmness. The door swung open and an elderly man's face poked out of shadow.

'I'm not on a magic carpet! Who are you? What do you want?'

Sophia was taken aback by the open anger in the voice.

'The flat. I've come to look at the flat. Number 10?' She spluttered her response tinged with momentary regret.

'And – who – did – you – speak – to?' The man paused between each word as if delivering to an imbecile.

Sophia straightened out the well-scrunched advertisement in her hand, her face filling in red.

'Frau Eckermann?'

The man abruptly closed the door leaving Sophia bewildered. Within the briefest of seconds the door reopened to reveal an elderly woman. The speed of the transformation made Sophia wonder if this was a second manifestation of the very same person. Her face beamed graciousness in complete contrast to the exchange immediately before.

'Do come in, my dear.'

The woman pirouetted, heading into darkness with Sophia following far more cautiously than entreatied.

'Herr Bruder mustn't be disturbed in the afternoons. It's really Frau Bruder.'

Sophia now stood in the cool of a musty hallway intrigued to be on the Coralena's inside. She had speculated whether it could live up to the bold exterior and she wasn't disappointed. Yes, there was a tired unkempt feel, but there was also something of an indefinable grandeur, the echo of a memorable past that encapsulated her instinct towards the Altstadt as a whole. In front of her sprawled a large mahogany staircase sweeping and twisting upwards, stagelit by refracted light descending from an unseen source above. Etched doors of the same reddish-brown wood hid to the side. The walls were covered in a rich burgundy colour patterned by twirls of gold. Wall lights rested behind frosted glass. A crucifix clung by the entrance next to assorted picture frames. And the muffled wheezing sound of accordion music could be heard adding a surreal finish to the scene.

'I'm Frau Eckermann. Your landlady.'

She firmly grasped Sophia's hand, as if a politician canvassing for votes.

'Remind me who you are?'

'Sophia.'

'Sophia?'

'Sophia Krauss,' Sophia replied more formally.

'Fräulein Krauss. Yes, that's right. I remember now from the phone call. Sophia's a lovely name. Italian. Are you Italian?'

'No.' Sophia gave a wearied response. Her sheer blonde hair hadn't saved her from Sophia Loren forever dogging her life. 'It was my grandmother's name.'

'A pretty name.'

Sophia realized that she was now being carefully examined, with the Frau literally looking her up and down. The Frau maintained her grip on Sophia's hand, which she endured with a growing awkwardness feeling it as more like a clamp fixing her for inspection. Sophia was at least pleased to have come straight from work ensuring her conventional dress of pleated skirt and blouse.

'You're so thin!'

Sophia instinctively placed her free hand across her waist, now confirmed in her discomfort. She wanted to wrest her hand away and, fortunately, that was what the Frau now did.

'And so young!' A smile warmed the Frau's face. 'Younger than you sounded on the phone. I hope Herr Bruder didn't scare you. He scares lots of people. This is a house full of characters!'

Sophia was beginning to sense this truth.

'That's the secret of how we all get on so well!'

Sophia calculated the Frau herself was probably in her mid to late sixties. She wore a conventional, well-worn but neat grey suit toning with her silvery white hair, which was pulled back emphasizing a plumpness of face that enabled her to carry easily an all-round bigness in features – eyes, nose, mouth. Dangling from her neck, resting on her chest, lay a cross with a yellow heart at its centre, emblem of the Sisterhood of the Immaculate Virgin dedicated to good works throughout the city. Sophia recognized it immediately because of her mother's affiliation.

Sophia was ushered to the stairs and they started to ascend. She rested her hand on the wooden banister feeling its sensual smoothness, gliding her hand along as she moved. High above, she could now identify the source of the light, flickering through mottled rectangular glass that made up the Coralena's ceiling.

'You'll have no problem with these stairs at your age.'

Frau Eckermann stopped to catch her breath on the first-floor landing set between two mahogany doorways whose silver numbers, 6 and 8, were the only discernible indications of distinctiveness. Sophia also examined the wall prints of romantic river scenes. The mysterious accordion music appeared to be gathering momentum, provoking Frau Eckermann into explanation.

'We made an arrangement. I made a concession. Herr Eckermann could play whenever I'm out. So now, the moment I leave the apartment, he begins!' She pulled an exasperated expression that also signalled her return to the climb.

'Wasn't it terrible, that bomb. You'd think after all we've gone through. To have it start again, I don't understand. I really don't. Do you?' Frau Eckermann stopped and turned to Sophia who, taking up her cue, shook her head uncertainly.

The Frau continued. 'Terrible. Just terrible. I just hope they catch the animals. And very soon.'

On arriving at the second-floor landing, Frau Eckermann paused again. From this new vantage point, Sophia followed the curling flow of the stairway downwards, admiring the exactness of its symmetry. She then looked at the two doorways, rapidly identifying the silvery indicator that marked their destination – number 10.

'It's good that you're young. We need a young thing to brighten the place.'

Frau Eckermann's preoccupation seemed to be about rules. Sophia vaguely heard them. No men in the flat after midnight, no unauthorized redecoration, monthly payments in advance, a deposit on account to cover damages, things about rubbish collection, noise and post. Sophia herself focused on just one sensation, both powerful and, in so being, somehow unsettling. The recognition that she had found her home.

To clear a sweet staleness in the air, Frau Eckermann had quickly opened the two windows in the main room. They were sufficiently close together to create a panorama effect and the view was simply astounding. Sophia looked down on the ancient streets of the Altstadt running to the Cathedral almost directly opposite, and then beyond, onwards to the River Rhine, stretching out before her as if she was its patron – ships at play in the water, the cranes of the Sterzenbach container port at stiff attention, the distant Prinz Georg bridge striking out across the waterway. Surely this had been her fantasy.

Frau Eckermann ticked off questions on Sophia's background – where she worked, lived, her family, her Catholicism. The Frau seemed pleased with her responses and escalated her marketing, talking up the flat's compactness, making intermittent promises about her son helping to fix this and that. The place would certainly require concerted fixing, including the sofa which failed to mutate to a bed despite repeated attempts, causing the Frau some embarrassment.

'She was the first to go, poor Frau Jodl.' Frau Eckermann joined Sophia at the window at the visit's end. 'Last in, first out. We called her the immigrant. She came from the East just after the war, from Danzig. She was lucky to get out with her life. The Russians!' The Frau guffawed, evidently expecting Sophia to appreciate the sentiment. She abruptly stopped. 'You're so lucky. Young people today shouldn't know about such things.'

Frau Eckermann was granted her prompt answer.

4

There are department stores that have such standing in the life of a city that they help define its very character. Bonhoffs had achieved such a status in Kussel right from its creation at the turn of the century. The store saw itself as the flagbearer of style and taste for the Kussel elite, thereby subtly creating its real market out of a mass of aspirants.

Bonhoffs had seen off its rivals by developing an acute sense of timeliness behind the cultivated guise of timelessness, and Sophia knew that she owed her job to that crucial event that had changed the history of mankind – the 1960s and the birth of youth. Bonhoffs had the wisdom to recognize the wider impact of the 60s and who better to help shape that timely response than the young themselves.

Sophia had gone straight to Bonhoffs from art college. Having worked there only nine months, she still relished that special awe every time she ambled along the ornate storefront, which took up a whole block, and walked through the palatial entrance flanked by 'Fidelity' and 'Integrity', the two bronze statues of Bonhoffs' very own Goddesses of Plenty. She would nod to the doormen, Hans Heinrich and Alphonse, bedecked in their distinctive Ruritanian red/gold uniforms straight out of Carnival, travel through the vast halls dedicated to every conceivable incarnation of merchandizing, past the rich aromas of Perfumes, the colorama of Cosmetics, being surveyed by a battalion of staff with too many names and too similar uniforms, all preposterously poised for nine o' clock in the morning. The sheer theatricality of the place made her feel that she had bluffed her way into some exotic farce.

Sophia had joined Bonhoffs as part of a uniquely large cohort of young trainees. Window dressing was not a job in her vocabulary before art college, but neither was the word *job* itself much in play. It was her college tutor who had planted the idea. He admired her work with fashion and textiles, and Sophia got that other message regarding his assessment of her core artistic ability. Still, he had made the connection with Bonhoffs on her behalf, with an embarrassingly enthusiastic reference he had insisted Sophia write.

The window design team was Sophia's principal world at Bonhoffs. Because their work was so specialized, they tended to be somewhat isolated from the rest of the store. Between them they had to conceive and prepare the ever changing window displays that presented the very best of Bonhoffs to the fine citizenry of Kussel. Their leader was Frau Margaret Fisher, a middle-aged American who had married a local Kussel man – twice. She was a glamorous daunting whirlwind of a woman who heretically demanded to be called by her first name. Her approach to work was equally unconventional. She effused about the need to be bold, and the adventure of risk. Every window display must reflect a 'living expression of creativity, drawing in and elevating the *very soul* of the viewer'. Sophia simply couldn't fathom her philosophizing and, as she reassuringly discovered, neither did any of her staff. She was usually spoken of as the Happy Hippy, although there were others who were far more brutal in their descriptive language. Yet, Sophia admired her flair for materials and acute sense of colour and composition which confirmed in its practice the merits of her enigmatic ways.

Margaret was her boss and her teacher, setting her work schedule and supervising her progress. But it was clear she would be nothing more. Her informality did not extend to breaching the strong traditions of hierarchy that pervaded the building. Sophia dearly wanted to know much more about Margaret's background, what she thought of Germany, whether she had met any film stars, why she didn't have children. But Margaret made it clear from the start that working together wouldn't lead to socializing together. She aligned herself with that august mysterious body referred to as 'the management', a standing evidently not to be compromised by mixing with lesser ranks.

The store's caste system led to a degree of solidarity amongst the new trainees assigned throughout the store yet still writhing in their collective initiate status. In time, as competencies and confidences grew, the ebb of integration pulled in the newcomers and fresh alliances were forged in the feverish heat of commercial enterprise. Sophia was fascinated by the distinctive personalities of each department. The men in Furnishings tended to be outgoing and aggressive, patrolling their department like detectives. The Food Hall was riven with personality conflicts that kept it a sombre, tense arena. Ladieswear was filled by women apparently dedicated to out-achieving their customers in snobbishness. And so it went on.

Sophia met Pauline Frisch, her closest work colleague and soon best friend, on her very first day at Bonhoffs, when all trainees were being given the mandatory orientation tour by Herr Stammer, the Personnel Director. In the middle of a hectoring on standards of staff behaviour, Pauline made her mark by asking where the foilets were. They ended up giggling in adjoining cubicles and soon began using each other as special confidante as they spied out the new land.

Sophia came to appreciate many things about Pauline. She liked her directness and her humour, the way she could laugh at herself and have everyone join in. She particularly respected the way she deployed the word 'fuck', with such assurance, the precise intonation to make an impact without its sounding ugly. It was something Sophia had never mastered, which was why she could only ever say it to herself, and usually long after it had lost its poignancy. Sophia also admired Pauline's appearance. Her dark swirling hair and olive skin which she proudly attributed to ancient Roman ancestry, certainly not to be confused with mere Italian. Sophia hated her own pale features, her gawky height and straight straight blonde hair that made her seem as if she was permanently exiting from a rain shower. Pauline had a natural womanly way about her that Sophia couldn't imagine herself ever achieving. But most of all, Sophia liked the ease of their friendship. The way Pauline had sought her out in such an unselfconscious manner, and had persisted through the silences.

Pauline worked in Cosmetics which meant her face required *brightening*, a task carried out with gusto by colleagues who evidently enjoyed saving her soul each morning. Sophia thought she looked amazing though Pauline compared her appearance to a prostitute's. She was envious of Sophia's more casual attire in keeping with her backroom role. However, as the months went by, Pauline did confess to enjoying her daily 'renovation', as she referred to it. Sophia soon also realized the status that the ground-floor glamour women had amongst their salivating male colleagues.

Pauline's contemplations on the subject of men dramatically intensified when she announced that she was single again having dismissed her latest boyfriend. She had even invented a code that she was willing to co-sponsor with Sophia whereby male grading would be achieved via a carefully calibrated 'scale of lust'. They were both on a *manhunt*, as Pauline was reminding Sophia with increasing frequency, linked to what was becoming a missionary zeal to have her address an evidently perilous lack of application, plainly as well as cosmetically speaking. And Pauline had already fled her parental home and so should Sophia, instead of whingeing on.

Pauline was in the staff canteen guarding their usual spot in the reserve for rebels and chain smokers, waiting for Sophia to arrive with hot property news. Sophia gathered herself for a triumphal entrance, and strode in beaming.

5

Sophia couldn't say that this was a tense moment. For if she did it would imply that there were moments without tension. It was more a question of degree. She was sitting in the living room with her mother and father about to embark on a family discussion. It was as ominous as it sounded. Sophia's routine response to looming conflict, particularly of the family kind, was conscientious objection, which meant her mother would now *arrange* such encounters. They had become events.

Her mother, as convenor, took the chair. This was both organizational and literal for she commandeered her favoured highest chair in the room. She reminded Sophia of that fish she had once seen on a television nature programme, the one that could puff itself up to stop being swallowed by predators.

Sophia sat on the big settee settling herself directly under the large Madonna and Child wall figurine with its portrayal of doting motherhood, her location of preference, her little joke. At another time, her father might have sat next to her. For this conversation he chose the neutrality of the rocking chair neatly equidistant from the two women in his life. He looked as he always appeared at such moments, stiff, emphasized by the fact that he was still in his manager's suit, jacket and tie tightly in place. He had recently undergone a cruelly indiscreet haircut, fully exposing a hairline in terminal retreat, a tragedy aggravated by a slight but noticeable imbalance, the left looping into his scalp outperforming the right.

Once, such occasions would have been conducted by her mother alone. She would enter Sophia's bedroom on a casual pretext, folded ironing in her hands, soon to reveal her true mission – to cajole, calm down, admonish. Her mother would have described such intrusions as indicative of compassion and involvement – nothing left painfully unsaid, everything sorted out. She always had her resolutions, if only Sophia would listen to reason, play her part.

'You've agreed to take the flat. We haven't seen it and already you've decided.' Her mother neatly proposed the problem.

Sophia paused. She really didn't want this. If an apology would suffice she would gladly offer it up. Sophia never had any difficulties with saying she was sorry, especially when she was in the right. But it was the ceremony that mattered. So she replied, and so it began. 'You wouldn't have liked it. You would have told me everything you hated about it!'

To have stated such grand intentions was one thing, but to have actually seen them through had taken her parents completely by surprise. Sophia had surprised herself.

'It's in a terrible neighbourhood,' her mother continued.

'That's what I mean! You didn't need to see it.' Sophia shook her head.

'Before the war it was different. But now? Who lives in the Altstadt now? I don't know why you want to live there. It's crumbling away!'

Her mother fell silent which Sophia knew was for pure effect. She was the master of the lingering pause, letting her comments sink in, adding gravitas, making her opposition stew in reflection. She just prayed her father wouldn't feel obliged to speak. She wished he wasn't there. Sophia distracted herself by looking at the Sisterhood of the Immaculate Virgin charity box on the sideboard with its reward of little yellow crucifix pins sitting beside. She tried to assess if there had been any depletion in stock indicative of brisk trade.

'It's on the other side of town. You couldn't have chosen somewhere further away from us.'

Sophia felt the ache in her mother's voice without flinching. She had dedicated too many years of her life to that agonizing vigil of pleasing parents. Then she discovered the delicious freedom of not caring. She wasn't abandoning them. She was saving herself.

Sophia took out a cigarette now grudgingly permissible throughout the house.

'How can you afford it? You've got to eat as well!'

It was the mention of food that got her mother turning finally to her father. Sophia bristled. It was so unfair. She knew where ceremony would now lead.

6

The bright morning sun gave the grey-white sandstone of the Coralena a distinctive sheen confirming its status as truly the anointed of the buildings on the Rheingasse. Sophia couldn't understand the casual way pedestrians passed it by. She wanted to stop them, as if they had been guilty of disrespect. She wanted to announce to them that today was the very day she was moving in. Then she longed to adopt their nonchalance that would signify she was already integral to the district routine.

This incredible fact of a new home, her very own, filled her with an overwhelming sense of achievement. She had pulled it off, confounding that great Doubter lurking inside her brain. It felt like a coming of age, another Confirmation, or like losing your virginity. There was only one first time. That was why she had insisted her parents drop her on the corner of Rheingasse. The parting had been swift. She couldn't bear her mother's restrained fearful expression that Sophia knew was more for herself. They would all learn to change. It was a moment to savour, standing opposite, surveying her new surroundings, baggage of essentials by her side, door key readied. On her own.

Actually opening the front door proved a trial. Frau

Eckermann had advised about pushing the key high into the lock, which she did several times under the increasingly sceptical gaze of the painted face above, before the door finally conceded. She gave a victorious nod to the watching maiden and dragged her cases into the hallway darkness, reacquainting herself with the scene. Ahead of her stood the magnificent coiled staircase. Behind, she now saw that the cluster of wall pictures next to the crucifix were thematic props of Cathedral iconography. Sophia recalled the Frau's invitation to join the Coralena's group excursion to Sunday Mass. 'Mostly the ladies,' she'd added seductively. It made her reflect again on the nature of the Altstadt's attraction. Pauline thought she was crazy – 'Geriatrics and tourists,' she had sneered. She wanted Sophia closer to her own flat shared with three girls, all sisters, in Ehrenfeld.

What precisely drew Sophia to the area, she didn't fully comprehend. Yes, there was the sense of history, a past, feeling connected to something far greater than one's own small life. But she knew there was more. An inexplicable urge to become intimate with this world, so different from her own in the new suburbs of the city's south.

The small nameplate on the left-hand door made its simple declaration: 'Family Eckermann'. The right one was even less forthcoming providing the coyness of a one-syllable surname – 'Schloss'. The first floor contained 'Herr and Frau Kuhn' on the left and, refreshingly, two first names opposite: 'Anna and Eva'. Sophia supposed for a brief moment that this reflected more youthful residents but then remembered Frau Eckermann's remark about the two widows.

On reaching the second, her own floor, she completed the ritual by checking the door across from hers. The name Bruder was written carefully in old German lettering and Sophia amusingly recalled that she had already made Herr Bruder's acquaintance.

The door to Sophia's flat opened easily, for which silent gratitude was expressed, and she poised herself in preparation for this momentous entrance. As she turned to pick up her bags, she heard an odd hissing sound, then again. Across the hallway, she identified spindly fingers protruding from the side of the opening door. Soon, she caught sight of the half-moon of an elderly woman's face.

'Pssst!' Frau Bruder repeated.

Sophia took up the summons and crossed the landing.

'It's so good to see a new face.' Frau Bruder spoke softly but audibly.

Sophia considered that her neighbour's face looked far from new. It was thin and drawn, almost ghostlike in its translucency. She was wearing an all white dressing gown, which she was clutching at the top. For some reason, images of the reclusive Marlene Dietrich came to Sophia's mind.

'You *are* young. Just a girl, I'm sure. I'm Frau Bruder. And you are Fräulein Krauss, from Bonhoffs. We've all heard so much about you.'

Had she conveyed *so much* to Frau Eckermann? Sophia considered.

'Frau Eckermann will give you good advice. She's an exceptional woman.'

Sophia was impressed that Frau Bruder had plucked the very name in her thoughts.

'And Dieter will help, her son. He helps all of us. We all help each other.' Frau Bruder paused. 'I'm sorry I can't invite you in. Today has not been . . . a good day for me.'

Sophia nodded. She was happy to be spared further detail.

'She got very old, Frau Jodl. I wonder who'll be next?'

Sophia could perfectly understand her personal investment in the wonder. Frau Bruder then stared hard at Sophia. It was as if she was properly acknowledging her for the first time. Her face seemed visibly to lighten.

'Look after yourself!'

Frau Bruder eased herself behind the door. By the time she was gone, Sophia realized that she should have delivered the Frau's concluding remark, and then she realized that she hadn't spoken one word throughout the exchange.

7

Housecleaning had been one of Sophia's least favourite chores and the state of the flat was such as to make even the most committed cleaner cower. But it was now her place.

Her very first action was to fling open the windows to escape a thick and disconcertingly sweet odour. She breathed in the air of the Altstadt along with the burgeoning crowds of Sunday visitors assembling below, swelling around the Cathedral, parading down the riverside boulevard. She reassured herself that there would be time for all this. Her aim was to achieve a basic inhabitability by the end of this first day for the simple reason that she was only going to leave home once.

Her next act was to extract from her baggage her most cherished 'Snowdrops' painting. She took off the only existing wall adornment, a beleaguered wooden crucifix, and replaced it with the picture, announcing solemnly to the apartment and the world 'May God bless Sophia in her new home!'

She changed into firmly discredited clothing, a pair of decaying jeans granted late reprieve, and a bruised old red shirt. Then, then she made her very first telephone call, and second and third to an unremittingly absent Pauline, before switching on the radio she had secreted from her parents' bedroom, and finally setting to work.

Soothed by the Moody Blues, Sophia made the bathroom her first assignment. At first she started timidly, dabbing around the sink, rinsing down the bath, careful not to get herself too grungy in the uncomfortable process of degrunging. Such caution vanished as she progressed and the enormity of the challenge sunk in. Soon she was gaily storming the bastions of grease and grime that had been allowed to fortify no doubt as the previous resident's health had deteriorated. She tried not to think of her predecessor, the poor Frau Jodl. What she most didn't want to contemplate was whether she'd actually passed away in the flat. She found the notion distinctly unnerving. Would she be sleeping in the very bed?

The kitchen such as it was, more an alcove set off the hallway, was in the worst state. The oven had evidently managed to elude any form of exposure to the purities of cleaning fluid and Sophia grimaced when she discovered a pile of rotting food beneath the fridge, along with a pungent sickly aroma that sent her reeling to the windows for recuperation. The cold tap seemed happy to oblige, flowing vigorously, but the hot water proved coy, dribbling intermittently even with the combination of the tap at full throttle and Sophia's heartfelt pleadings. As the rubbish bags filled, she was beginning to take the long view.

Sophia did enjoy the discovery that the wardrobe contained a full-length mirror. As she stared at her unkempt self, pondering how she might preserve such a moment for posterity, the internal doorbell rang. Sophia had assumed Frau Eckermann would pay her a visit at some point in the day. She had been so persistent in wanting to know the precise timing of Sophia's move. Hence her surprise with the stranger at the door.

'Hi, I'm Dieter. Dieter Eckermann. From downstairs. Well, I used to be from downstairs before I escaped, sort of escaped.'

Sophia was still confused. From somewhere below she heard the pumping sound of accordion music.

'My services are freely offered by Frau Eckermann, my mother, your landlady, which makes me her assistant, as well as her son.'

Sophia hesitated, unsure how to respond, then she came to the realization that he was expecting her to invite him in. Sophia hadn't anticipated meeting any young faces in the Coralena. She peered down at herself. The fact that she looked untidy was understandable. But there was something more significant in her self-consciousness, which wasn't merely about being caught in such a state, but was also about who was doing the catching. What she was registering was a jolting attraction for the man now before her, entering her flat. It was the type of instinctive reaction one might have in any situation, like an intuition, but because it was in such unexpected circumstances she was concerned she had been too unguarded.

'Your mother mentioned you.' Sophia was keen to get the measure of this first caller, Frau Eckermann's son. He headed straight for the window view. His long curly black hair rested on a denim waistcoat over a baggy bright blue T-shirt tucked into ridiculously tight, ridiculously flared hipster jeans with flower patches stuck like fried eggs on each back pocket. He was tall, tall enough.

'You've got one of the best views in the city, d'you know that?' Dieter turned and Sophia re-experienced that first response – tumbling jet-black hair, a long boyish face with sharp clean features, a sort of Jesus look, and, yes, she could identify them clearly now, eager blue eyes. For the briefest of seconds, Sophia felt him reciprocate her scrutinizing stare. He also registered something.

'Frau Jodl became blind. Ironically,' he continued.

Sophia was dreading what he might reveal of her end.

'She told me she could still look out the window and see everything.' Dieter moved across to examine Sophia's 'Snowdrops' painting on the opposite wall.

'She was a hoarder. That's why the place became . . . like it was. Kept hold of everything. Manic about it. You couldn't imagine the junk we threw out of here.' Sophia held her breath until the topic shifted to her painting.

'Did you do this?'

'Yes!' Sophia didn't like the tone of suspicion in his voice, but that quickly dissipated with his following comment.

'You're a real artist.' She could indeed warm to this man.

Dieter seemed perfectly willing to oblige with Sophia's various requests. For certain tasks, Dieter's role was simply crucial. There was no way Sophia would have mastered the mysteries of coaxing the sofa into a bed without his expert instruction. He seemed to curse it into submission. He also explained its origins as a recent second-hand purchase because Frau Jodl's old bed had collapsed in sympathy with its owner's – precious news! Dieter also helped her slide the fridge facilitating a substantial victory for hygiene. Sophia appreciated Dieter's willing manner, which made her exploitation of him guiltless. She also quietly admired his fearlessness when he had to lean out of the window to release a stubborn catch.

Sophia desperately wanted to confront him with a barrage of all sorts of questions, but making conversation was proving difficult. She knew it was more than her usual diffidence. Despite herself, she was feeling overawed by his presence. Perhaps it was simply the intimate context – he was after all in her bedroom! What she did learn emerged largely from his own remarks as they worked. He was the only child of the Eckermanns, born and brought up in the building. He had moved out a few years ago but still lived nearby because of his infatuation with the area. He was a lawyer, taking on Legal Aid work only, he had quickly stressed, as if tainted otherwise. The Unique Café on Isabellenstrasse made outstanding Italian ice cream, a richer experience at the beginning of the week than its end for reasons never divulged.

Sophia wondered how long he would stay but didn't want to enquire in case it sounded presumptuous. So she was thrilled when he volunteered to venture downstairs on a forage for refreshment. He would be around for a while more. In opening the front door, bursts of accordion music signalled up from below and Dieter warned Sophia of the implications, the need to beware his prowling mother.

Sophia stood by the door following Dieter as he strode to the stairway. She was thinking how she had just arrived in the Coralena, and this fantastic place had been his home all his life. He suddenly turned.

'Have we met before?' His face was crouched in a quizzical expression.

'No,' Sophia replied. His look remained. No, she would have remembered.

Sophia, now alone, thought about changing out of her old clothes but feared it would be too blatant a move. She was now so regretting her earlier selection. She did however wash herself, brush her hair, and generally tidy her appearance fully exploiting the revelation of the wardrobe mirror. Dieter did a slight but noticeable double take when he returned, bottle of wine and plate of pancakes his spoils; spanner clenched pirate style in his teeth.

8

'Ho. Uncle Ho!' Dieter was getting excited, stretching his T-shirt as wide as possible with his left hand, while his right held onto a swaying cigarette.

'It looks like a spider. I don't see anything like a face.' Sophia thought how unfair it was. Her father had blue eyes like Dieter's, yet she had been allocated her mother's greyish-green.

'See, there's his beard. See it. Come on!' Dieter gave Sophia his cigarette, now freeing both hands to assist with the illustration.

'I just don't.' He was a beautiful man. But it wasn't just that. What she couldn't understand were her feelings of pride. Maybe it was simply that he appeared genuinely interested in her. He had stayed after all. She was trying to douse such appealing thoughts because she knew where they must inevitably lead. She was never pursued by the ones she found attractive, the ones *she* wanted. Sophia had learnt to make do with the attentions of men she would convince herself were acquired tastes.

Dieter was re-examining his T-shirt, despairing at the thought of Ho Chi Minh fading from his chest. Sophia dragged on the cigarette.

The men Sophia desired were usually identifiable from the barrier of awkwardness she would immediately erect in a neat act of sabotage. It made her appreciate the disarming circumstance of their meeting. Her timidity had been outmanoeuvred.

Dieter took the cigarette back from her. 'Did I tell you that they persecute smokers?' he announced. 'It's all in the house rules. Make sure you air the place before inspections.'

'What inspections?' Sophia replied suspiciously.

'Do you think they'll leave you alone? They'll be keeping a close eye on you. That's what rules are all about – spying.'

Dieter raised his long emptied glass with an air of smugness. Sophia considered that he'd deployed that demeanour with sufficient frequency to make it a definite character trait. He'd oozed smugness when he'd lectured her on the workings of the central heating, dismissing her questions on the confusing time switch.

'You look like a follower of rules.'

And then he would end his posturing with a mischievous grin, a quest for forgiveness in acknowledgement of possible misdeed, and his intimidation would be checked.

It was now mid-evening and what had begun as a work break had stretched into something more final. Sophia was content to settle the first day's account on what were considerable achievements of transformation, considerably eased by Dieter's unexpected assistance.

Pancake consumption had commenced at the flat's small wooden table. However, the painful cracking sound that had been emitted when Dieter leant back on his chair had sent them both scurrying to the sofa, actually the sofa now turned and remaining bed, lest Sophia fail to execute the manoeuvre on her own.

Dieter had originally divided the pancakes evenly but Sophia conducted a well-received redistribution based on the principle of need, and Dieter happily consumed the bulk. The wine was more evenly apportioned, although its effects apparently less so.

Sophia's light-headedness did succeed in emboldening her in the burgeoning flow of conversation. She still hadn't pinned down precisely Dieter's age. He looked young but was a practising lawyer. She put him at six or seven years older than herself, around twenty-eight or twenty-nine. He was conclusively unmarried and she had been closely monitoring his speech to pick up any references to girlfriends. She didn't ask him outright because that would have been too intrusive. She was trying not to be, while being as intrusive as she felt possibly able.

He spoke about growing up as the only child of the Coralena, which he described as a lonely experience. 'No siblings, many parents.' Which he went on to rephrase as 'No playmates, many bosses'. He became far more animated when talking about the neighbourhood itself. Sophia came to realize that she had unknowingly signed up to some kind of introductory course on the delights of the Altstadt covering everything from laundry to bakeries to beer halls to tram routes and where to avoid walking at night. Sophia let him continue, enjoying the vigour of his presentation having long lost the capacity to retain what was being conveyed. He even took her to the window, pointing out boats on the river as if old friends at a party.

Dieter must have recognized the waning of his audience because he suddenly, simply, switched off. They both stood before the window in silence absorbing the soft evening light.

Soon, Dieter was announcing his departure and Sophia was expressing her gratitude. He offered to return.

'It's safe! No accordion music,' Dieter joked as he stood on the landing. He had a final question. 'You haven't told me your politics.'

'I hate politics,' Sophia replied with a swift honesty. Politics held one primary association for Sophia, the rantings of her father. 'And you?'

'The Stones, Streetfighting Man.' Dieter paused. He looked disappointed. Sophia sensed she'd been asked something of significance and was regretting her offhand reply. She had given the wrong answer. 'So you're a bystander.' Smugness, then that redeeming smile.

Sophia's exhaustion was now overwhelming. She undressed placing her clothes carefully on one of the wooden chairs, now under deep suspicion. She bathed in the cold water, hopeful of Dieter's promise to fix the thermostat. The lumpiness of the bed contrasted with the familiarity of the sheets brought from home, her former home.

Next morning, Sophia awoke to her alarm's characteristic hysteria. She surprised herself by instantly recognizing her new surroundings. She had had a restless first night. Her mind was on the previous day's visitation. She was experiencing sickly-sweet sensations of the wildest fancy that brought her back to every teenage crush she'd ever had. The powerful glow of light from the windows was a welcomed distraction reminding her of the need to pursue the acquisition of curtains with Frau

Eckermann. She got to her feet and walked to the window excited about demonstrating her solidarity with her new neighbourhood as it woke to a new week.

Marked on the window's inside, something caught Sophia's notice. It appeared to be some form of lettering plainly visible in the light condensation that clouded its periphery. She peered closer and made out a word – *RAGE*.

9

Sophia often reflected on the basis of the rapport that had been so readily established between herself and Pauline. They were so completely different, which in a way provided explanation in itself, for Pauline represented so many of the things Sophia wished for herself. And the fact of their friendship gave her hope.

Sophia had once compiled a list of attributes formulating the adult she planned some day to become. She imagined a moment when she would reach the requisite maturity that would enable her to metamorphose into this wonderful super-being, free of the anguish that had blighted her youth, free of the guilt that weighed her family down.

When she started at college, she was sure that this must herald the dawning New Age, and was shocked to discover how much it was merely an extension of school. She was still the nervous schoolgirl, struggling to win teacher's approval, reticent with her peers yet resentful of the attentions lavished on the popular. And now she was in her first job, and living independently. When would it come?

It had not been a good day for Margaret. One of the new buyers in Ladieswear was objecting to a window layout because not enough prominence was given to her bolero jackets. She had made the mistake of going directly to Margaret to make her 'constructive comments' and Margaret went wild, calling her a jumped-up *sonofabitch*, made all the more ferocious delivered in its native tongue.

Sophia had quickly understood this major pitfall in her department's work, namely, that everyone had opinions on it, and they were too often voiced. Even the doormen, Hans Freidrich and Alphonse, would debate for days the merits of each window, monitoring which ones were most admired, forwarding on their findings. Sophia also learnt that they had given names to the types of mannequin used, and they would say things like 'Beate really doesn't have the legs for those culottes,' or 'You pushed Kurt behind Werner and you know he won't be happy.' She even caught herself unconsciously using their coding with Margaret, who would look bewildered when Sophia recommended a choice between Ulrike and Luise.

Margaret's team tended to bear the brunt of the criticism because very few would dare to express anything but fulsome compliments to Margaret herself. That was certainly true of the lower ranks with whom Sophia mixed. What happened higher up the organization was not something she ever had first-hand experience of, but she understood Margaret similarly suffered at the hands of her own peers. She would regularly return from board meeting summonses spewing contempt for her philistine colleagues who 'couldn't dress themselves never mind a window'.

Margaret herself was always immaculately dressed although certainly not in any conventional way. Her style was more a reflection of Margaret the artist, or rather, the artiste. She was an ideal resident of a Carnival city. Her most recent adoption could be encapsulated in the one word *ethnic*. At various times she could be seen in an Afghan coat, zigzag poncho, or even her unashamedly outrageous harem trousers. Her Indian jewellery spread from head to – literally – toe, weather permitting. And she adored scarves, which she would drape decorously around her neck and over one shoulder. Margaret also had expectations of her staff and Sophia found such scrutiny the most trying aspect of her job. With customary bluntness, Margaret accused Sophia of wearing clothing that 'suffocated' her femininity. For several months, Sophia found herself being regularly fixed by one of Margaret's contemptuous stares signalling the launch of a deeply intimidating lesson in dress sense that felt more like a form of cloning. Pauline became quick to tease if Sophia revealed any drift towards the Frau Fisher look. And Sophia avoided scarves of any description.

While window display generally followed a well-structured planning cycle mirroring the flow of the seasons, there were the occasional one-off projects and Margaret had just announced the latest. Nineteen seventy-two was Bonhoffs' seventieth year, and the approaching anniversary was to be marked by special celebrations. The windows team had been asked to come up with birthday concepts and Margaret wanted *feisty* suggestions for the next team meeting.

Sophia's mind was on this urgent challenge as she stood at the store's entrance waiting for Pauline. She had come to appreciate through painful experience that the noisier you were at staff meetings the more Margaret could be relied upon to ignore you. Anonymity required tactical conspicuousness! Sophia gazed up at the two glamorous Goddesses of Plenty, Fidelity and Integrity, with their outstretched arms. Hans Friedrich had told her that the Goddesses were the only surviving remnant of the original Bonhoffs building destroyed in the war. They were carefully hidden, then restored with the reconstruction. Sophia found herself toying with notions of continuity.

'Surprise!'

It was always a surprise to see Pauline in her street clothes, out of her severe white uniform, yet incongruously still plastered with her full-on cosmetic cover. In the beginning, Pauline would have ensured that every last drop of make-up was creamed off her face before exposing herself beyond the confines of work but, as she'd grown accustomed to the look or, more correctly, the effect, it now tended to linger.

Pauline wasn't particularly familiar with the Altstadt. She had visited in the past, confessing to Sophia that she'd found the place 'dingy and grey'. Sophia started her missionizing work as soon as the tram entered the neighbourhood, glamorizing the veneers of distinctive buildings, pointing up the famous beer houses, the approaching Cathedral.

Pauline did seem finally prepared to revise her assessment

outside the Coralena itself, describing it as fantastic and spooky which Sophia took as a concession. Pauline repeated both sentiments as they made their way up the stairway, including some humorous reference to a vampire film set. Sophia did understand what she meant. She knew *objectively* that the building had an eerie atmosphere, especially at night when the dark hues of the interior easily overwhelmed the meagre lighting. Yet, for Sophia, it was all part of the drama of the area, the very rationale behind her choice. And, by living in the Coralena, she was no longer spectating, she had become a player.

Pauline was the most unreservedly positive about the flat itself. She now fully appreciated why Sophia had chosen it. She described the view as spectacular. It was small but conceptually on a different plane to being a lodger in someone else's home. 'It's all your own place. It's a real apartment.' Sophia was grateful for this final vindication. The decision was a substantial one and what had caused Sophia most anxiety was the unprecedented lack of anxiety that accompanied her decision.

Sophia changed out of her despised work skirt and slipped into jeans. Pauline produced a house-warming present, which proved to be the inevitable collection of cosmetic applications. Much to Pauline's annoyance, they were quickly despatched to a wardrobe shelf. Sophia had already got that particular message!

She put cold meats on the table and some yellow bean salad, warning Pauline to sit firmly upright on the chair. Pauline uncorked a bottle of wine she had also brought to commemorate her visit. She considered herself honoured to be the very first guest. Sophia didn't disabuse her. That prize had already been taken.

'I got a moving in card from my parents. My dad told me it took them ten minutes to settle on which one to send me. You know what my mother described in it? What it felt like to carry me in her womb!'

'At least she cares. I have to remind my mother I'm still around,' Pauline said.

'It's always got to be about her, whatever I do.'

Sophia carefully lifted a single slice of meat onto her plate. She then cut the piece up into precise small squares. Pauline, by now only too familiar with Sophia's eating rituals, struggled to ignore the distraction.

'I don't understand why you do this. You're the skinniest person I know!'

Sophia maintained her concentration, rolling up a small slither of meat into a tight cylindrical ball and placing it delicately in her mouth. Pauline returned to her own meal with spiteful vigour.

'Don't you want boobs?'

'You only need them for breastfeeding,' Sophia casually answered. Pauline stared at her.

'So are you going to introduce me to your neighbours, the nearly dead people?'

Sophia chuckled. 'Sssh. They might hear!'

'Isn't hearing the first to go?' Pauline assumed a mock contemplative air. 'Or maybe it's teeth?'

Sophia hadn't actually encountered any more neighbours

despite her occupancy of a few days. A note had however been thrust under her door from a mysterious Frau Bitzel containing an overly effusive message of welcome edged with child-like coloured drawings.

The conversation turned to work and a flurry of gossip was exchanged with Sophia as usual receiving more than giving. Pauline envied Sophia's ability to have legitimate dealings with departments throughout the store and would often interrogate her about staff members and, being single again, she had become particularly interested in Sophia's skills of reconnaissance. The focus of her current ambition related to two salesmen in Leather Goods, both of whom had scored highly on her 'scale of lust' now up and well and truly running. She'd conversed with one of them in the canteen although her enthusiasm was more for the other.

And what about you, became the tone of the next conversation piece with Pauline pressing Sophia needlessly because there was nothing to squeeze out.

'You can't just give me that Sophia look of yours. You have to say something!'

There hadn't been anything on that front for over a year, ever since she had finally extricated herself from the hapless Walter, her fellow art college student, with whom she had stupidly involved herself simply because she confused her admiration of his attentions with their source. 'Not for the moment,' Sophia declared, attempting to salvage some dignity, swatting from her brain the recurring image of her intriguing visitor, Dieter Eckermann.

Sophia now enjoyed an avenging reprimand, reminding Pauline that she had attached an offer to her visit, and soon plates were being piled in the sink. Sophia had managed to charm her father into handing over his beloved toolbox and they both fiddled with its contents – cutters, cramps, pliers, chisels – trying to discern tasks that could usefully employ such awesome devices. Pauline swung a mighty hammer and dared Sophia to point her in a direction.

Sophia chose to wipe down the bland white painted walls, her least favourite feature of the flat, while Pauline took a scraper to tackle staining on the wooden floorboards. While Sophia fiddled with the radio, Pauline launched into her own musical renditions, with enthusiasm overwhelming any suggestion of melodiousness, and they were both soon in full voice competing to outdo each other in the recollection of various pop song lyrics.

Sophia was standing on the bed attempting to extend her reach when she suddenly stopped and called Pauline over.

'Look!'

Pauline peered up at the wall.

'The old pattern underneath the paint. Isn't it beautiful?' Sophia was delighted with her find – distinctive wallpaper defiantly visible under an area of thinning paintwork.

Pauline readily agreed, appreciative of any break, and proceeded to sit down on one of the chairs, which let out a tortured screech as she leant back.

10

Having brought Pauline to the flat, Sophia was keen to introduce another work colleague although in this case it would be more as a permanent resident.

Taking the Monika mannequin out of the store proved more troublesome than expected. She was usually highly amenable within the confines of display posturing. As a commuter, she was far more trying.

Getting her on the tram was a challenging question of geometry, which Sophia managed to overcome, all the while resenting Monika's inflexible constitution. The task was not helped by Sophia's growing awareness of her nakedness, albeit sexless, which called for a degree of propriety. Monika forced Sophia to stand with her for the full journey. Fellow passengers were clearly baffled by the couple. An elderly woman stopped in front of them apparently uncertain whether to turn back or move past. A group of children made a point of sitting nearby and giggling, and Sophia indulged them by passing the occasional remark to Monika, even leaning forward to catch her reply.

By the time Sophia arrived at the Coralena, Monika was being dragged more than carried. Sophia pushed the front door open with her knees and entered Monika's head first. In front of her stood the buoyant figure of Frau Eckermann, and behind, a gaggle of half-hidden figures.

'There you are! We've all been waiting for you.' Frau Eckermann studiously ignored Sophia's companion. 'Everyone's here. All here to welcome you to the Coralena. Follow me, my dear.'

Frau Eckermann headed into her ground-floor flat pursued by the unidentified 'everyone' formed into a shuffling queue. Sophia quickly engineered the propping up of Monika in the hallway.

Inside, Sophia appreciated for the first time the true impact of being in a home of the elderly. Her neighbours clustered around her while maintaining a strange silence as if natives first encountering a traveller from another world. Sophia felt profoundly uneasy. Her thoughts turned to whether she could pass off Monika as an ailing friend to whom she must urgently return. The only faces she recognized beyond Frau Eckermann's were those of the sickly Frau and sombre Herr Bruder.

Frau Eckermann took command of the situation and began introductions, which Sophia soon realized were following the order of the building.

Herr Eckermann was a towering moustachioed man with a soft-spoken voice betraying his Bavarian roots. The Schlosses 'across the hallway' saluted their greeting in unison, made all the more impressive by their similar height. Frau Schloss had a refined, delicate appearance contrasting with her husband who had a ruddy face, almost babylike in its roundness, with a bulging waistline poised to assault the last notches of his belt.

The first floor brought forth Frau Kuhn, a petite sparrow-faced woman with thick spectacles exaggerating her eyes, which seemed to be fleeing her face. Herr Kuhn at first stood behind his wife and then directly in front of her when introduced himself. He started firing questions at Sophia in quick succession until cut off impatiently by Frau Eckermann.

The widows were next. Frau Bitzel scurried forward to embrace Sophia as if she had been given up for lost. 'You got my note, you got my note!' she repeated feverishly. Her face was so laden with make-up that Sophia struggled to identify firm bodily contours. Frau Mueller, her apartment companion, was a tiny waif of a woman who stood at Frau Bitzel's side staring up at Sophia in silent wonder.

'I'm so excited you've joined us,' Frau Bitzel continued. 'I'm right below! I've been listening to you cleaning away up there. I wish I could have helped you.' She then leant forward lowering her voice to a whisper. 'We're the only young ones here, you know. We need to stick together.'

Sophia unnervingly thought of herself as a third Coralena widow.

Frau Eckermann moved Sophia on. 'You've already met Herr and Frau Bruder.' Herr Bruder nodded correctly. Frau Bruder gave Sophia a knowing look and touched her arm in a suggestion of affection.

Frau Eckermann finally let Sophia loose and she was grateful to be able to retreat to a side wall to escape the attention. She distracted herself by considering the appearance of the Eckermanns' apartment. What made the most immediate impression was the dramatic swirling wallpaper, which was similar to the pattern she had discovered under the paintwork of her flat. A fine lace tablecloth covered a dining table off to one side, with a silver bowl sprouting flowers at its centre. Matching green armchairs were similarly draped with lace across their brows. Ornate dishes glowed behind a glass-fronted teak cabinet. Da Vinci's *Last Supper* adorned a wall beside the obligatory crucifix marking out every good Catholic, Catholic home in the city. On a sideboard next to her, exotically coated fish gently cruised in a large bowl. Sophia calculated that the number of fish correlated exactly with the number of people in the room, and she began matching fish to neighbour. And which one was she?

'Now, Sophia, you mustn't be shy!' Frau Eckermann emerged from the kitchen holding an extravagant cake. She leant it forward to reveal to Sophia her name misspelt across its top in carefully etched icing. A flurry of activity then commenced, which appeared to be a well-honed routine.

Frau Schloss took charge of distributing cups and saucers, while her husband poured the coffee, trailed by Frau Mueller mournfully clutching a sugar bowl and milk jug. The Kuhns took charge of cake distribution, passing around plates and then equitably allocating slices. Frau Bitzel commandeered a plate of biscuits facilitating her presence at the rear of the Carnival procession.

Sophia noticed that no one actually sat down, which she thought was particularly odd given the age of the assembly. Perhaps it was all part of protocol at the Eckermann court.

Frau Kuhn, with her rolling eyes, declared herself once a regular Bonhoffs shopper until they changed the store layout and she couldn't find where anything was any more. Herr Eckermann was interested in where Sophia had moved *from*.

He had been a civil engineer and had worked on various post-war projects in the city's south before his retirement. Sophia admired how his bushy moustache precisely followed the ebb and flow of his mouth adding its own commentary and emphases. Frau Schloss wanted to understand why she would want to live on her own as an unmarried woman. Herr Schloss expressed his surprise that she'd chosen the Altstadt and, lowering his voice, confessed he would have left long ago if he could have. There was something in his syrupy manner which, if it wasn't for the proximity of his wife and the natural barrier of his girth, Sophia would have been convinced was flirtatious.

Frau Bitzel hovered in the background ominously waiting for her moment to re-engage, which ensured that Sophia did her best to maintain lively conversation with the others. The Bruders seemed content to keep their distance, although she could see that Frau Bruder was observing her progress. Frau Mueller stood apart from everyone. Her unchanging vacuous expression suggested that she was in a place far removed from the confines of the Coralena.

Sophia's youth was an unexpected source of celebrity and what she came to realize was that, incredibly, she was the first new resident in the Coralena since Frau Jodl herself just after the war. It made her feel as if she had entered a time warp, bringing word of the future to this lost outpost of Kussel's past.

Frau Eckermann took Sophia aside to break the news that she had been assigned a post tray by the entrance, adding the fine advice that she should check it daily. A letter was already there from the Frau with the rental agreement for her signature. Sophia thought it odd she hadn't simply handed it to her and concluded it was a training exercise.

She then led Sophia to admire family photographs arrayed along the sideboard next to the fish bowl. Sophia was indeed interested to see the Eckermann family in younger days, and they appeared almost as caricatures of what they should have looked like. She was taken by how attractive Frau Eckermann once was, especially in one striking picture where she posed like a pouting film starlet. Herr Eckermann surfaced in surprisingly few, suggesting his primary role as recorder rather than participant.

Sophia was particularly engaged by the images of Dieter, a similar youthful demeanour she had met just days before acknowledged her, eating ice cream, lying half buried on a beach. In each, he deployed the same exaggerated, pained grin as if he hadn't quite mastered the technique of the smile. There was also baby Dieter, looking delicate and vulnerable, being held aloft in one by an exultant Frau, whose expression reminded Sophia of fishermen with record catch. She tried to identify which parent was most realized in his appearance, but his darker features seemed more of a contrast. Perhaps he had his father's mouth.

It made Sophia bring to mind her own brother, Rolf, and she tried to place him against the photographs of Dieter. She recalled images of country cycling and the air thick with summer, racing to gather mushrooms and beechnuts in the forest, splashing in crystal-clear lake waters – her own family photographs swept from the sideboard. Had Rolf been able to enjoy the simple pleasures of childhood?

A sudden silencing brought Sophia back to the room. The tribe was once again assembling around her. She was once again their prize.

'Sophia, we really are so pleased you've joined us.' Frau Eckermann was smiling broadly. There was genuine affection in her voice. 'Treat us like family. We are your new family. If you need any advice or help, anything at all, everyone is here for you.' The Frau turned to Frau Bitzel who stared blankly back before springing into action like a suddenly released mechanical toy, thrusting herself forward to present Sophia with an elegantly wrapped parcel.

'It's a welcome *home* gift from us all!' The Frau stepped forward and kissed Sophia on the forehead. It was like an anointing, and it prompted within her a strange surge of elation, as if this rite of passage was receiving its due ceremony. It made Sophia wish her parents had been somehow involved.

She quickly gathered her thoughts and managed to proffer brief words of thanks, primarily directed at Frau Eckermann. Frau Bitzel clapped at its end. Frau Kuhn enquired if she played cards. Herr Schloss successfully communicated his profession by magically turning his wife's conversation on houseplants into a discourse on dental hygiene. More cake was passed around.

It was then that Sophia heard a commotion behind her. As she swung round and caught sight of Dieter, she felt her whole body involuntarily seize, her face singe with redness.

Fortunately, he was now the focus of eager attention and her indiscretion went unnoticed. Frau Bitzel was buzzing round him, Frau and Herr Schloss combined to pour him coffee. Even Herr Bruder seemed to become animated, slapping Dieter on the back. He was like a prince returning to his people.

Sophia didn't have to wait long for her own audience. Dieter approached clutching what she now saw was a bouquet of flowers, presenting it to her while engorging on a mighty slice of cake. 'I couldn't find snowdrops,' he remarked in cute reference to her prized painting. He leant forward as if he might be about to kiss her and Sophia froze.

'Do you want to escape?' he whispered.

'Oh yes!' Sophia was experiencing the strain of celebrity but had resigned herself to having to see through to the end what was after all an event in her honour.

'I promised to help Sophia sort out her water problems,' Dieter solemnly announced. 'You don't mind if we go. She's not washed properly in days.'

The goodbyes were swift, probably made swifter by Dieter's declaration, which brought both sympathy and a discreet distancing. Sophia recognized that Dieter's departure was the far greater loss. Herr Schloss complained that he'd only just arrived and he owed them a visit. Frau Bitzel grabbed hold of his arm for as long as she could. Frau Eckermann insisted that he return as soon as he had 'concluded his business' upstairs.

Sophia exited the unexpected bearer of two gifts. In the

hallway, she introduced Dieter to Monika now slipped to a slouch in an apparent huff.

'Did you need to explain it quite like that?' Sophia tried to appear annoyed. They were going to spend more time together. He'd given her beautiful flowers. She was working hard to still a racing mind.

'Don't worry. You don't smell.'

Dieter and Sophia carried Monika up the stairs like a hopelessly drunken friend. Sophia was convinced it wasn't just what Pauline would quickly diagnose as *lust*, her term of the moment. The energy she could sense between them was something else, and yes there was lust!

'They'll be discussing you now.'

'And how did I do?' Sophia enquired.

'Well, let me put it this way. No one wanted to ask Frau Jodl back.'

'You're sick!' Sophia couldn't stop herself giggling. She was excited.

Dieter handed Monika over to Sophia and took her door key. Sophia found his familiarity curious. She joked to herself that she should feel flattered that the person who was so obviously the building's idol had chosen to spend such valuable time with her. And Sophia made sure it was used productively, getting him to work first on the thermostat and then on an erratic light switch in the bathroom. He also reacquainted Sophia with the involved procedures for changing the bed back to a sofa, which this time were committed to writing.

Dieter's rewards were meagre – a share in Sophia's herring

salad eaten with careful composure at the table. A dessert of apples served up on the sofa. Sophia decided to open her present from the neighbours, revealing a set of kitchen utensils.

'Very sensible. They like you!' Dieter concluded.

'But I'm not as popular as you,' Sophia wryly observed.

'I've lived with these people all my life. The Bruders lost two sons in the war. The Schloss's daughter moved to Hamburg. I became everyone's child.'

Dieter chewed on his apple core. Sophia took out a cigarette.

'They've got old. But they're basically decent people. They don't have much. All they have is each other.'

Sophia reflected on the assortment of faces she had just encountered. Weathered, bruised, yet there was also liveliness, an impressive exuberance. Her neighbours were survivors. Yes, she could imagine herself identifying with Dieter's compassion. She certainly admired it.

Dieter then told her a series of Coralena tales, the most memorable of which being when he took Frau Bitzel on the back of his motorbike and they were cautioned by the police for indecent exposure. Sophia was in hysterics.

'I also have another very special parent,' Dieter declared in more sombre tone. And she's called Coralena. You saw her face when you came in, above the entrance. You know Coralena is the name of a Rhinemaiden, a river mermaid. Coralena lives! And if you listen out for her, she'll visit you.' Sophia liked how he anthropomorphized the building. It was the only way to explain what she sensed, the profound personality embedded in the construct.

Dieter stared at Sophia as if she was required to give his insight some sort of acknowledgement, as if he needed to confirm she could. Everything about him appeared exceptional. Sophia thought about the boy she had met in Frau Eckermann's photographs, and how that boy hadn't much changed. And then he kissed her.

Sophia woke the next day to catch Monika peering down at her. She wondered what was being construed behind such a determinedly expressionless demeanour. Had she been unwise, too willing in her response? But he liked her. He liked her! It was so thrilling!

She hadn't let it go beyond gentle caressing and she appreciated the way Dieter had let her pace the embrace. His restraint suggested a confidence that she had longed to find in a man. She thought of Walter climbing on top of her like he was a mountaineer on a mission. But there was definite passion behind Dieter's exterior of affected cool. She considered why it had felt so *comfortable*, and all she could conclude was that it was because he was. Dieter had left without her asking. And she wished he could have stayed.

She speculated on whether he had returned to the Eckermanns as the Frau had requested. Had he matter-of-factly announced to them that he'd fixed her water problem? It made her think of herself back in a teenager's bedroom, with parents on patrol beneath.

Sophia got out of bed and lazily stretched. Yet again she had slept restlessly, waking before her alarm, and she resolved not to forget to bring up the matter of the curtains with Frau Eckermann. Her thoughts turned to the day ahead and the preparations now under way for the autumn displays. The dreaded word Christmas was also lurking in the air. Sophia had arrived just in time to experience its mania the previous year. And she had to think up ideas for the anniversary project lest she provoke another of Margaret's 'window dressers must be dreamers' speeches.

She wandered over to the table, to the makeshift vase that contained Dieter's flowers. She noted their striking beauty against the plain white walls. She smelt their aroma in a sub-conscious search for Dieter's own. She then glanced down and saw that her diary, which she kept in her shoulder bag, was open on the table's surface. She looked more closely and saw it was turned to that day's page. Across it, she read the word *RAGE*, written in studious script.

11

At that precise moment, the three of them were in different worlds.

Her father was totally absorbed by that day's news. The teenage son of Judge Eggert was missing. Eggert had been the trial judge in the Krombach war crimes case and the link was confirmed when the Red Revolutionary Front released its state-ment announcing the abduction. Chancellor Brandt and President Von Hassel had been in the city for most of the day.

'What are the politicians going to do!' her father railed from the window.

Sophia was preoccupied with the diary entry. Its presence had deeply disturbed her. It was the very same word she had seen spelt out on the window condensation, something she had dismissed at the time as the remains of earlier playful graffiti. She'd obtained Dieter's work number from Frau Eckermann on the pretext of following up a problem with the flat. He denied any knowledge of the diary and resented the implicit accusation.

As for her mother, she was sitting erect on the sofa shrouded in an aura of abstention. She had toured the flat, straightened wardrobe clothing, sniffed at Monika, opened the fridge, finally made vaguely complimentary remarks that were restricted to minor features, suggesting she had an overall opinion being kept firmly at bay, and then had resorted to her current position.

The plum tart Sophia had bought from a nearby bakery sat forlornly on the table, next to Dieter's fading flowers. Her parents had declined her offer of coffee and Sophia was beginning to feel edgy about the cake's continuing presence in the flat following their departure. She had switched on the radio, fiddled, and switched it off.

'Coralena is the name of a Rhinemaiden.' Wrestling with the novel responsibility to *entertain*, Sophia attempted to revive the conversation.

Her father obliged. 'Do you know the sailors' tale about the Rhinemaidens?' Sophia shook her head appreciatively. 'They demand a quota of human sacrifices every year as a price for keeping the river navigable. In the old days, if a sailor fell overboard those on deck wouldn't try to save him. They'd tell him not to struggle, to simply give in to fate and let the Rhinemaidens take him down.'

'What a terrible story! Terrible.' Her mother pulled a disgusted face. Her father waved his hand dismissively.

'My Coralena wouldn't do that. She's been tamed,' Sophia reassured.

This prompted her mother to speak on far more sensible matters such as the latest tally from home – three confirmations, one wedding, an operation pending, an engagement anticipated – Sophia wondered if the couple themselves knew. True to the spirit of conscientious hostess, she did try her best to feign interest in the roll-call of familiar names, the world from which Sophia had felt ejected, and in turn grew to reject. What was now a physical reality had long ago been her emotional state. Sophia loved being in the Coralena.

'I just hope you'll look after yourself here. Promise me you will.' Her mother suddenly leant forward.

'Why wouldn't I?'

'You'll eat properly?'

'Ye-es.' Sophia replied sternly, answering *that* question yet again. Her mother couldn't just leave it alone for once. This was their first visit! If Sophia had the means, she would have stocked the fridge with all manner of goods. Unfortunately, deception came at a price. Instead, she had offered up the paltry cover of a plum tart.

'If only you weren't so thin. You look just like the people after the war!'

How often? Sophia grumbled to herself. All her mother's stories of post-war poverty, scrambling for rotten potatoes. The martyrdom of her generation, her martyrdom. Her mother was a saint, a blessed woman. Sophia should feel so proud, and grateful. And how often would Sophia be expected to communicate with them? There were no rules for their new situation. Does she telephone once a day, a week? And when do they visit, and when will she visit them? What would be sufficient for its purpose? It was the sort of advice she would have sought from her older brother Rolf if he had still been alive. He would have established the precedent and she would have followed in his trail. Sophia knew of several contemporaries who'd enjoyed freedoms hard won by older siblings. It was yet another resentment to add to the tally.

After her parents left, Sophia observed them from her window. They walked along the Rheingasse in silence. Her father with his longer stride was sufficiently ahead of her mother to suggest to any onlooker that they were not actually a couple. Her mother, in her heels, was finding it increasingly difficult to negotiate the cobbled street. She called on him to slow down. He showed his impatience. She wouldn't ask for his help, nor would he offer it. In earlier times, she might have been between them, holding onto their hands, forcing them to walk at her pace. And now she was staying away.

There was a test Sophia was keen to conduct with Monika, whom Margaret considered the skinniest, most androgynous-looking, of all the svelte models in the collection. She placed Monika in front of the wardrobe mirror. Sophia then undressed herself until completely naked and took up a position next to Monika, elongating her own thin limbs to replicate Monika's coquettish pose, comparing their two unmediated forms – narrow shoulders, small breasts, tapered waists, slim hips. Sophia turned Monika sideways, swivelling herself to the new angle, and then concluded the exercise from the back, the two rear body shapes evaluated in the mirror from behind one shoulder.

Sophia was pleased. She was alone and she felt pleased. She got hold of the plum cake from the table and merrily licked off the jellied topping.

12

Sophia was hoping it wouldn't be a history lesson. Neither facts nor figures had ever held particular interest for her, and she didn't want to have to think up intelligent questions to impress teacher. She derived pleasure from the atmosphere of the Altstadt, not the dates of the buildings. But she didn't want to offend Dieter. He had made the offer of a Sunday tour and she had accepted. She trusted he saw it as she did, as purely another means of being in each other's company.

They had arranged an early rendezvous in Marienplatz, the central square of the district, the location of Carnival launch. Dieter was waiting for her, casually draped across the foot of the fountain marking the square's centre. She was late because she had experimented with every possible permutation of clothing before settling in the end on her original choice, a simple cheese-cloth blouse and jeans. Her white moccasins, with their non-existent heels, were a strategic suggestion once advised by Pauline.

His greeting was a polite *correct* handshake, which Sophia found disappointing, and it got worse. He told her how attractive she was. It was the way he said it, coldly, as if it might somehow be a cause for suspicion. The compliment, the manner of its delivery, unnerved her.

Dieter began like a boy scout leading a field trip, explaining that the square was originally the main market of Roman Kussel, the city's founders, whose legacy was being dug up at an excavation site on the Altstadt's edge. They moved down a side alley and on to opulent houses on Ritterstrasse with Dieter talking about the grand merchants whose wealth once flourished in earlier centuries. Herring, wine, tobacco – Kussel, the Altstadt, had dominated Rhineland trade and, with the building of the railways, became a major staging post into Germany's hinterland.

Dieter went on to show Sophia his Catholic elementary school on Joachimstrasse and contemplated the trauma of short trousers. In Kaiserplatz, he boasted of a night of underage drinking that took in every beer house, and then insisted on revealing the very spot where he threw up. Sophia had by now confirmed he was definitely the taller, but it was close.

At some point Sophia asked Dieter about his legal work. He described it as 'helping the helpless'. He had just completed a case of tenant eviction. A family were in arrears with rental payments and the landlord hired thugs to drive them out. Dieter had managed to secure a court injunction. He was trying to appear blasé, which felt more like a reined-in conceit. Sophia, suitably intimidated, struggled to provide the requested 'typical day' at Bonhoffs.

Berger Allee, with its fine and not so fine antique shops, was a street Sophia had become acquainted with when she'd worked on her period fashion project at art college. In one store, Sophia pointed out a porcelain chamber pot she was convinced Dieter urgently needed, although she was concerned about its small size. In turn, Dieter balanced a grotesque set of antlers on his head, which he insisted Sophia would be craving for her hallway to help overcome homesickness.

Throughout their walk, the Cathedral remained a brooding presence. It kept appearing and reappearing as corners were turned or streets crossed, as if monitoring their very progress. Sophia hadn't been inside the Cathedral for years, so she decided to succumb to her pursuer, persuading a reluctant Dieter to make this adjustment to the itinerary. However, she first needed his assurance that the Coralena delegation would have attended an early Mass and would be long gone. Sophia had received a further colourful missive from Frau Bitzel suggesting an intimacy Sophia wasn't looking to encourage.

As they made their way to the Cathedral entrance, Dieter led Sophia into trespassing across the trim lawns, as if the building's imposing size warranted this humble act of defiance. He asked Sophia if she thought the Cathedral had been saved from destruction in the war through divine intervention, or because the British preserved it for the purposes of aerial reconnaissance to guide their bombing runs.

The late morning service had just ended and pious-looking congregants were trying to exit from a narrow doorway, doing battle with the inflow of strikingly less than pious-looking tourists. The only tranquillity in the scene lay with the rows of saints making a gentle angular ascent in the arches above the entrance. At their apex sat St Julien, patron saint of Kussel, in benign contemplation, whose status was achieved through his ruthless suppression of local paganism.

Inside, Sophia was immediately struck by the sheer magnitude of the structure, an impact she had forgotten from her previous visits. The huge vaulted ceilings with their soaring lines, like some vast Gothic spaceship about to lift off to the heavens. It was dazzling.

Dieter gave his curious reaction. 'Doesn't it make you feel so small, like an insect?'

As they walked around, Dieter talked about his experiences as a child. The Cathedral was his local church. It was where he had received his first Communion and had dutifully attended weekly Mass with his parents until finally permitted to give up the pretence after lengthy and acrimonious dispute. The Cathedral was an intimate, borne of familiarity rather than affection. Dieter seemed to have a commentary on every window, mural and chapel despite Sophia's persistent efforts to catch him out. She finally quizzed him on the name of the woman selling the postcards, and he answered with such astonishing swiftness, including a listing of implausibly numerous children, that Sophia had to laugh, far too loudly for the austere surroundings.

Dieter was keen to show Sophia 'as an accomplished artist yourself' his favourite painting – *The Betrayal of Our Lord* by Stefan Cornelius. It portrayed the Last Supper just as Jesus declares he will be denounced by one of his disciples. The faces reveal shock and bewilderment, except for the figure of Christ himself. He is calm, resolutely serene in his demeanour. Dieter admired the work because 'Jesus doesn't allow himself to be a victim'.

Sophia decided to light a candle for her brother Rolf. It was something her mother would have performed that very day in their local church, as she did routinely every week, and Sophia felt it was an opportune moment to conduct her own memorial – her protest. She stood in front of the flickering mass of candles, illuminating the Golden Virgin shrine behind, and added another to their fiery display. She brought to mind an evening of tree climbing in the garden. She had fallen to the ground. Rolf had jumped next to her and they lay, heads touching, looking up at the fiery display of a dazzling star-filled night. Rolf aimed his finger at the brightest and declared that was where they would one day meet. He would wait for her there. She knew that's where he would be now, bathed in a brilliant heavenly light, whatever others might say. That was her prayer.

When she turned, Dieter was standing far across the central aisle, almost lost to the vastness of the space. But she was sure she could still make out his eyes, that he was staring at her, and she now understood what he meant about feeling small.

Outside the Cathedral, they picked up street food – fried potato pancakes and apple sauce. Sophia made Dieter finish hers.

The warmth of the day was holding and soon they were entering the Rhinepark by the river. They stopped to observe local children foraging in a landscape of swings and slides, the pleasure on their faces suggesting that remarkable ability to relive each turn as if their first. Model boats were being put to sea in a nearby pond. Dieter brought up his own childhood visits to the park and Sophia sensed he was watching himself amongst the busy players of today. Yet his remarks seemed curiously detached, as if he was a watcher even then.

Dieter asked her about the candle lit in the Cathedral and, when Sophia disclosed she had lost a brother, it had a palpable effect. Dieter gripped her hand, held her, and something in his behaviour made her think they were comforting each other.

A troupe of ducks weaved amongst boats in the pond and a boy started throwing stones. Dieter shouted and the boy ran off.

It was beyond the pond that the real ships could parade. They continued to the pedestrian walkway adjoining the Rhine and, in silence, gazed out across the river. Its massive scale experienced so intimately was stunning, as if in the end the river was really all that mattered, a blue grey slithering behemoth with Kussel mere clutter on its banks. Sophia wondered if this was where he would kiss her.

It was a short walk to Dieter's apartment. He lived in a block close to the river. He said the Coralena was fifteen minutes away but, by now, Sophia had completely lost her bearings. A gleaming silvery motorbike was parked beside the building and he took her across to admire it. While extolling the bike's virtues, he caressed it reassuringly. Sophia felt flattered.

Dieter described his flat as a commune, which he shared in a variety of ways with three friends, two male, one female, all of whom he expected to be out on a Sunday afternoon. He proved to be two-thirds right when they discovered Alex and a male friend enveloped in a haze of illicit smoke and the raucous sound of the Grateful Dead.

On seeing them, Dieter expressed his surprise, which Alex must have taken as a signal for they both soon disappeared either out or into Alex's room, Sophia wasn't sure which. She came out of the bathroom, the noise had stopped, and they were gone.

Dieter explained Alex was a student doing a doctorate in sociology at Kussel University. 'Permanently,' Dieter added. Sophia immediately assigned to him the parka in the hallway. Dieter's other flatmate Bernard worked in his law firm. He would be at his girlfriend's in Bonn. As for Marita, she could be anywhere.

Dieter went to make coffee in the separate kitchen area, giving Sophia the opportunity to inspect the place. The living room might have felt spacious if it hadn't have been swamped by an odd assortment of furnishings and general debris. She could identify a matching pair of battered leather armchairs, a wheel-less drinks trolley hosting a record player, LPs stacked against its side, a white plastic table patterned by burn marks, a punctured wicker chair, and some kind of camp bed. A telephone clung to the side of an avalanche of comics. What appeared to be a mangled trumpet lay on floor cushions beneath the one large window. One wall was a tribute to the poster industry – anti Vietnam war, anti-nuclear, pro-abortion, pro-peace, a bikinied Jane Fonda with a haunting Che Guevera positioned provocatively between her legs. On the opposite side, deep creviced shelving brimmed with books.

'So what do you think?'

Sophia hadn't noticed Dieter's return, cups of coffee in hand.

'Now you know how I'm able to advise you so expertly on interior design.'

Sophia's eye caught the grin of a toothful vampire beckoning her from a poster on the back of the living-room door.

She thanked Dieter for the tour. 'You like history, don't you?'

'History is all there is. These very words are slotting right into history as they leave my mouth.'

Sophia scanned the room for somewhere to sit and Dieter casually proposed that they retire to his bedroom. For privacy, he added as justification, exacerbating Sophia's dilemma. She paused, caught in that moment between the grinding wheels of confused feeling, what she wanted to do, and what might be the most prudent. In her mind, she had anticipated this scenario from the day's beginning, from when they had first met, and she had played with the conflicting responses. She looked at this man in front of her. She had watched him all day long, move and talk – earnestness, sarcasm, sensitivity, humour. And now who was this Dieter? He had adopted a soulful, enquiring expression that portrayed such an absurd intensity. What did he want? He was a mystery. And yet. And yet, there was something so persuasive about him. He touched her arm, and they kissed.

Dieter suggested his motorbike but Sophia preferred that they walk back to the Coralena. The cool evening air suggested the growing vulnerability of summer. Sophia didn't have a favourite season, but she loved the transitions, one season on the cusp of the next.

As they journeyed, Sophia decided to raise, in order to promptly re-bury, the ritual 'previous relationships' topic. Dieter admitted to a number, a couple serious, one very. 'She got fed up with me. I left her before she kicked me out.' 'I think what I really need is a sister,' he concluded with a wide grin, putting his arm around Sophia as if she was offering herself as a candidate. Dieter never enquired about hers.

The walk did take around fifteen minutes as he had claimed. On reaching the Rheingasse, Dieter slid his arm from her shoulder. Sophia wouldn't have thought the adjustment odd if it hadn't been for the deliberate manner in which he executed it. Outside the Coralena, they talked of next meetings and he kissed her lightly on the cheek. Sophia supposed that Dieter was taking her relegation to sisterhood seriously. And then, having completed their farewells, he unexpectedly entered the building alongside her, approaching his parents' door while Sophia proceeded upstairs.

Sophia experienced a particularly troubling sensation in that final act. Hearing the Eckermann door close, she started to wonder if Dieter might now be filing his report, as if their day had been some form of contrivance. She had moved into the Coralena and Frau Eckermann had arranged for her son to call. He was a complimentary benefit attached to the apartment. And now Sophia could also claim him just as the others in the building so readily did. Or maybe it was the reverse. Maybe she was the youthful arrival served up by the Coralena to its cherished son. Sophia found her sudden paranoia disturbing.

13

The kidnapping of Judge Eggert's son had an immediate impact at Bonhoffs. It had not been forgotten that the Red Revolutionary Front had made its name in the late 1960s from the firebombing of department stores. Nerves were not helped when the fire alarm mysteriously went off on the very day of the kidnapping, causing the complete evacuation of the building for most of the day.

At the entrance, the genial faces of Hans Heinrich and Alphonse in their benign costumes were bolstered by severe, grey-uniformed security men, creating an absurd contrast. And there were other measures, some overt like the new staff identification tags that had to be permanently on display, and some allegedly undisclosed, like plainclothes detectives, which became the subject of much speculation. The informal news networks were buzzing.

Sophia had come to appreciate how it was the staff in the relatively junior positions that acquired the most astonishing intelligence on what was really afoot at Bonhoffs. For it was they, and only they who, beyond management, actually got to meet the elite owners, the Von Scheiben family, and often in disarmingly informal situations. They were the maintenance men who fixed electrical plugs and office shelving, and frequently had their roles extend to private homes; the canteen crew who served up the meals in the hallowed Executive Suite; and the company chauffeurs, especially them, who enjoyed the unique access of many hours spent toing and froing – journeys to meetings and airports, picking up wives, dropping off mistresses. Such an impressive array of informants ensured the swift flow of gossip long before the official company politburo brought out its truth on events.

One of the stories circulating was that the chairman of Bonhoffs, Herr Otto Von Scheiben, had employed two bodyguards, one of whom bore a close resemblance to him and was required to dress in similar fashion to confuse potential kidnappers. This caused much amusement and was used as further evidence of his weakling image summed up by the aphorism scathingly applied that he had the good fortune to have been born after his father rather than before.

Sophia had spent the day caged inside the windows rushing to finish her particular responsibilities for the autumn displays. This had entailed positioning props, cajoling mannequins, wearing down ladders, angling lighting, stretching great swathes of PVC fabric everywhere, pinnings galore, all in the sweltering heat of the glasshouse windows. It had been the designated completion day and window deadlines were always always adhered to, with perfection minimum standard. The pressures had exhausted her.

It was in the toilets, as Sophia washed her bloodied fingers, that Margaret descended, declaring more definitively that she had liked her proposal.

It was hard to discern genuine enthusiasm from Margaret especially appreciating that she was at work on the looming Christmas season, which was acknowledged even by her to be her most unbalanced. There was also the ongoing language problem, which meant that Margaret had her own unique Americanized German whose subtleties sometimes defied unravelling. When Sophia had made her suggestion for the Bonhoffs' anniversary project, at the time Margaret had described it as *considerable*. Sophia was also aware of the sensitivities surrounding subordinates with good ideas, which may have explained why Margaret was more fulsome in the privacy of the bathroom than at the staff meeting itself.

It was the story of the Goddesses of Plenty that had given Sophia the theme, that the windows fronting the store be dedicated to the decades of Bonhoffs' existence, 1902 to 1972, demonstrating through period display its historic and continuous commitment to 'Fidelity' and 'Integrity'. The other windows would then become a complementary showcase portraying how the store was maintaining its unique role, providing Kussel with the very best in product and produce.

Sophia had casually proposed it at the staff meeting amidst a flurry of noisy suggestion and hadn't minded the equally casual response. She was more concerned merely to prove to Margaret and the rest of the team that she was able to speak up with her own ideas, and hadn't given the discussion further thought until Margaret's approach.

Margaret now needed Sophia to prepare rough workouts of window scenarios to develop the concept. It was only after Margaret had left that Sophia recognized the enormity of what had just transpired. Her proposal was being considered for what had to be the most prestigious windows assignment of 1972. She couldn't contain her excitement and rushed to find Pauline, who duly proclaimed her a genius.

14

Frau Eckermann was proving a regular visitor. Sophia was learning the distinctive tapping sound that would announce her presence. She never used the doorbell, as if to accentuate her special status. And Sophia would often open the door to the sound of the accordion, adding its own salute to the unique personage that was her guest.

'Are you settling in?' 'Is everything okay?' 'Do you need anything?' Sophia was overwhelmed by the Frau's attentiveness, which also warranted a degree of special vigilance in having to anticipate the masking of her smoking. Any matters that Sophia raised with the Frau were carefully noted down in what appeared to be an old school jotter, and remedies swiftly sought. With the curtains, Sophia was consulted on their selection and Dieter had them installed on the very day they arrived.

The Frau also had plenty of advice on the riches of the Altstadt. She even insisted on escorting Sophia personally to the neighbourhood shops, calling away the local greengrocer from a perplexed customer to effect the introductions. 'You look after her now, she's one of mine!' The owner nodded wearily as if beaten down years before by this irresistible force.

Sophia found the Frau's maternal cosseting strangely endearing. She began to joke with herself that she was now a Coralena child, indeed the sister Dieter had missed out on, and adoption papers were being readied.

Sophia also started to notice that the Frau had a tendency to include in their encounters some kind of counsel or moral of the day. Sophia thought of it in the context of the Sisterhood of the Immaculate Virgin, with its yellow-hearted cross forever featured on her chest. She informed Sophia of an upcoming Coralena collection for the poor to be distributed at the time of Carnival. On a second occasion, she asked Sophia to be especially mindful of Frau Bruder and offer her any assistance. 'She's never been so poorly, and winter's still to come.'

In the face of such evident selflessness, Sophia resoundingly quashed any feelings of cynicism. The Frau was even the prime mover behind what Sophia discovered were occasional *house* events. The Frau promoted the latest as Coralena's farewell to summer. 'We're taking to the river. It'll be such fun.'

The formal invitation was awaiting Sophia when she swept her letter tray that same day. The Coralena emblem emerged from a pink envelope, the note lavishly filled with the Frau's correct geometric handwriting. She had seen the emblem first on the rental correspondence, the one made memorable by its long list of rules covering every eventuality from hanging washing to the fire drill – and smoking. It was the face of Coralena's very own Rhinemaiden. Sophia imagined Coralena as the true instigator of the occasion, enticing her residents to join her for some sport on the river.

Sophia had by now met both the other males of Dieter's commune. The one woman, Marita, had been out each visit, which meant Sophia was left to speculate on her character from the displays of her washing that forever decorated the bathroom. Bernard had come back from Bonn with his girlfriend, Gabriele. They were both friendly but clearly too engrossed in each other to be much interested in anyone else. The other flatmate Alex proved to be too much the opposite, and Sophia found his repeated questioning of her uncomfortably intrusive. He had pressed her about her student life in such a way that it was as if Sophia had to admit to something, what she couldn't fathom, before he would deign to leave the subject. He also wanted to know all about her work at Bonhoffs, but she soon realized it was not out of any genuine interest. He seemed to be playing with her. And he had also provoked her into revealing her easy capacity for blushing, her embarrassment of embarrassment. Dieter would laugh off his behaviour telling her just to ignore him. 'He's crazy.' Sophia heartily agreed with the assessment without sharing the amusement.

Sophia was also learning about the collection of passions that filled Dieter's life. There was his 'mother' the Coralena, of course, to whom he gave boundless loyalty, forever tinkering in the building on some obscure assignment. His motorbike, an old British Norton, which he used to commute to work and escape the city. Then there was his dancing. Sophia was bemused to discover that he had a fascination for American jive, an addiction he regularly indulged at a Monday nightclub on the river. And there was Writers Night.

Writers Nights were held fortnightly in the Barbarossa Bar on days set by Alex who acted as the group's convenor. Dieter explained that the original members had collaborated on the Kussel University magazine, hence the title, competing with each other over who could get the most stories banned by the University authorities. What the group had become he described as a social and political forum.

Sophia experienced her first Writers Night on a wet Thursday, made all the more damp by journeying on the back of Dieter's bike. Some of the group were already assembled around a back table topped by an array of drinks in various stages of consumption. Alex was sporting a cowboy hat with a feather pasted on one side, which he tipped in silent greeting. Strangely, Dieter didn't actually introduce Sophia to anyone, which made her feel already a known quantity, and then she wondered whether this signified her status was still being determined. They sat between a woman in a long floating dress and a large man nicknamed the Prussian, wearing a bright kaftan and sporting an overly lush beard. Yet Sophia could make out far more of him than his startling neighbour, a man whose face was wrapped in a black kefia completely obliterating his face except for a slit to accommodate large darting eyes. Sophia considered whether she was about to discover that Carnival was the true purpose behind the gathering. Soon there were twelve, nine men and three women, most of whom seemed to be intimately acquainted with each other. It was like a school reunion and Sophia was acutely aware of her inadequate heritage.

The conversation was initially light. The meagre start to the football season of FC Kussel was the first grievously intoned topic, somehow drifting into a debate on the colour of a cat, which became strangely heated. A man in a bright orange tie-dye shirt asked Dieter some legal question about a squat he was setting up and the Prussian offered Sophia a marijuana joint which she declined, trying to appear as if she couldn't possibly have another.

Someone brought up a recent sit-in at Kussel University to protest 'the Vietnam war and American imperialism in the Third World'. The media coverage had been 'brilliant' and Alex was toasted as some kind of leading figure. He was the last to speak on the subject, standing to deliver a tirade that Sophia found largely incomprehensible. Having struggled to digest his first sentence which finished on the dubiously poetic flourish, 'the ugly twins of capitalism and fascism', she took to speculating on how steadfast the hat feather would prove.

The approaching visit of US Secretary of State Kissinger neatly proceeded with talk of ominously sounding 'preparations' being co-ordinated by Berlin. Names and events followed in quick succession referred to in a shorthand that Sophia couldn't even attempt to decipher. She thought of herself as having joined a play far into the story. She was meeting characters already long established, and had yet to figure out the plot. The colour of the cat came up again with someone threatening to settle matters by bringing it to the bar. Sophia wondered when Dieter would speak.

The Eggert name came up obliquely, which led Sophia to presume that this was already an established topic. Someone talked about the pending release of the war criminal Krombach from prison and how 'even the bourgeois press' had acknowledged Judge Eggert's wartime membership of the SS. One of the women then described as 'utter shit' the statement on his son's kidnapping issued by the Red Revolutionary Front. A venomous argument erupted, but Sophia appeared to be the only one alarmed. Then a couple at the table's end announced the police had questioned them. Alex said he was expecting it. Sophia swiftly turned to Dieter, finally abandoning the pretence of coolness that had been her own primary aim for the evening. He said he would explain later.

Sophia felt he never really did. He talked about living in a police state and how all groupings on the Left were routinely monitored. How Alex was the most vulnerable because he was the most active. Sophia asked him if it had been a successful meeting. Dieter shrugged. She wondered if she'd done something wrong.

15

Pauline wanted them to go out on a double date. She was still tracking the two salesmen in Leather Goods and, on the basis of not having yet to commit herself to either one, she needed Sophia's assistance. If it wasn't for her persistence, Pauline might not have discovered Dieter's existence for some while longer.

Part of Sophia was relieved it was now out in the open. She had sensed a certain reticence in Dieter's behaviour towards her, and she didn't want to collude by responding with her own.

Pauline still wanted her for the double date. She even threw in as an incentive her 'professional' assistance in helping Sophia learn how to apply the assorted cosmetics that were Pauline's recent gift – evidence of which had yet to appear, she added scornfully. 'Come on! Don't you ever do anything even a bit bad?!'

The downside to the announcement was the inevitable interrogation that followed.

Afterwards, Sophia considered how she would have answered if she'd been more forthcoming. 'There's a lot going on in his face.' That response given as a sop to Pauline was certainly true. Dieter was clearly someone with principles, some sort of idealist with beliefs that she was still trying to comprehend. He could also be cynical and yet curiously deferential, as she had witnessed in his Coralena dealings. There was humour and fun and caring, but there were moments of moodiness that she suspected were also characteristic. He was intelligent, at times arrogant, yet there was also gentleness and vulnerability, like when his eyes would sometimes search her out, as if needing to own her attention. This was enhanced by his youthful looks which she found deeply attractive, almost despite herself. She had a recurring and worrying image in her head of wanting to mother him although she had never remotely acted it out, or so she sorely hoped. Maybe she wanted to feel superior to him because he could be so infuriatingly intimidating. She was particularly baffled by how implausibly intense he could be with her, and yet, on occasion, seem so unsure, almost wary. And beyond all this contradictory front, she hadn't encountered his soul. And solving that mystery had become compelling.

She wondered if she saw anything of her brother Rolf somewhere in Dieter, but he wasn't really there and she was relieved. She was sure that her affair with the despised Walter had had a lot to do with that. When she had first encountered him at college she'd constructed a romanticized image of an older Rolf out of his energetic style and quick tongue. And she was so lonely. His attentions became a drug. She hated herself most for losing her virginity with him. Why did she go and tell him? He became so pleased with himself, as if it was a badge of honour he would graciously carry throughout his life. If she'd only had Pauline's mouth.

Sophia and Dieter had never stayed overnight together, nor had they made love. He hadn't put her under any pressure, and Sophia didn't want to feel in any hurry. They had once joked about whether she would be permitted to break the Coralena regulation of no visitors after midnight if he bore the

Eckermann name. And then last week the subject of contraception came up. They were discussing the latest storm caused by the pro-abortion campaign that had leading celebrities 'confessing' their abortions in advertisements carried in every national newspaper. Before Sophia had had time to think how the topic had moved on, Dieter asked if she was on the pill.

It was Pauline who came up with all the advice, told her what to do. Sophia had never spoken to anyone about such an intimate subject before and was full of admiration when Pauline referred to conversations with her mother on the subject. Sophia tried to imagine such a moment with her own mother, thumbing through her great rulebook on right and wrong, her dreams of Sophia remaining at home until a whiter than white wedding already shattered.

Somewhere inside their discussion, Pauline also made what for Sophia was a startling announcement. She ever so nonchalantly revealed that she no longer considered herself a Catholic, because of the Church's 'perverse' attitude to sex. 'How can it possibly be a sin?' She had even gone so far as to remove herself from the Church Tax Register!

Religion was another topic Sophia had never raised with Pauline. It was not something one would. It was like discussing being German. It was simply what you were, whatever you actually did about it. Sophia herself hadn't taken Communion for years. It ended sometime after Rolf's death. But the idea of declaring oneself an actual ex-Catholic had never occurred to her. She found the notion shocking.

'Don't you *think* about these things?' Pauline protested.

Sophia felt herself shrinking. They were the same tinglings of anxiety she had had at school, when she felt that she should have known something, but didn't. When she felt stupid. It was how she had reacted to Writers Night with Dieter, cocooned in silent bewilderment. It made her wonder what Dieter thought of her. Was he also disappointed?

16

The Coralena river outing began with Frau Mueller's disappearance before they'd even reached the cruise ship, which was then held up while the men of the party went in search of her. She was eventually found trying to board a vessel heading in the other direction.

The ship finally set sail, the rain drizzled, the women played cards, the men drank and sang prehistoric songs. Sophia and Dieter tried to outsmoke each other at the ship's rear.

Sophia had anticipated that Dieter would be guarded towards her in front of the Coralena gallery, but he seemed distant, almost hostile. Sophia couldn't understand why spending time in each other's company, as the Coralena's two 'young ones', should arouse suspicions of there being anything more between them, if that was in fact his problem. It wasn't hers. He made her feel like an intruder.

Dieter started talking at length about the help he was being required to give his parents. He began in a tone of complaint which seemed to shade into some sort of excuse. Sophia asked why he made himself so available to the Coralena and he responded with a peculiar reference to having always had to 'earn his way'. This caused Sophia to quiz him about his childhood to which he answered with so determinedly little that Sophia wondered if she had made an unreasonable demand, as if he didn't want to own up to a past.

Dieter went to buy drinks. Sophia put on her jacket and went out onto the deck to spy for Rhinemaidens, meeting up with a promenading Frau Eckermann. From a bar somewhere inside, they could hear the sounds of the gentle *Nightingale Lullaby* being robustly massacred by the Coralena men.

'Girls become women, but boys . . . boys are always boys,' the Frau sighed.

Sophia took in the riverbank view, pine-covered slopes enveloped in a watery haze, a sliver of yellow beach, two small boats meandering towards a remote pier. Sophia saw herself at the end of the pier, sitting with Rolf, him jumping into the lake, her swimming so hard to keep up, always trying to be his match, always.

'Even in the rain it's a beautiful view.' The Frau squeezed Sophia's hand. 'I'm so pleased you could come along.'

The Frau mentioned the ailing Frau Bruder and her concern that she wasn't well enough to join the trip. 'The biggest frustration is knowing there's nothing we can do. It doesn't feel the same if one of us is missing.'

Sophia looked down at the racing waters. 'Do you think Coralena is with us?'

'Coralena had to give up her swimming days,' the Frau

answered. 'You should ask Dieter. She was one childhood *friend* of his he kept from me. Boys are always boys.'

The Frau enquired if Sophia was still having difficulties with the sofa bed. She also mentioned the new curtains, if they suited. 'We hope you'll stay.'

Dieter approached with drinks and the Frau coolly departed just as Dieter arrived. Sophia was startled.

'What's happened?' Sophia asked him.

'It's nothing. Nothing unusual,' Dieter replied in a resigned tone.

They went for a stroll along the deck. A girl dressed from head to toe in harmonized shades of blues was throwing bread. River gulls swooped around her, squawking their gratitude in an effusive clatter.

'Your mother said you would know if Coralena was travelling with us.'

Dieter looked at Sophia. She couldn't think what she'd said now.

Sophia abandoned trying to engage Dieter and returned to the river gulls. She was upset. The birds were enveloping the little blue girl in a flurry of white. Sophia realized how vulnerable she had allowed herself to become, far too quickly for her own good. It all had to go disastrously wrong. Because of how she was already feeling about him. And it was bound to be all her fault, bound to be. That was what was making her scared.

They spent some minutes overseeing the women engrossed in their cards. Sophia was grateful for the diversion. At that precise moment, if she could have swum to a bank, she probably would have. Frau Kuhn was amassing a fortune in small change. Sophia realized that her exaggerated eyes behind her thick glasses were perfect for the game, every hand appearing a winner. Frau Bitzel pleaded for help. Frau Schloss wanted complete quiet while she plotted. Frau Mueller, with apparently the least to lose, had lost and was now a forlorn onlooker. The only one who seemed relaxed was Frau Eckermann, treating the vagaries of each hand with statesmanlike equanimity. She insisted that Dieter stood next to her, and she put her arm around his waist. He whispered advice on her play. Sophia felt witness to some sort of discreet reconciliation.

Towards the end of the trip, Herr Eckermann assembled the group in the ship's lounge, but it was the Frau who provided the address, delivered in a commanding schoolteacherly way. She kept an eye fixed on Sophia and Dieter for most of it, speaking of the different personalities that constituted the Coralena, yet everyone so agreeable because of 'our respect and tolerance of each other'. 'Everyone plays their part.' Her rousing conclusion was on the importance of loyalty and friendship, and how she'd found that 'in abundance from the people I care about the most, my Coralena family.'

Sophia was reminded of the photograph on the Eckermann's sideboard, the one of the Frau as a pouting starlet. There was something truly exceptional and magnificent about her. Frau Bitzel clutched Sophia's hand as if she could only survive the emotion of the moment with her support. The men started singing 'For she's a jolly good fellow', at least most of them did, for Herr Schloss had expended his capacity for celebration and was laid low in a toilet somewhere below.

Sophia's company, largely absent, had been so much appreciated she'd received various invitations to visit. Frau Eckermann wanted her to come for dinner 'very soon' and then talked of Frau Bruder and a surprise birthday party in preparation. 'It will mean so much to her, the poor soul.' It made Sophia suddenly contemplate all the Coralena birthdays, anniversaries and assorted special occasions stretching out ahead of her. 'She's got all her own teeth you know,' the Frau added.

17

Sophia would join them on a Sunday every fortnight. She would arrive for Mass and remain for lunch. Her father had conducted the negotiations. He had wanted her to make her stay weekend long but Sophia stood her ground despite his irritated tone. Whatever she did agree to, she would no longer sleep over.

Dieter offered to take her on his motorbike, which she readily accepted. It was the sort of image of her new city life she was delighted to parade before her former neighbours who, she prayed, would be peering through their suburbia curtains. In contrast to her own necessarily conventional church attire, she had insisted Dieter wore his one leather biker jacket despite the warm weather.

Even with the lift, Sophia was still late, one of her endearing family traits. As Dieter's bike roared up the street, her mother was waiting on the porch. Sophia watched the subtle twisting of her face as the realization dawned that the noise busying towards her was the delivery of her daughter. For a moment, Sophia thought about introductions, then thought better of it. As Dieter drove off, her mother called inside to her father.

'Who was that?' Sophia knew her mother would be aching to know the identity of her chauffeur. Her mother hated any feeling of exclusion. Sophia fancied that she would now be conjuring up all sorts of ideas about her daughter's accelerating waywardness.

'A new friend.'

Her mother took out a comb from her pocket and started tugging at Sophia's hair, often the first stage of churchgoing ritual. Her mother couldn't simply advise her to brush it, or give her the comb. 'It needs to be longer. You mustn't get it cut like that again.' Sophia viewed her dogmatically straight hair as irredeemably bland but had the obvious difficulty in explaining such sentiments to her mother, whose own hair revealed her role as progenitor. Sophia had often considered the impact on their relationship of their physical similarity, how it had been treated as an implication. Indeed, her evident recruitment to the maternal line had been further emphasized by her very name, being as it was that of her mother's own late mother.

As usual her father drove speedily through the streets because they were as usual late. As usual her mother would urge him to slow down in ascending tones, and he would tell her to relax with corresponding levels of assertiveness. From the rear, Sophia silently observed the performance, sinking in to the familiarity of home. In the car park, her mother succeeded in having him remove the 'for sale' sign taped to the car's back window – 'really so undignified'.

Their entrance at the rear of the assembly coincided with the entrance at the front of Father Scholtze leading a procession of altar boys. They quickly found seats as the congregation rose and the organ bellowed its summons to voice.

'O Lord, let our hearts hallelujah sing, and praise be to you, our mighty King.' The mix of voices wrestled with harmonization. Sophia took in the familiar surroundings. The church was laid out in customary simplicity. Rows of pews fanned out from a central marble platform on which the altar table was positioned. The emaciated figure of the crucified Christ floated high above, his gaze as ever purposefully upwards as if unconcerned by such earthly adulation. His alter ego lay in a statue below, resigned to a bloody demise in the arms of his anguished mother, the Blessed Virgin.

Sophia noticed that they were sitting near Herr and Frau Stern, old friends of her parents, who nodded amiably in their direction. This encouraged Sophia to peruse the congregation in search of other recognizable sights. The Lennard family had been old friends of her parents until the 1969 elections, which saw the first ever victory for the Socialist Party. Her father could tolerate Herr Lennard and his views only as the underdog.

Erich Beer was also there in a rare visit accompanying his sister and her new husband. He had once been Rolf's best friend. As children, all three had performed together in a church nativity play. Erich had played Joseph, Rolf a donkey, and Sophia had been one of the Three Wise Men. She remembered the play embarrassingly well because she had resented not actually getting to hold the baby Jesus, and threw a tantrum. So the script was eventually amended to add the swift passing of the doll to each of the Wise Men. She felt sad seeing Erich. He used to be round at the house all the time.

Father Scholtze went to the podium to deliver his homily. Sophia was still finding it difficult to adapt to his absurdly youthful face after so many years of his predecessor, Father Hubner. Sophia had become hopelessly conditioned to consider his grey chiselled features as a more convincing representation of God on earth. She recalled her first experience of confession as a seven-year-old being prepared for Communion. Her mother had tried to explain the nature of sin, and how she must repent to feel better. Sophia couldn't understand. She wasn't ill. At school she started hearing the tales that children adore tormenting themselves with, stories of the ground opening up and the very jaws of hell swallowing the wicked. How she had cried and cried in complete terror at the thought of what God in the guise of Father Hubner might so unjustly do to her.

The bells rang out calling attention to the central drama of the Eucharist. Sophia watched as the priest held up the Communion wafer and intoned, 'Take this, all of you, and eat it: this is my body which will be given up for you.' Moments later, he raised the wine-filled chalice. 'Take this, all of you, and drink from it: this is the cup of my blood of the new and everlasting covenant. It will be shed for you and for all so that sins may be forgiven. Do this in memory of me.'

'Christ has died, Christ is risen, Christ will come again,' the congregation boomed.

Sophia remained in her seat while her parents went forward to receive Communion, to consume the Lord's body and blood, to 'unite with God' as Father Hubner had taught her. She viewed again the church's two contrasting presentations of Christ, the images that had been so central to her childhood devotions, Jesus that she had once walked between – the mysterious deity she had never understood. And she thought about Dieter's comment on his favourite Cathedral painting, about Christ not allowing himself to be a victim.

What about Rolf? Sophia quietly demanded of these twin tortured enigmatic figures – soaring above, dying beside. What about him?

After the service, Sophia was approached by a friend from her childhood, Gerda Hahn. She was with her square-jawed fiancé who, following his introduction, appeared content simply to decorate her side. Sophia amused herself with her recollection of their wedding preparations so enthusiastically divulged by her mother. She wasn't keen to hear a reprise. As with previous encounters, they struggled to motor beyond an exchange of bleak pleasantries. Their relationship had never survived Sophia's move to her new school.

Sophia then watched as her mother conducted her moment of private ritual as she did every week, lighting a candle before a desolate Virgin in memory of her own dead son. Her parents would then hug each other, brought briefly close through the grief that was killing them. And Sophia would be sought out to embrace their chill, and she would fight back her anger.

It was on the journey back from church, as her parents bickered over the sermon's merits as if it was genuinely their topic, that Sophia thought more about Pauline's declaration. It suddenly made perfect sense. Sophia was an onlooker in the proceedings, a bystander. She would no longer categorize herself as a non-practising, or even lapsed Catholic. She was an ex-Catholic, a non-Catholic. It was yet another rite of passage. She was growing. She was free!

In the kitchen, Sophia and her mother were a well-attuned team. Sophia slid easily back into the role of captain's mate as lunch was prepared. She had performed the function for as long as she could remember, to the extent that they had made language between them largely superfluous. Her mother would look in a certain direction, or nod in a particular way, and Sophia would instantly know what was required of her.

Returning to her mother's kitchen reminded Sophia of her extraordinary passion for neatness and order. Drawers, shelving, fridge, larder – all space carefully assigned, labels deployed lest implausibly she forget. The kitchen was her mother's sanctuary where she had constructed the soft padding of a predictable environment. Her father didn't have one. That was why he liked going out. And Sophia? Sophia was too young. She wanted to bring Rolf back.

At lunch, her father spoke of the regional conference he had just attended and the depressing speculation that Germany's post-war economic boom was drawing to a close. It was the first time that the steel mills had ever considered laying off workers and the Union was preparing for a showdown. Her father was unambiguous in apportioning blame. He spat out the word *socialists* like it was poison, focusing his disgust on 'the Swede', his most cherished term for Chancellor Brandt, pointing up his choice of exile during the war. Sophia pictured her father meeting Dieter and his friends.

Sophia ate slowly and self-consciously, recognizing in her parents' overly relaxed manner that she was being studiously monitored. She did finish most of the cabbage soup and consumed more of the salad than the schnitzel, having successfully engineered the potatoes onto her father's plate.

Her mother wanted to hear about the Altstadt in the context of Sophia 'making new friends', a reference to her mode of transport that morning. Sophia spoke about the Coralena river trip and the multiple offers of hospitality from her neighbours. She added Frau Eckermann's wish to meet them both.

'I'm pleased you spoke with Gerda in church,' her mother added, as if the exchange, such as it was, had been accomplished through her will. They *spoke* and said nothing. Sophia considered the simple notions of parents, reassuring herself that there would come a day when she would reveal to her mother the exact choice of words Gerda had once used to describe Rolf, and Sophia would be finally excused that particular comparison. Sophia resolved to move the conversation on by disclosing the incident that was still causing her the deepest apprehension.

She had attempted to put it out of her mind but the more she had tried, the more her anxiety had grown.

Her mother was dismissive. Sophia must have merely forgotten that she'd been doodling in her diary. Her father at first came up with a joke, the *RAGE* note being the sentiment of an understandably disappointed burglar, but he soon grew more engaged by the puzzle. Having discounted the presence of anyone else in the room, he came to a bizarre yet, for him, the only feasible conclusion.

'You got up in the night and wrote the word yourself,' he dramatically proposed. 'Some sort of sleepwalking.'

Her mother produced her distinctive scoffing laugh. 'What! So she'd remember in the morning?'

Sophia shared her scepticism. She did however try to recall any similar incidents from the past, with the only nightly sojourns she could bring to mind being the occasional childhood expeditions into Rolf's room, conducted with full consciousness.

'Was it in your handwriting?'

Sophia wasn't sure.

'Are you feeling angry?' her father casually enquired.

What a question! Sophia wouldn't take it seriously.

Her mother seized on the opportunity provided by the conversation to talk up the Coralena in all its apparent weirdness. Sophia asked her if she considered the building haunted, essentially to expose what her mother was proposing, but the idea had crossed her mind more than once. At one mad moment, she had even accused Monika of the deed.

After the meal, Sophia went upstairs to collect some more things from her bedroom. It was her first trip back since the move and she reflected on how civil her parents had proved. She wondered how they were with each other, but didn't want to dwell on it.

She passed Rolf's old room and considered entering. Since she'd left home it was no longer a daily sight, but she resisted knowing it would still be wrong.

Her bedroom was eerily neat having been carefully tidied by her mother. Sophia lay on the bed for a while imbibing the surroundings that had been until so recently her most intimate. Restored to the walls were a series of pony prints that Sophia had pleaded for at eleven and ruthlessly discarded somewhere in her teens. Laid out in an orderly row on the dresser were all her old paraphernalia – hand mirror, make-up box, hairbrush. Sophia thought about Rolf's room next door, its similar trim clean finish, and she suddenly froze.

A familiar noise rose up outside her room and Sophia quickly got to her feet. She gazed out of the window, onto the rear of the house. Her father was ensconced in the garden, tending to his beloved plants, now being pared back and readied for winter.

PART 2

AUTUMN 1971

1

Sophia was convinced Monika was upset with her for sleeping in late on a workday. Indeed, Sophia wondered whether, now that she had been able to supply her with a flowing brunette wig, Monika was getting above herself.

From her bed she faithfully explained that she had been given permission to take the day off to work on the seventieth anniversary proposal. At this stage, all she needed were illustrative images and contexts on a period theme. Her day would largely consist of a return to the Altstadt's antique shops to acquaint herself with original materials. Margaret was asking for an outline but she also knew Margaret's expectations of thoroughness. 'A window display is like a painting and, just like in a painting, *our* canvass has to be completely filled with paint.' Another enduring Margaret-ism.

Sophia got out of bed and instantly regretted her failure to reset the heating timer. Being more exposed to the elements on Coralena's uppermost floor, autumn's march was being too keenly followed. Sophia mused that she had discovered the explanation for Monika's mood.

Sophia was fairly certain where Berger Allee was located

although, with her poor sense of direction, overconfidence was her frequent downfall. As she walked away from the Coralena, the rain upped its tempo, making her gamble more poignant. She eventually found the street sufficiently to the right of where she had anticipated it to be to provide her with two excursions around Marienplatz. She was soon shaking out her umbrella in the first antique shop of the parade.

If the store had assistants, they didn't appear available to give assistance. Sophia was anyway content to meander on her own. A face popped into view as soon as she started picking up items but she wasn't challenged. It was only when she began sketching that a saleswoman approached, conveying a finely honed bonhomie that startlingly evaporated when she realized Sophia wasn't paying custom.

The next shop was a welcome contrast. A refined if somewhat dusty man of late middle age seemed pleased that he might be of service to a store of Bonhoffs' standing and he gave Sophia the run of the place while he followed horseracing on the radio. It proved to be an Aladdin's cave of bric-a-brac and Sophia imagined herself as a deep-sea diver as she explored its nooks and crannies, digging out odd pieces of furniture and porcelain, glassware and art. Whatever appealed had its form added to her growing compilation of period drawings.

The Evergreen Emporium, with its unique specialization in antique clothing, was a shop Sophia fondly remembered from her research for the art college fashion project. The elderly owner enthusiastically advanced from the store's rear, which Sophia mistook for recognition. Certainly Sophia recalled her distinctive rotund appearance and mass of greying black hair.

'I was working on a college project and you helped me pick out clothing.'

The woman was obviously willing to reciprocate the recollection but simply lacked the capacity. 'I get so many people,' she apologized. 'And my memory . . .'

Sophia introduced herself and explained the nature of her visit – this latest project.

'I'm Frau Mayer, but please call me Edith. I find I sell more when people do that.'

Frau Mayer was wearing a bright purple blouse and long flowing Gypsy dress. Sophia pondered whether this was her usual appearance or an act of promotion.

Frau Mayer explained the system of clothing along the shop rails, in that there wasn't any particular one, requiring Sophia to conduct a broad sweep. Another customer came in and the Frau left Sophia to her mission, sifting through a tumult of garments that she was certain could clothe Kussel.

When the customer left, Frau Mayer re-engaged, pressing Sophia to explain her work at Bonhoffs in more detail. In so doing, she also began helping Sophia haul back the clothing on the rails, and was soon making her own selections for Sophia to consider. 'You want period clothing? Well, I've seen more of the period than you, unfortunately.'

The counter began to fill with an impressive array of fashions, a 1920s black evening gown – 'Chanel,' Frau Mayer commented reverentially – a gentleman's tailcoat, a spectacular silk wedding dress, a two-piece bathing costume to which the Frau added a bright pink cap. Layer upon layer of discoveries that Sophia began sketching while Frau Mayer rummaged on.

Sophia enquired about accessories and the magician was soon producing ostrich feathers, diamante tiaras, bead necklaces, sequined bags, even a monogrammed pocket handkerchief – 'an old boyfriend!' The shop was now completely given over to her quest, with Sophia drowning at its centre.

Frau Mayer insisted on a pause to the proceedings. 'I want you to do something for me. I want you to try something on.'

Sophia was initially reluctant. 'I don't really wear dresses.' She listened to her own feebleness, and the Frau was persistent. Sophia certainly didn't want to offend the woman who was being so overwhelmingly helpful.

The Frau flung before her a large exotic corset. 'A joke. Just a joke!' she exclaimed in response to Sophia's wide-jawed expression.

The Frau went through to the back of the shop and returned with a gleaming slender red satin dress, which she said was from the 1930s. The Frau spun it to reveal a daring V-neck back.

'Try it on. It'll look great on you. You've got that flapper shape, which if you ask me is no shape at all.'

While Sophia changed, she heard the 1930s melody 'Dreaming in Winter' strike up from what she saw when she re-emerged was an old gramophone Frau Mayer had wound into action for the impromptu fashion show.

The Frau gasped with delight, heightening Sophia's

discomfort as she stepped forward, rather overdressed for the setting and distinctly uncertain as to how far the V-neck plunge plunged. The Frau placed pearls around Sophia's neck and a lace stole. She then turned her to face the full-length mirror.

'You're the first person I've managed to get into that dress. And just look at you! Welcome to time travel.' The Frau beamed.

Sophia twirled in front of the mirror doing her best catwalk imitation, her movement unconsciously in time with the chirping rhythm of the music. The sensation of wearing such a tight-fitting outfit made her feel as if she was indeed being literally embraced by the past. Sophia was astounded by the transformation. She looked like nobody she knew. She looked like a woman.

'Show you in that dress to any man and he'll never let you out of his sight.'

Sophia laughed. 'Will he have to be in his seventies?!'

While Sophia changed back, Frau Mayer put on a kettle and dealt with the intrusion of another customer looking for lacy underwear. 'We get those types as well.'

Over coffee, Sophia talked of her recent move to the area and when she made reference to the Coralena the Frau's mouth gasped open. 'My best friend lived in the Coralena! That was before the war. I see Frau Eckermann on the street sometimes, with her son.'

The Frau herself had lived in the Altstadt since her twenties. 'Except for the war,' she added matter-of-factly, as if there was an assumed 'of course'.

Sophia finished up her drawings and warmly thanked Frau Mayer for her generous assistance.

'Maybe you'll even want the dress,' the Frau replied with a naughty twinkle.

Sophia returned to the Rheingasse delighted with the success of her Altstadt outing. She decided to take advantage of a break in the drizzle to add one final drawing to her collection of period looks. She stood across from the Coralena and quickly sketched its striking form. As she worked on the detail of the façade, she realized that the tear stain feature down the wall curiously began from under one of her very own second-floor windows.

Her last touches were left for her most enigmatic neighbour, Coralena herself above the doorway. She moved closer, staring hard at the face like any true artist dedicated to revealing the essence of her subject. Coralena was a striking young maiden, wispy curls, thin round face, straight straight nose. A seriousness of purpose was conveyed through the mouth which was simply a construct of three almost parallel lines. The eyes were marked by a series of light grooves which, as well as giving them an unusual prominence, made them appear incongruously old.

Sophia heard her name being suddenly hailed and turned to witness Frau Eckermann struggling up the Rheingasse laden with supplies.

'Good timing, my dear. Could you please get the door,' the Frau gasped.

Sophia took several bags and also opened the doors to her flat and her kitchen. The Frau talked about how a beggar had just accosted her, and how the neighbourhood had become so run down and 'positively shabby'. 'No one takes any pride in where they live any more. When we first moved into the Altstadt, it was maintained so beautifully.'

The Frau laid out the fulsome shopping on her kitchen table and insisted that Sophia accept a reward of refreshment. The Frau left Sophia sitting on kettle watch while she distributed purchases to other rooms. By the telephone, Sophia noticed the same Sisterhood of the Immaculate Virgin charity box as her mother, with its bundle of little yellow cross pins readied to honour passing philanthropic trade.

When the Frau returned, Sophia, aware of the Frau moving behind suddenly felt the sensation of her hair being lightly held.

'You've got such fine hair,' the Frau said. Her touch changed to long sweeping strokes with her fingers.

'I've never liked it.' Sophia was appreciating the relaxing tingle brought on by the Frau's caress. It reminded her of her mother's when she settled her down for bed as a child.

'I wonder what it would have been like. To bring up a girl instead of a boy. I always wanted one.'

'Why didn't you?' Sophia asked, then regretted asking, fearing intrusiveness.

'You have to accept what you're given in life.' The Frau sounded oddly contemplative. 'I'm sure girls are so much easier than boys. You've been getting to know Dieter, haven't you?'

Sophia was suddenly jolted from her daze, feeling an immediate onrush of embarrassment. She wished she could just see the Frau's face, read it.

'He's been very helpful,' Sophia anxiously replied.

The Frau continued to stroke her hair but the sensation now felt awkward, inappropriate.

'Yes. He's a good boy. But be careful. He's not all he seems. Don't let yourself get involved with him and his nonsense. I know him too well. Remember, I'm his mother.'

Sophia was taken aback. She tried turning in the chair but she still couldn't catch sight of the Frau's expression.

'The Altstadt's different in the autumn, you'll see. It's the river. It all comes in from the river. You're such a thin thing. There's not a lot there, is there. You've got to start dressing properly for it, my dear.'

2

As soon as Sophia had returned from her parents, she had sought out the *RAGE* diary entry. Before she had even started writing, she knew the answer. That was part of the shock of it at the time, but she hadn't consciously realized. She filled the sheet with lines and lines of *RAGE*, all perfect copies of the mysterious first that headed the page.

In desperation, Sophia had turned to Monika, the only witness to whatever this bizarre occurrence had been, but she remained committed to her infuriating inscrutability.

Dieter was equally perplexed by the note, and equally dubious about her father's sleepwalking proposition. But he was fascinated by the conundrum. He took the approach of lawyer-cum-detective. He asked a flurry of questions that had positioning as their theme. How had Sophia woken, had anything else in the room been altered, what were the whereabouts of the diary the day before? This didn't prove fruitful and his determined curiosity was making Sophia regret she had confided in him.

Rage was the driving conviction behind Sophia's second Writers Night event, her first *exhibition*, held on a cool Saturday evening. Dieter had told her that the prison release of the acquitted war criminal Krombach was being delayed, and the 'fascist' National Freedom Party was threatening a protest rally in Kussel. The Nazi past of Judge Eggert had been exposed. Writers Night was joining a nationwide campaign for justice – and punishment. What began as explanation rapidly turned to lecture. Dieter had evidently committed himself to Sophia's enlightenment. She wasn't grateful.

There were around twenty-five people mustered outside the bruised exterior of the Central Courthouse, all dressed in similar striped prison garb. The clothing had apparently had its first outing on some sort of student anti-Carnival float and, even with the belt, Sophia was still struggling to keep the ill-fitting garments on her body.

Dieter's flatmate, the cowboy-hatted Alex, was very much in charge confounding the theory that the permanently stoned were made meek. He orchestrated the preparations like a fox harrowing sheep, barking orders, flailing his arms about as he went as if constrained by language.

Having languished on the sidelines, Sophia was delighted

finally to be given her own task that even exploited her artistic skills. It also meant she could escape the suspicious glances of her co-conspirators patently uncertain of the pedigree of this innocent in their midst. She soon found herself squatting on the pavement with a fellow convict drawing the one bold word *LIES* with coloured crayon onto large pieces of card. Dieter had deserted her long ago, and she eventually witnessed his reappearance straining behind a large metallic barrel being bounced up the Courthouse steps.

Sophia recognized some of the participants from the Writers Night evening in the pub. The Prussian, his face still half submerged by his luxuriant beard, was affixing yellow stars to costumes. His presence reminded Sophia of the mysterious kefia-wrapped figure that had been his neighbour. She examined the faces around her to determine if this character might on this occasion have deigned to surface, but no one appeared to possess his strange flitting eyes.

The group eventually assembled in one long row at the bottom of the Courthouse steps with Sophia between Dieter and a girl who looked barely eligible for studenthood. Sophia took comfort from her display of colourful bangles that so effectively defied the grim attire. The Prussian went along the line adding the finishing touch of interlinking mock chains. Banners were now unfurled. One in dripping red paint proclaimed, 'The Dead Cry Out For Justice!' Someone held aloft a sign with the number of Krombach's victims presented as the odds of convicting a Nazi in a West German court – 90,000 to 1.

'Killer Krombach', 'Traitor Brandt', 'Nazi Judges in a Nazi

Germany'. From the highest Courthouse stair, Alex led the concentration camp in rhythmic chanting set to a fierce drumbeat. It was fortunately of such simplicity that Sophia was easily able to partake, although her voice felt meagre in the swell of enveloping passions. Fists were raised in sync with the throb of sound. Some of the group began handing out leaflets to bemused passers-by. A small crowd of onlookers settled across the street and sporadic shouts could be heard.

When the first of the media arrived, Alex led the group in a repetition of the word that was the event's thematic core, delivered in punching mantra style, 'Lies! Lies! Lies! Lies!' Against this driving tumult, the barrel was stuffed with papers and set alight. Dieter turned to Sophia with an expression of relish that reminded her of a child anticipating Christmas. Alex picked up a coloured *LIES* card and held it aloft.

'There are no Nazis in the Judiciary!' he declaimed.

'Lies!' was screamed in unanimous response. The drum thundered its own concurrence.

'There are no Nazis in Big Business!'

'Lies!'

'There are no Nazis in Government!'

'Lies!'

Alex paused and a drum roll built to theatrical climax. He then ceremoniously fed the card to the flames to the accompaniment of an enormous cheer.

The prisoners now marched round the smouldering vessel in a slow-beating procession. Louder catcalling rumbled in from across the street. Sophia looked up at Alex, catching his stare, which was unashamedly, disconcertingly sustained. She wondered if this was some sort of loyalty test. Maybe he could already detect what Sophia felt. That it was all meaningless pantomime. She was the rogue performer. Would Sophia ever be in a position to reveal to Dieter her darkest thoughts, that she was amongst a merry band of egotists. She had turned up because Dieter had asked that she did, and, yes, it had felt like a test.

Sophia's biggest fear was that someone would pass whom she would recognize, and be recognized by. This sweetly changed when the first contingent of police arrived. The bonfire was stoked and a further colourful *LIES* card readied for sacrifice.

'There is freedom of speech in Germany!' Alex bellowed.

'Lies!'

'There is justice in Germany!'

'Lies!'

'There is democracy in Germany!'

'Lies!'

Another set of amens were concluded to the evident satisfaction of the preacher, and another of Sophia's *LIES* was consigned to the flames to general applause.

The police looked on without interfering, until their numbers grew. A group of them then casually climbed the steps and began engaging with Alex, soon becoming the focus of more aggressive chanting. 'Fascist scum – Out! Out! Out!' The drum banged on, upping its tempo, matching the shifting mood. Pig sounds were followed by jeering anti-capitalist and anti Vietnam war slogans, confirming the police's status as the eponymous

Enemy. Dieter was to the fore in the barracking, venting an anger punctuated by expletives that Sophia found excessive and disturbing. She had performed enough. Some in the crowd across the street were making Nazi salutes. The girl beside Sophia launched into a hysterical diatribe directed at a stone-faced policeman inches from her face. Shouts in support of the Red Revolutionary Front were followed by someone yelling out the name of the abducted Frank Eggert, which was taken up more generally as a more cruelly effective taunt. That's when the scuffles broke out. Someone started jostling Sophia from behind. More police moved in with batons raised. Cameras began flashing furiously. Sophia was now very nervous. She couldn't believe what she had allowed herself to be talked into. And she was furious, with Dieter firmly her target. He was clinging tightly to her, and she suddenly caught sight of his face, the utter panic it revealed. The image both shocked and sobered her. Instinctively, she held him close, as if trying to shield him from the fray. The Prussian was attempting to calm the situation and, just as it looked as if pandemonium was about to erupt, Alex's voice could be heard above the noise calling on the group to disperse. The exhibition had concluded.

The later gathering in the Barbarossa bar was celebratory. Dieter had apparently forgotten his earlier moment of distress and talked enthusiastically of the event's success and Alex's consummate skills of manipulation. 'It's all a game with the media.' Sophia had felt from the beginning that it was all a game. She couldn't conceive what had been achieved for the glorious cause.

'But how are you feeling?' Sophia asked. Dieter didn't appear to understand.

3

Sophia began thinking more deeply about Dieter's politics when he took her to his Monday night jive club. It was the sheer incongruity of the two pastimes.

The fact that Dieter and his friends were on the Left didn't fundamentally bother Sophia. The art college had become as political as any other campus in the late 1960s and, while finding it all supremely tiresome herself, Sophia understood that Left was as far Right as any self-respecting student activist could be. But what she objected to was the way Dieter assumed her lack of interest was purely a case of an ignorance that he could quickly cure. And there was something else that disturbed her even more. A nationwide hunt was under way to find Frank Eggert. It was filling the media every day. The most recent speculation was that the army would be mobilized. What was worrying her was that Eggert was part of Writers Night discourse.

In a triumphant manner that Sophia, true to her evident condition, decidedly failed to grasp, Dieter had presented her with the local newspaper article portraying the exhibition as something approaching a mass riot. Sophia was at least relieved not to have made the photograph, a pose of contorted heads during the brief moments of altercation with the police. Sophia had

drawn Dieter's attention to the adjoining article on the escalating search for Eggert.

'Don't believe everything you read in the papers,' was his
maddening response.

Dieter had been threatening for some time to take Sophia to one
of his jive sessions and, despite initial resistance, she had
relented assuming this to be one of his *safer* pastimes. He then
announced that she was required to forgo her beloved jeans for
a dress. Sophia was onto her next costume affair with Dieter.

He picked her up from the Coralena, once again insisting
that they meet outside on the Rheingasse, much to her irritation.
Only Coralena herself was seemingly permitted to witness their
rendezvous. The club was situated on a large riverboat moored
off the Altstadt, marked out by garish lights. It was close to
where Dieter lived, hence sparking his original interest quickly
turning to addiction.

When they arrived, a mix of people were already making
their way down the illuminated gangplank. Some were dressed
in distinctive 1950s clothing – emphatically feminine women in
flared party dresses and white socks, men in slim suits and
slicked-back hair. Sophia stared into the black Rhine waters
swirling below as they shuffled downwards. From inside, blasts
of rock and roll music made their raucous greeting.

Dieter explained to Sophia the routine of the Monday night
class – the first hour would be devoted to beginners' steps, the
second was for the more advanced, when she would sit out,
and the evening would conclude with 'open dancing'. Sophia

marvelled at the way Dieter talked the terminology of the dance club regular. She was entering another of his peculiar worlds, with a whole new set of codes and personalities to endure.

Women and men were separated into facing rows and Dieter and Sophia duly squared up. Sophia perused the eager faces surrounding her. From the flirtatious glances, she knew many had come for motives far removed from developing dexterity on the dance floor. A pair of teachers stood on a stage and proceeded to take the group through a number of basic jive steps. It began with 'the Crossover' move, which was a fairly simple switching places procedure, effected with a twirl. Dieter moved Sophia through it expertly. The step was repeated several times before the men were required to move down a partner, placing Sophia opposite a nervous weedy man who bowed politely while taking her hand for the next move ominously called 'the Lady's Drop' for reasons Sophia was now obliged to discover. This process continued until several steps had been learnt with several men of varying abilities and body odour.

Sophia endeavoured to monitor Dieter's progress as he headed down the line. He seemed to be enjoying himself with his partners, demonstrating a mastery of basic steps he had clearly long ago absorbed. Soon, driving music struck up, synchronized to a machine spraying coloured lighting, and the couplings were made to perform the acquired steps repeatedly and in sequence. Sophia's height proved awkward for her diminutive final partner making her feel at moments that they were wrestling more than dancing, but they struggled valiantly on until eventual reprieve with the music's end.

Sophia thanked her partner – for what she couldn't think. As she turned towards the bar area, she saw that Dieter was already ensconced with seat and drink in a way that suggested he'd been there for some time. She wondered how long he'd been staring at her.

'Did you enjoy that?'

'Yes, it was fun.' Sophia tried to disguise insincerity with breathlessness.

'Takes a while to get the hang of it. There's a system.'

Dieter got to his feet and took Sophia by the hand. Extending his arm above her, he spun her around, then leant her back gently in his arms.

'Romantic, huh?'

Sophia giggled while trying to restore her balance. 'You're a complete mystery!'

'And you're a puzzle!' he replied with a swiftness that suggested it was the opinion he had just been mulling over. 'You know the difference between a puzzle and a mystery? Puzzles are always solved.'

'That's not fair!' Sophia protested. 'I'm changing you to a complete puzzle.'

Teacher announced the start of the advanced class and Dieter, the conscientious pupil, sauntered off. Sophia lit up a cigarette while watching him go through the more intricate dance steps with effortless poise. It was obvious that his partners delighted in him. They smiled and laughed. He could be with any of them, Sophia mused. Did he really want to be with her? She followed him through his manoeuvring of twists and twirls. The idea of

Sophia routinely turning up at such a place was as conceivable as her joining Alex's next exhibition. She and Dieter were so completely different. Yet why did she sense this incredible feeling between them. Lust! she heard Pauline boom in her head. Sophia inspected the rouge-lipped women on lustful display along the row. Maybe she should let her hair grow longer again. She quickly concluded that what she needed most of all was a cooling walk!

She managed to find an exit onto the deck. A fresh river wind whipped around her. Sophia looked out across the expanse of water; a cloth of tranquil black except for reflections of coloured light and the low hum of music emanating from behind her, an intrusion of which she was self-consciously apart.

Sophia thought of the legend of the Rhinemaidens, longing for victims to fall into their watery laps. She reflected on how they might regard the club booming forth above them, whether they viewed it as an opportunity, quietly joining the queue, luring unsuspecting prey from the dance floor. From the predatory appearances of some of the women, this felt highly credible.

Sophia walked up the deck and came to a window through which she could once again survey the dancing. Against the muted sounds, the scene of locked couples gyrating through a range of bizarre postures seemed abruptly ridiculous. There was also something disquietingly manic in its energy. At first she couldn't locate Dieter, but then managed to spy him at the far end spinning one of the white-socked women, her dress fanning out luxuriously around her. Sophia then looked up to behind the boat, shoreside, at the outline of triangle-topped tenements with the Cathedral beyond, a striking silhouette perforating the night sky. As her eyes picked up the flicker of reds and oranges from the window, she suddenly saw an incredible image of the city in flames, a vision of crumbling buildings, searing heat and desperate desperate cries. For an instant, it was as if she could have seen it all.

The voice of Dieter brought her back. He was behind her complaining about the cold. The evening's programme had reached the open stage and he was keen to show off to her his prowess, now fully unfettered.

Dieter escorted Sophia onto the dance floor. He firmly gripped her hand asserting his role as lead, and tensed his body. In time with the music's lively beat, he began by forcefully pulling her to him, their bodies immediately close, his hand on the small of her back, scathing blue eyes locked on hers. Dieter had a demeanour of absolute seriousness that Sophia quickly adopted. He spun her, then pulled her to him, again, and again. Each time she was made to press hard against his body, each time they lingered in a tight embrace, his hands on her waist, then dropping to her hips in a sensual glide. He extended their arms and they turned together. The music's pace was now quickening. She just knew that all eyes were on them. They were moving with an ease and grace that was exhilarating. Dieter was saying something. He was now behind her, his hands on her hips, making her swivel in sync with his body and the music's compulsive rhythm. He whispered it again and this time she heard him. 'Who are you?' he was saying. 'Who are you?' They were whirling and she was feeling giddy. He was kissing her and they were spinning, around and around.

Dieter walked Sophia back to the Coralena. She told him about the contraception.

Sophia wasn't allowed to have visitors after midnight. She broke the rule.

4

Sophia woke first. The heating was working well, which she put down to its honouring a special occasion. She got out of bed and poured herself a glass of water. Her legs were sore from the dancing and she stretched them, holding onto Monika for balance. She looked towards the bed and experienced a twinge of angst as she realized what was ahead – an unprecedented morning encounter with Dieter, first thing, the time she considered her most bloated.

Sophia came back to the bed and knelt in front of the resting Dieter. She admired the perfect symmetry of his face. Everything so neatly aligned, his oval eyelids, slim nose, the light groove dividing his chin. It was a perfect face. She wondered if she would ever feel secure with him, certain that he wouldn't leave.

Asleep, he looked even more like a little boy. She had slept with a boy. She delicately touched his hair, careful not to disturb him. She wanted hair like his, deep natural curls set like waves across his forehead, down one cheek. It had been a gentle, loving night. And it had been more than that. She considered why they hadn't reached this moment earlier. It felt so *essential*.

She went to the window. The sun had commandeered a cloudless sky. She tried unsuccessfully to locate the direction of the dance club. And then she turned.

'Wake up! Wake up!' Sophia shook Dieter who quickly came to and leapt from the bed.

'What is it?!'

Sophia pointed to the table.

Dieter made his way across while still trying to master consciousness. His eyes fixed on the open diary. As he approached, he began to identify the lettering at the top of the page. Sophia cautiously joined him, peering from behind his shoulder.

The single word *ALONE* in the same recognizable hand stared up at them. Sophia was suddenly gripped by numbness.

'Oh shit!' Dieter exclaimed.

He picked up the pen by the diary and wrote *ALONE* underneath the original. His A was too narrow, his L too squinted, his word more a scrawl. He gave the pen to Sophia, gently pressing her. She felt like a serial killer in an identity parade. Sophia's was a perfect copy. She wrote one, then another, and another – *ALONE, ALONE, ALONE.*

They went over all they could remember from the previous night. They even clinically reviewed the stages that led up to their lovemaking. Nothing indicative stood out. Sophia had no recollection of awaking, nor could Dieter recall any disturbance.

Dieter was sliding further into investigative mode with more questions that Sophia was starting to resent. He wanted her to focus on any similarities between this manifestation and the first. Sophia began to wonder if he thought she was hiding something, and there was something else in his behaviour, as if he was wary of her.

'Maybe this is more a mystery than a puzzle,' Sophia declared trying to draw a close to the process, reminding Dieter of their previous evening's conversation.

He had to leave and they embraced. Sophia tried to catch his eye in a desperate act of retrieval, to convey something of her feelings after their special night together, but the diary incident had cruelly moved them on. Dieter left, and the abruptness stung, exacerbated by his sudden reappearance at the door. He had met Herr Kuhn coming out of his apartment below which had forced him to switch directions with the covering claim that he had just *arrived* to fix Sophia's bath. He sat awkwardly for some minutes before making his departure a final time.

Sophia was by now in no mood to go to work. She had expected to wake to a moment of renewed intimacy with Dieter. His questioning of her had made her feel like a freak. She was concerned that that was indeed Dieter's conclusion, and he feared being tainted by association.

Pauline found the whole business amusing and blown completely out of proportion. 'Say it is sleepwalking. You walked a few metres to write a word.' She talked of a friend whose mother used to sleepwalk. 'She once ended up in a petrol station!'

'What if it is an expression of how you feel,' Pauline went on. 'Who doesn't get angry or feel lonely? What's the big revelation?'

Sophia wasn't so convinced. There was something deeply

troubling in it all and she was finding it difficult to distinguish the Dieter aspect from the rest. Pauline was also eager to keep a focus on Dieter. She wanted to know *everything* about what she considered the far more important landmark in Sophia's eventful night.

Sophia had been trying to seek out Margaret for most of the morning. She gave up her search when she discovered her location, ensconced with Herr Johannes Voss, the Marketing Director, ostensibly assisting him with Father Christmas interviews.

Their twosome had been the first piece of gossip Sophia was exposed to, confirmed when she had entered the mannequin storage area at an inopportune moment. In many ways they were a perfect match. Both were talented and creative, with a flair for self-presentation. However, Herr Voss's central handicap was the basic material he had to work with. Sophia found him simply the ugliest man she had ever met – small and squat, square-faced and featureless. His tragedy was the way he would cultivate his appearance, always immaculately dressed, meticulously groomed which, for Sophia, simply brought the central problem into greater relief.

The affair diminished Margaret's standing in Sophia's eyes. She had higher expectations of her extraordinary boss. Pauline saw the relationship in more tactical terms. Herr Voss was on the Bonhoffs' board and had most influence over store visuals. Pauline viewed it as a shrewd move.

Sophia did finally corner Margaret after lunch, full of the spirit of Christmas dread. The board had embraced a traditional look for the store and she had just discovered that her trusted reindeer manufacturer had closed down. Margaret was not someone who handled misfortune at all well and Sophia would have retreated if it wasn't for an unusual cheerfulness in the way Margaret presented her difficulties, which Sophia put down to earlier consolation from Father Christmas.

Sophia was awaiting feedback on her anniversary display sketches and Margaret had promised a quick response. Sophia had learnt that several colleagues had been approached to work up their own preliminary ideas and, given her attitude to all matters that demanded faith, she was keen to get the disappointment over with.

Margaret pulled out Sophia's portfolio of drawings and they studied them together, with Sophia trying to mask an itching apprehension. It was *the* prestige project of 1972! Margaret liked the wedding concept, and praised even more the Carnival piece. The bathing scene was the weakest, 'in her view', she added, in a show of rare humbleness that Sophia found deeply unsettling. Margaret then made brief asides on ideas for the complementary contemporary windows. Sophia started to entertain the unthinkable.

It was the overall principle that concerned her at this stage, Margaret concluded on. 'And it works. It has power! Sophia my darling, I'm going to go with it. I'm going with you!'

Sophia waited for her to say it unambiguously a second time before she would allow the decision to register fully. All she wanted to do was jump up and down, which was exactly her routine in a later embrace with Pauline. Sophia was particularly thrilled because, although the original proposal had been put forward more to demonstrate her existence than anything else, as she had developed it, delving into the fashions and styles of the century, so had its merits truly come alive for her. And to have it adopted by the department was a moment of real achievement.

Margaret stressed the importance of the undertaking, being the definitive visual statement on seventy years of Bonhoffs trading. She advised her to conduct research in the City Museum to build the concept, and to work meticulously. Sophia would have to transform her sketches into detailed *mood boards* laying out themes, colours, and textures for each window display, which in turn Margaret could present to the board. She then paused and cocked her head, which Sophia knew was Margaret's way of indicating she was about to be inspirational. Sophia hovered pen over pad – the required response.

'This is about continuity,' Margaret gave a pained expression as if her insights were achieved through great suffering. Sophia dutifully wrote. 'This is not about specific products because the ones we will select, we're not trying to sell. This is liberating. The approach is exclusively about conveying an image. And what is that image? Excellence!' Margaret was pleased with her response. Sophia wondered if she had ever failed to answer her own questions.

'And let me give you another word – energy! Excellence is what the audience should see. Energy is what will draw them in. We must have both.' Sophia highlighted her summary words – *excellence* and *energy*.

'Sophia, I want to raise something else with you, about

confidence.' Sophia felt the word's sharpness in her ear. 'I'm going to make what may seem like an odd request. I have chosen you to do this project because I believe in your talents. I want you to believe in me, because if you believe in me, you'll have to believe in yourself!'

Sophia held herself. She wished she could simply appreciate the gesture, but instead it was the catalyst for all her familiar anguish to come tumbling to the fore. Margaret was only too well aware of her lack of self-assurance. Sophia must have communicated that expertly. The problem was significant enough for her to raise it. Margaret must be uncertain whether Sophia would manage. The project was some sort of test. Perhaps Margaret had also given the go-ahead to other team members in case she failed. Sophia was being provided with this opportunity more as an act of compassion.

Why was it always in her moments of triumph that the demons came to call? Sophia quickly scribbled two more word pairings across her pad – *RAGE* and *ALONE*.

5

Sophia just assumed he'd be there, and he wasn't. She had been so certain of it she hadn't even asked him. She was having dinner with the Eckermanns minus one. Where was Dieter? She longed for the sound of a motorbike.

But the Frau offered no excuse for him, suggesting he had never actually made it onto the invitation list. This was emphasized by the location of the dining table under the window. Herr and Frau Eckermann sat at either end, with Sophia in between, facing her partner, the Altstadt itself, beyond the glass. The positioning made Sophia conjure up the image of a courtroom, with herself in the centre as judge.

'You're so thin, my dear. I don't want your parents thinking we're not looking after you here. They must worry.'

The idea of Frau Eckermann pleasing Sophia's parents had arisen a few times ever since she had revealed that the Frau shared with her mother the calling of the Sisterhood of the Immaculate Virgin. The Frau had cooked a substantial meal and was finding Sophia's reluctance to eat hard to grasp.

'I had such a big lunch,' Sophia lied, trying to control an increasing anxiety.

The Frau still filled her plate – 'Go on!' – and Sophia nibbled and shuffled the fare as best she could.

Service was firmly in the hands of the busying Frau, and she firmly rejected Sophia's offers of help. 'Not at all! You're here as our guest.' Herr Eckermann didn't budge from his place throughout the meal, which came across less Lord of the Manor, more as a mark of enfeeblement. However, when his moustache twitched into action and he spoke, he did so with a surprising authority which Sophia recognized from their previous meetings.

The news of the day was uppermost in the Herr's mind. A letter written by Frank Eggert, in which he pleaded for his life, had been released to the media by his captors. Herr Eckermann was indignant. 'Imagine his family, what they must be going through, and now they have to read this in the newspapers. They're the scum of the earth!'

The Frau was equally appalled. 'How dare they! What do they think they'll achieve? I hope they bring back the death penalty for them.'

'As soon as the Reds get into government, the country falls apart,' Herr Eckermann continued. 'And they're giving Brandt the Nobel Peace Prize!'

Sophia looked to the window and wondered if they'd stopped inviting Dieter. It occurred to her that she must have been sitting in his seat.

The Frau requested lighter conversation with an appealing glance to Sophia. She talked about her Bonhoffs work and her excitement over the anniversary project. 'This country has too many anniversaries!' was the Frau's odd response.

Sophia continued, describing her day of research in the antique stores of the Altstadt. She then remembered a connection to the Eckermanns, how Frau Mayer knew them, 'of the Evergreen Emporium?' But the name didn't register.

The Frau regretted not getting into the city centre as much as she used to, and complained that, unlike Bonhoffs, the shops now changed with such frequency that, by the time you'd become familiar with one, it would close down. 'We have all we need in the Altstadt,' she declared as if they lived in some remote outpost, touching Sophia's hand reassuringly.

When the Frau departed to the kitchen to seek out dessert, Sophia asked Herr Eckermann about his accordion playing. He was grateful for the interest and talked with an unprecedented enthusiasm that only faltered with the Frau's reappearance.

Sophia took her return as an opportunity to excuse herself. Herr Eckermann pointed her in the direction of a corridor with a bathroom at its end. Instead, Sophia discreetly opened the corridor's very first door. Taking in the size of the bed and the nature of the scattered clothing, Sophia quickly retreated and moved across the hall. This next room had a large bureau and some storage boxes along one wall, but it was also unmistakably a boy's bedroom. Sophia jumped onto Dieter's old bed, rolled across it, smelt the sheets. She rummaged through clothing in a cupboard and slipped on a sweater. She opened drawers and searched shelves. It was a noise outside that brought her to a stop. She returned the sweater and cautiously peered from the door. She slid into the corridor, and went back to the table.

The conversation turned to house affairs. Frau Eckermann was getting very concerned about Frau Bruder. She wasn't sure how well Herr Bruder was coping either. 'He's a real soldier, but he's getting on.' She requested that Sophia exercise vigilance. She alluded to a difficulty over lack of information about Frau Jodl's demise but Sophia thought better than to enquire further.

Frau Eckermann was anxious to hear about her dealings with the other neighbours in the building. Sophia talked about her regular encounters with Herr Kuhn at the tram stop. She didn't elaborate that she was learning not to ask how he was, because he was so rarely fine. 'You really must visit our widows. They are so keen to get to know you.' Sophia was only too well aware of Frau Bitzel's never ending quest, a persistence she found completely unnerving.

The Frau raised a problem with a neighbourhood dog and its fondness for defiling the Coralena's doorstep. Any form of fraternization was strictly forbidden. When observed, it must be rudely chased away. She also requested that Sophia ensure she cleared her rubbish earlier for the Thursday collections. That apart, 'everything has been fine'. Sophia amusingly imagined those words written in the Frau's precise hand at the bottom of her Coralena report card.

Dieter's name arose in the most roundabout fashion. Something the Frau said, that Sophia didn't catch, linked him with troublesome leaves and the clearing of drains. There then followed a series of assertions delivered in a peculiarly provocative way. The Frau began talking about Dieter wasting his law training on down and outs, when he should be developing his career in a 'proper law firm'. She then criticized his appearance, how he dressed, even the length of his hair. She mentioned dubious friends, eccentric interests, and a dangerous motorbike. 'It's not been easy for us!' she concluded as if her accumulated evidence was now overwhelming. The Frau's behaviour made Sophia deeply uncomfortable.

For the finale of coffee, the diners decamped to the armchairs with Sophia guided to the one under the supervision of the crucifix above, next to the sideboard with its goldfish, her Coralena motif, and esplanade of family photographs. Sophia again searched out the portrayals of the earlier Dieter models. She noticed that the record appeared to close in early teenhood and she wondered if this was the moment his life slipped beyond the pale. And there was something else she realized. He never appeared with other children. He was either on his own or dangling below parents.

Frau Eckermann directed Sophia's gaze to a certificate at the sideboard's far end, the acknowledgement she had received marking the end of a lengthy teaching career. Sophia considered how the Frau was a perfect example of how people become absorbed by their professions, and it made her surmise that she may yet become a Margaret clone, swathed in outrageous scarves that she would come to make her own.

'Your work must have been very satisfying,' Sophia remarked, supposing that it was the right thing to say, and a good finale. Not having actually visited the bathroom, she was now burning to leave and keenly anticipating her moment.

The Frau asked Sophia about her schooling and became intrigued when Sophia revealed in the course of an otherwise undistinguished reply that she had moved schools. The Frau pressed her and Sophia, aware of her error and trapped by its consequence, explained that she had faced some difficulties. This caused the Frau to lean forward. She had the same inquisitive look as before, when she had been voicing her litany of Dieter's crimes. Sophia just had to leave and this could now be turned to her advantage. There was a time when she had been forbidden to talk about it, and for a long time she couldn't talk about it. But she had made a recent *adult* resolution to confront it directly whenever it came up. And then it could be over with.

'My brother killed himself.'

There. It was done.

*

Sophia had taken to sitting out on a number of occasions by now. She would position herself at the top of the magnificent Coralena stairway, always late at night when she could rely on being undisturbed, and could smoke her cigarettes with impunity.

And so she returned to her spot, her post, in the exotic light, the characteristic musty smells, and the rain patting the skylight above, the noises of the building's residents now settling.

The Coralena was at its most alluring at night. She thought of herself as a Jonah cocooned in the belly of some great mothering beast. It was a moment she could use for reflection, and listening. If Coralena was a spirit, Sophia communed with her there.

RAGE and *ALONE*. Sophia knew she wasn't sleeping well and the curtains provided by Frau Eckermann hadn't had the desired effect. She was also undergoing the sensation of dreaming in ways far more powerful than anything she'd previously experienced. At the precise moment of waking, it was there with an immediacy that would jolt her but, like the air of a burst bubble, the images and their memory instantly disappeared with the kick of consciousness.

She wouldn't have speculated on it – moving home entailed inevitable disruptions – if it hadn't have been for *RAGE* and *ALONE*. She was now reflecting on anything and everything that might offer a rationale. This had never happened before. It was disturbing.

And she was thinking of Rolf. *RAGE* and *ALONE*, brother Rolf. Is that what you felt? You never told us why, Rolf. Do you want to tell me now?

Sophia listened hard to the beat of the rain on the skylight.

Are *RAGE* and *ALONE* how you're feeling now? It wasn't a sin. What you did. You mustn't upset yourself. We miss you so so much.

Do you want to talk to me, Rolf? Or do you want to leave it to our meeting on that heavenly star?

6

Dieter visited Sophia the very next evening. 'A quick visit,' Dieter warned. He was on his way back into work on some urgent legal affair and she didn't hide her disappointment.

Sophia soon established that she was on the receiving end of a condolence call, somewhat belated, she mused.

'You didn't say!'

Sophia wasn't surprised that the story of her brother had been so speedily transmitted. It had after all been revealed in Coralena HQ.

'I'm so sorry.' There was genuine emotion in his voice.

Sophia wrestled Dieter's jacket off him and then went for more clothing but she could tell he wasn't to be persuaded out of his plans. Instead he sat her down on the sofa and started asking questions about Rolf. All she could give him was her mother's summation, that he was a 'sensitive boy'.

'I was too young at the time. And we don't talk about it now.' Sophia paused. 'I so much wanted to be like him. He loved the outdoors. Boys seemed to have much more freedom.

He was just older I guess. I remember I could only go cycling in the neighbourhood if he accompanied me. Of course he hated that. I went through a phase of wanting to copy him. I would watch how he ate at the table and would imitate him exactly, how he held his fork, the way he chewed. I wanted to be his twin! Rolf hated that even more. He got so angry with me once, he made me undress so he could demonstrate how I had the wrong shape to be a boy.'

Dieter put his arms around Sophia and held her.

'I'm sure as a teenager I would have fought with him all the time. Sometimes I wish he'd waited until I was older! I know it sounds . . .'

Sophia noticed that Dieter's blue blue eyes were now filled with sadness. She was regretting the effect of her words and started stroking the side of his face. His hold of her tightened, and then he said softly, 'We both know about death.' The remark instantly sparked thoughts of her parents' relationship, and Sophia got up from the sofa.

'Why didn't your mother invite you to dinner yesterday? Wasn't that weird?' Sophia could hear the unusual pace in her speech.

Dieter leant back on the sofa. 'She's treating you like a neighbour. Anyway, I wouldn't have been able to join you. I had to help out the Schlosses.'

'What! You were in the Coralena last night? Why didn't you visit?'

'Because you were out!' Dieter replied indignantly.

'You could have said hello. And what about after? You could

have stayed over!' Sophia was furious. 'Don't you want to be with me? Or were you worried someone, one of your many *parents*, might catch you!'

Dieter shook his head. 'It was late. I was tired!'

'You don't trust me, do you?' Sophia suddenly announced.

'What are you talking about?' Dieter sat up.

'I don't know. It's something I feel about you.'

Sophia went on to give Dieter a run-down of his mother's criticisms of him. She wanted them to sound as if they were her own, but they were so outlandish she couldn't achieve the effect. He didn't seem concerned. In fact, he seemed surprised Sophia felt it worthy of mention.

'How long do you think I've been hearing this sort of thing?' Dieter said. 'I've had my head filled with their expectations, believe me!' Dieter lit a cigarette. 'I was supposed to be their clone, but something got screwed up in the mix. You can safely ignore whatever you hear about me.'

'What else am I going to hear?'

'That I slept with Frau Bitzel.' Dieter said it with such a dead-pan expression that Sophia couldn't help but choke.

'Unless you hear it from Coralena herself, it's not true!' Dieter smugly added.

Sophia returned to the sofa, and he put his arms around her. They soon had their arms round each other.

'Can I have a photo of you?' Sophia asked.

'Why?'

'So when you're not here I won't miss you so much.'

Dieter asked Sophia to help him off with his sweater.

7

While the Bonhoffs' public basked in the store's autumnal hues, the windows team was being rallied to the cause of that approaching monster – the Christmas season. Herr Voss had brought Margaret together with Bonhoffs' leading buyers to have a final run-through on product positioning. Margaret hated anything that smacked of accountability and viewed the buyers with particular contempt. Sophia was grateful to be excused the brewing drama.

Sophia had to change trams to get to the City Museum located on Kussel's north side. The second tram grew busy with passengers. Sophia gave up her seat to a grateful mother clutching a tiny baby. It appeared just weeks old. With this discreet bond of self-sacrifice, Sophia allowed herself to fix on the little creature unexpectedly before her, becoming quickly mesmerized as it contorted and twitched, its head thrusting forward, mouth gaping, eyes wide open and eager. It was as if all the world was on that tram.

When the seat next to the mother and child became available Sophia took it, and the woman duly offered her the baby. Sophia carefully positioned her hands around the bundle and pulled it to her. Through its puffed clothing, she could feel the baby's incredible warmth. Sophia was embracing a willing live being that only weeks before had been unimaginable. It was so pure, and so vulnerable. And it made her think how impossible it was to live up to the calling of motherhood, to give such a precious thing all that it deserved. She handed the baby back.

Some faded memory of a school outing returned as Sophia skipped up the Museum's steps, past the stone lions in gentle slumber by its entrance. Her research commenced with a diversion. Sophia wanted to emerge into the twentieth century from the appropriate direction of Kussel's past, and she resolved to embark on a quick overall tour beginning from the beginning with *Section A – Rome*.

Sophia was pleased that the Altstadt received due recognition throughout the centuries, the district used to pinpoint the current locations of much of medieval Kussel. As she passed displays on trade routes, coal and herring, tobacco and sugar, Sophia was reminded of Dieter's accomplished commentary on their Altstadt tour. She particularly enjoyed examining the displays of clothing, fascinated by the bizarre contraptions of the evolving high society, and the surprising constancies.

The twentieth-century room had been split rigidly by theme – economics, social and cultural, politics, etc. – and, being the only one so designed, Sophia fleetingly questioned the wisdom. She began with costume, taking out her pad to draw turn-of-the-century clothing casually draped on featureless models. Margaret would be outraged, Sophia mused.

She moved on to other display cases, sketching period photographs that she deemed might help her formulate window themes which conveyed that essential 'energy', ever mindful of Margaret's advice – determined tennis players, a Carnival scene of great revelry, bustling café society, exuberant celebrities.

In the display on Kussel's economy, Sophia felt an immediate pride in acknowledging the Goddesses of Plenty beckoning her from an image of Bonhoffs taken in the 1930s. Sophia realized that this building must have been the pre-war original, which enabled her to confirm that the current structure was indeed an exact replica.

The political section included the rise and fall of Nazism. One display had pictures of mass rallies alongside portraits of anti-Nazi martyrs. However, Sophia's eye was drawn more to an image on the wall behind this section. She was now certain that she had visited the Museum before, because the effect of the enlarged photograph was definitely a re-experience. It was a picture of the city's utter destruction.

There was something awesome in the completeness of the devastation it portrayed, almost beautiful in its horror. The aerial shot was taken on the day the war ended. Street after street, block after block of rubble and ruin from the river to as far as the eye could see. Only one building was still standing, the Cathedral, stark and inspiring, a glorious remnant.

Dieter had asked her on their Altstadt tour whether she believed the Cathedral was saved by God, or by the British. From this photo, Sophia concluded that God had clearly won. She examined the picture closely. From the angle of the shot, the Altstadt was mainly behind the Cathedral but she could just make out indications of other buildings. She couldn't begin to calculate which pile of rubble would have been the original Bonhoffs. Sophia thought how amazing it was that anyone in the city survived. Neither of her parents had been caught in the bombing. Her father was recovering in a military hospital, her mother evacuated to a farm.

She had never considered how the Coralena residents had managed. And she remembered that Frau Jodl had been a refugee from the East. It made her wonder who had lived in her apartment during the war. Evidently someone who had moved out by the end.

The final Museum section dealt with post-war reconstruction and Sophia saw familiar scenes of Kussel's modern city centre in the process of being built, displays on the dynamism of new industry, the reassuring faces of post-war politicians, and a finale on the European Economic Community as the great way forward, as if the whole journey had been one natural progression to this very point.

By the time her tour ended the library section was closing, and Sophia was grateful.

Her growing confidence in her knowledge of the Altstadt streets was such that she felt sufficiently competent to tackle the route to Dieter's on her own. She wanted that photograph of him. She was missing him.

8

Sophia assumed Dieter would be home. So did his fellow communard Bernard. He invited her in to wait. 'Shouldn't be long.' Bernard sat with her for a few minutes then excused himself. 'Help yourself,' he said with the assuredness of a man dedicated to the principles of sharing. He pointed to the kitchen then disappeared behind a bedroom door.

Instead, Sophia visited the formidably stocked bookshelves, which she discovered were mainly filled with heavy academic tomes. Politics, law, society; big grey books of the type that she found so intimidating. There was also history, and some fiction. She scrutinized the names of the authors, longing for just one she might actually have heard of. As an exercise, Sophia decided to select one at random. She ended up with *The Drowning Man* by someone called Manfred Ley.

'Excellent choice,' she heard from somewhere behind her. Sophia's insides churned in recognition of the voice.

Alex was smiling broadly from under his ubiquitous cowboy hat, its feather neatly perked. Beside him stood a woman whom he introduced as the 'fourth musketeer', Marita, the commune member Sophia hadn't so far encountered. She was wearing a trim denim jacket, short black skirt, black tights and long long boots. Her demeanour was one of grudging curiosity. She was smoking a joint, which she offered Sophia. She declined.

'Do you know what that book is about?'

Alex motioned Sophia to sit down. She wondered if she could go straight to Dieter's room, but it seemed too indicative a move, more likely just to provoke Alex. As she reluctantly took a seat on one of the battered armchairs, she prayed for Dieter's swift appearance. At least they were not alone, and Bernard was somewhere in the apartment. Marita lay across the armchair opposite, her long legs dangling over an arm. Alex remained standing.

'The smothering hand of consumerist society.' Alex smiled.

'A good day at Bonhoffs?' He was relishing the moment. He

glanced conspiratorially at Marita while Sophia's face rapidly betrayed her discomfort by burning red.

'The argument he puts forward is that the so-called German economic miracle is merely the power elites buying off the masses with cheap goods to create an illusion of happiness so they can pursue their exploitation. Interesting, don't you think?' He paused for breath. 'That's why the Red Revolutionary Front started burning department stores. Dens of commerce! Remember that? It was to shake people out of their apathy. I mean, in the war the Allies burnt down whole cities to get their point across!' Alex was talking to Sophia but looking more at Marita, who was now giggling.

'Do you think we really need so many things?' Alex continued. 'Take Bonhoffs. A store I happen to know well and, this will surprise you, a place I often go to. All those sections. Things for the feet, things for the face, things for the kitchen, things for the children, things for the car. It must be so carefully worked out. You couldn't just invent somewhere like Bonhoffs, could you?'

Sophia just kept telling herself to stay calm. She was Dieter's girlfriend. How far could he go?

'Do we need all these things?' Alex took off his hat and tossed it to the floor. 'Things!' He started unbuttoning his shirt. Marita put a hand to her face. Sophia couldn't believe what he was doing. His shirt soon joined his hat on the floor. 'Things!' He tugged his vest over his head, baring a thin wiry torso. 'Things!' He then proceeded to unzip his jeans.

Sophia heard them roaring with laughter as she ran out. She

slammed the door with all the force her humiliated state could muster.

Dieter telephoned later that night. He had a court-imposed deadline and had worked late. He wanted to know what had happened. Alex had told him about some joke they had played on her. He then said something about not taking Alex too seriously. Sophia was not in the mood.

9

No, Dieter couldn't turn on the radio because she couldn't concentrate with music. At one point, she even threatened to abandon the project altogether if he didn't keep still on the chair. Dieter retreated to polite conversation.

'What's the difference between a photograph and a drawing?'

Sophia lowered her sketchpad and leant against the window. She was resigning herself to a lengthy process.

'One is an image, the other an interpretation.' Sophia was abruptly pleased with her reply. She had made herself sound unusually authoritative.

'Isn't a photo just as much an interpretation?' Dieter replied. 'It's no more real than a painting.'

'Can't you talk without moving!' Sophia invoked increasing irritation, although in truth it was more a cover for her profound enjoyment of the task. She was combining her two enthusiasms – drawing and its subject.

Sophia had put herself in the position of being able to gaze upon Dieter with unfettered scrutiny. Seeing him struggle to keep still reminded her of how rare it was to capture him so close to rest. He had too many passions in his life. Sophia was now required to ask herself who *was* Dieter when he wasn't disguised by action? What translation might she bring to the portrait about to emerge from the page – *her* face of him that she had been empowered to bring forth? Once again, she felt drawn to his eyes. They defined him more than any other feature – his soulful, searching, restless eyes.

'Is the Snowdrops painting your best?'

'No.'

'So why did you hang it?'

'It gives me the best feelings.'

'Why haven't you hung more stuff on the walls?'

'I hate white walls,' Sophia answered. 'They remind me of a sanatorium.'

'So change them!'

When Sophia ended the session, Dieter rushed to free himself from the chair and the rigid posture he had been forced to maintain due to the twin concerns of the task in hand and the seat's fragility. Sophia also stretched, placing on the table the picture that Dieter was now anxious to view. She was in turn anxious for his reaction, while exuding a perfect air of indifference, which she assumed was the pose of a true artist. He swung round and gave her a big bear hug, lifting her off the ground. 'It's magical!' his verdict.

She wondered what he saw, if he could see it.

Dieter's attention turned to demonstrating again how to change the sofa to a bed and he was soon dragging Sophia onto him. She joined Dieter willingly. For two very different people, this was one common ground that had been effortlessly established. It was through their physical relationship that Sophia felt in closest rapport with Dieter. He became with her someone so needy, as if Sophia was fulfilling a vital purpose that she alone was able to provide. And there was the strange ease of it all, something she'd never encountered before, which sometimes gave Sophia the feeling that their relationship was a form of re-enactment.

She had attempted to explain these sensations to Pauline who had responded with all sorts of foreboding. But Sophia couldn't think like that. Whatever she experienced with Dieter when they made love conveyed a rationale that transcended the ordinariness of boyfriends and girlfriends, of every affair she'd ever had, or ever would. That was magic for her.

Afterwards, Sophia could sense in Dieter a growing restlessness. She noticed that he had stopped looking at her. He then proposed going to a local bar in a way that sounded like an urgent SOS. Dieter seemed lost to a strange anguish, as if he'd conceded something he now wanted to take back. They put on their coats. Dieter smiled coyly, and Sophia tried to relax. He then began hauling Monika to the door until Sophia pulled him off her.

As they reached the bottom of the stairway, they heard a rattling noise from behind the Eckermann door. Sophia sensed

Dieter's whole being suddenly stiffen. Frau Eckermann emerged, her face instantly given over to an expression of complete surprise. She gestured a warm greeting, but exchanged a look with Dieter that could best be described as suggesting they were both acknowledging a large stain down Dieter's front. When Sophia asked him about it afterwards, he replied, 'She thinks I'm taking advantage of you.'

Dieter and Sophia travelled through Altstadt alleyways in the direction of the Cathedral, its blackened red stone fiercely lit against the reigning darkness of an evening sky. A restrained river wind provided gentle escort. Sophia took hold of his hand.

She talked about the photograph she had seen in the City Museum, the 1945 picture of a ravaged city. She asked Dieter about the Coralena residents. How they had managed to survive the devastation. Dieter explained as far as he knew. Who had lived away. Who had hidden in the bomb shelters dug deep in the ground.

'I'm so grateful I wasn't alive then.'

'Do you want to be alive now?' Dieter smirked in reply. The comment incensed her.

He started explaining a case he was taking on linked to an anti-Nazi demonstration outside the prison where the war criminal Krombach was awaiting the end of his incarceration. There had been clashes with National Freedom Party supporters calling for his release and the scene had become bloody. He described the violent response of the police 'in support of the fascists' in such horrific detail that it seemed to border on relish.

'What about Eggert!' Sophia expressed her exasperation. She

had heard all about Krombach. She had heard all about 'the fascists'. Dieter was making sure that she was receiving regular doses of such *education*. 'What about that other crime!' she now wanted to know, the one that was never given any acknowledgement in Dieter's prodigious collection of condemnations.

'The so-called Judge Eggert should rot in hell! His son will be fine,' Dieter responded dismissively.

To illustrate what sounded 'not fine', Sophia brought up his fellow commune member Alex and his apparent enthusiasm for the burning of department stores.

'He's a big talker. You got his apology.' Sophia was not grateful to Dieter for *that* phone call, being forced to listen to oozing insincerity while Sophia went through the time-honoured torment of a fury unspoken. 'It's all a show. That's what he does best.'

Sophia's ballooning frustration finally broke through all her diffidence, and she managed to blurt out the full collection of anxieties over Dieter and his politics. She demanded he explain whatever was the complete story, Writers Night and the rest. What was he really trying to achieve? Why did it make her feel so scared? Sophia didn't know which of them was more taken aback by her strident tone. They were standing by a busy junction next to Cathedral Square, against the halt sign of a red pedestrian signal. People gathered for the crossing were watching them.

'Listen. Basically, what we want is simple – we want equality and justice for all, and we promote this by protest.' He was talking fast. 'We have a socialist government that lost its memory as soon as it got into office. If you want society to change, you have to challenge the status quo, right? You have to force people to think, provoke them, otherwise nothing will happen, everything will just stay the same, right?'

Sophia was trying to evaluate the right of Dieter's rights. He continued. 'People just don't think! Shall I show you the *state* of Germany today?' Suddenly and without warning, he walked straight into the road. Sophia was completely flummoxed. Someone immediately shouted, another grabbed at his shoulder and drew him back. Dieter jerked his arm away and scowled.

'See what I mean! We wait for the green man of the authorities to tell us what we can do. We don't think for ourselves. And look how the people react if you do. That's how they built Auschwitz!'

Everyone was now staring.

'If we let things just carry on as before, if we're silent, aren't we also guilty?'

Dieter took Sophia's hand and, from their pavement spot, started guiding her through several jive steps. He was humming a tune to himself as he made Sophia follow his lead, pulling her under his arm, then swinging and spinning her.

10

Her father's punctuality was a constant source of amazement. It was a disposition that had clearly failed the generational leap.

Sophia was still getting dressed when the buzzer went precisely at eleven. It also meant that Sophia was impertinently unable to help him carry the old television set up the stairs. She left him to urgently needed recovery time.

The television's aerial proved temperamental, and her father's efforts to coax it along forced Sophia into revealing her abduction of his beloved toolbox. Fortunately, the subsequent discussion on the set's positioning seemed to distract him from any thoughts of reacquisition. That the television shouldn't be by the window was a point of consensus, agreed by all except the aerial. It refused to countenance Sophia's preferred corner, where it served up a spiteful blizzard. In the end, its intransigence won out, and Monika was politely escorted sideways to accommodate the new arrival.

Her father wanted to see both the diary words, *RAGE* and its accomplice *ALONE*. Having previously uncovered the identity of the messenger, her father was now in pursuit of the message, if two odd words could be considered as such. Sophia wasn't inclined to encourage him. She aspired to adopt the Pauline 'so what' approach to the mystery, which reflected more the fact that she was still deeply troubled by the occurrence, and was attempting to banish it from her mind. A regular pattern of sleep was continuing to evade her, and the added angst of what waking might bring didn't help. She left him to his detective work and went to put the kettle on.

When Sophia returned with drinks, her father was by the window holding up her drawing of Dieter. He was delighted she had resumed her sketching. She solicited his opinion. He liked it.

He was impressed by its intensity. 'But I hope you didn't have to spend too much time with your sitter!'

'Why?' Sophia enquired, intrigued by the comment.

'Look at him! He's so miserable.' Her father scrunched his face. 'No, it's more . . . heartbroken. Am I right?'

'Yes,' Sophia said. 'You are right.'

'Who broke his heart? I hope it wasn't you.' Her father smiled.

Sophia looked at the drawing. She had recorded a face that was fixed on its viewer. Her scrutiny of Dieter had been reciprocated. 'I don't know,' she answered. 'I really don't know.'

A tap-tapping at the door interrupted them, announcing the presence of that most singular of women. Frau Eckermann entered dressed in distinguished Sunday finery, greeting Herr Krauss like he was a bishop, and expressing a choice selection of prearranged utterances on Sophia's behaviour that would have reassured the most paranoid parent. She included the one failing that Sophia 'doesn't join us for Sunday Mass. It's such a beautiful service,' which, in its exception, perfectly proved the rule. It was a strategic masterstroke. Sophia could once again confirm that performance brought out the very best in the Frau. 'Herr Krauss, in the Coralena Sophia has a group of people who respect and love her dearly. While she is with us, she is with you.' The Frau winked at Sophia as she left, leaving her father flabbergasted in her wake.

The delivery charge for the television was a neighbourhood foray, and Sophia was happy to play the role of Altstadt old-timer. Sightseeing began with their very first steps outside the door with Sophia insisting that her father take in the great vista from the top of the stairway. He remarked that the Coralena reminded him of his childhood home. Sophia recalled its oft-repeated description as that 'stinking tenement'. 'What the parents escape, the children seek out,' her father quoted from somewhere.

As they came out of the Coralena, Frau Kuhn was hurrying in, eyes all at sea behind her thick glasses.

'Have you seen Herr Kuhn? He was supposed to meet me on Hadrianstrasse.'

Frau Kuhn marched up the stairs and Sophia pondered the Herr's fate.

'Shall we wait for the screams?' her father wondered.

An autumnal coolness was asserting its hold, but at least it wasn't raining. Her father made affectionate reference to the weather. Sophia had long come to appreciate that such expressions were proffered in the context of his precious garden. Sophia bade Coralena farewell and took her father's arm. They were heading off and she could once again assume the mantle of 'daddy's girl'.

The weather had confirmed Sophia in her resolve to direct their outing to as many indoor locations as she could quickly bring to mind. The first required little imagination, immediately presenting itself, and they were happy to acquiesce to its summons.

With the tourist season well and truly over, the resultant calm gave the Cathedral an enhanced feeling of sanctity. A mild aroma of incense sweetened the air, the sensuous remnant of earlier services. Visitors huddled in modest clusters and conversed in hushed tones. A group of nuns floated down the nave, as if on cue.

Her father sought out the glittering shrine of the Apostle James whose body was believed to be encased within it. It was more accurately most of his body because the Prince who had brought the relic as booty from the crusades had shared body parts with a chapel in Mainz. It was in reverence of the shrine that the Cathedral was originally built, accommodating the thousands of medieval pilgrims who flocked to the site.

Sophia's thoughts were on Dieter. She pictured him as a naughty child, dressed in his Sunday best, trailing behind Frau and Herr Eckermann, all the while dreaming of escape. She returned to his favourite painting, *The Betrayal of Our Lord*. She examined the face of the Christ figure. One of his disciples had compromised him. He foresaw his own death. Yet he was calm, strong. He knew that ultimately he would triumph. It made her recall the Cathedral in the Museum photograph.

Her father joined Sophia by the painting and she mentioned Dieter. She had already given her parents his name but not much else. She could tell her father more because whatever she revealed on this sort of subject was generally all he wanted to hear, which she suspected was indicative of his struggle to combine his two contradictory notions of daughter and adult.

Her father was impressed that Dieter was a lawyer and she carefully avoided mention of the type of law he practised. The fact that his parents, the very same Eckermanns, were living below, caused her father much amusement. 'Now I know why Frau Eckermann said all those things. You *will* have to behave yourselves!'

'So when will we meet him?' he enquired.

Sophia hadn't considered it.

'You like him?'

'I like him.'

She was in love with him. She had made that announcement to herself a long time ago. Maybe from the very moment they first met, as bizarre as she realized it was. You know when you know, she had once been told by Pauline, who had apparently *known* on numerous occasions. Well, now Sophia knew.

Sophia took her father to Marienplatz. Despite the weather, the cafés and bars still paraded their al fresco tables for the brave of heart, and odd groups, that her father considered were of Eskimo stock, had taken up the challenge.

Sophia reminded her father that he had introduced her to the Altstadt on their Carnival outings. Her mother hated the festivities and refused to take part. She considered the gaiety and boisterousness demeaning. As a child, Sophia herself had found the outrageous masked costumes and atmosphere of manic exuberance quite terrifying. But it didn't stop her wanting to go. She wouldn't have countenanced her father and Rolf going off without her.

Her father reminisced on the infamous occasion when Rolf went missing. They had spent a frantic afternoon battling against the throng of people in hopeless search. A mischievous older teenager had plied him with beer and, when he finally resurfaced by the car, he had lost his centurion helmet and was too drunk to speak.

It was an event Sophia recalled vividly, for the fear that Rolf was lost, but more for the fury of her mother when they finally arrived home. Her father couldn't have forgotten. He was the only one who had mastered that ability to introduce Rolf stories in the most benign of contexts, with such blandness of tone, as if he would confirm his recollection with Rolf himself later. But he wasn't introducing a conversation. He was simply emptying out what had fleetingly entered his head. 'Rolf is dead!' he had once had to tell a little girl who idolized her brother. It was a moment they would always share. She could still remember the precise detail of her father's face, the shape of his reddened eyes, the tremor across his mouth. But most of all, she remembered that stunning guilt-absorbed look, as if he was offering himself as the perpetrator. It was the day that changed everything.

Sophia was shivering with cold and proposed taking her father to the antique shops in Berger Allee. Like every true man of Kussel, he loved any excuse to dress up and they were soon in the Evergreen Emporium with Frau Mayer as effervescent as ever. 'So now I get to meet the father, I'm honoured!'

Sophia showed him examples of period clothing she had selected for her Bonhoffs project work, teasing that, for him, these would be a lot less historic. She then appropriated Frau Mayer's role and cajoled him into trying on a tailcoat. The Frau was impressed to have such a resolute assistant. 'English tailored,' she whispered to Sophia, with an expectation that this would be passed on.

Frau Mayer also dug out a top hat but her father's head proved deliciously too small and it plonked down onto his ears, sending Sophia into great whoops of laughter.

The Frau insisted that Sophia atone through an act of reciprocity, by putting on the red satin dress she was now 'keeping aside' for her. Her father became curious and Sophia felt suitably obligated.

Frau Mayer helped her on with the dress, muttering a critical something about Sophia not wearing enough make-up. Sophia amusingly thought she was hearing Pauline. Once again, the Frau added accessory finishes, and also brushed up Sophia's hair 'to give it some body'. The reaction of her father was something akin to paralysis. Sophia spun in front of him, now more confident about the propriety of the revealing V plunge, parading in her party dress before daddy.

'Didn't I tell you,' Frau Mayer was beaming in the same enthused manner as before. 'Will you look at this lady!'

Sophia turned to the mirror and greeted once more the mysterious implausible woman she had managed to summon from out of nowhere. The transformation was as astonishing as before, with the corroboration of her father's expression.

As Frau Mayer helped Sophia off with the dress, she asked after Frau Eckermann. Sophia gave a fulsome report, including her latest circular in pink in which she all but implied that there was an internal collaborator feeding the stray dog now notorious for its repeated desecration of the Coralena doorstep.

'Who was your friend who lived in the Coralena?' Sophia carefully stepped out the dress using the point of the V as her exit.

'Such a long time ago. Erica Litmann. Before the war.' Frau Mayer was concentrating on carefully gathering up the dress. Sophia slipped on her jeans which the Frau disparagingly described as standard issue of the young. 'Why would boys and girls want to dress the same?' she complained to Sophia's father.

'You're one of the few people to get Sophia willingly into a dress,' her father replied, embellishing with tales of tomboy exploits that confirmed Sophia was ready to leave.

Her father was now hungry, 'so hungry' he was *grudgingly* prepared to treat Sophia to lunch. They made their way back to the eating places of the Marienplatz. As they walked, her father came out with a request. He asked Sophia to be in more regular contact with her mother, and to be 'friendlier'. Sophia's departure had been 'especially difficult' for her and Sophia should show 'sensitivity'. To bolster his case he chose to remind her, though it was Rolf's shadow that loomed large, that her mother had grown up virtually motherless. Sophia considered the disturbing irony, given that she had been made to carry her late grandmother's name.

'One day you'll be a mother,' he concluded.

'No I won't.' Sophia gave an immediate response. That was an easy one, resolved long ago. She would never be a mother because she knew all that it entailed. She wouldn't allow herself to fail children, ever.

But her answer was also an overall response. Sophia could see his disappointment, but all she could think of was the tragedy of their situation, that through her very absence from home, they were still treating her as its panacea. It was what she had feared most. That she would leave, establish herself independently, yet stay the same, that they would all just stay the same. They had to let her go. And no more guilt, please, no more guilt. They could fill the Rhine with it. That's what she would have said, if it wasn't for the fact that she couldn't speak such things to her parents, because she loved them both so much.

They found a café and, while they assessed the menu, her father requested a first beer. He was annoyed with her. Sophia took out a cigarette. After they'd ordered, he began to question her closely on how she was coping on her own. Right from the beginning of her search, her father had indicated his preference that she found lodgings in a house with owners locked into routine supervision. Sophia wondered whether Frau Eckermann's visit had backfired, appearing too obviously a contrivance.

Sophia was soon sizing up her herring salad, but more looking on at her father as he tucked into rubbery liversausage. She marvelled at how he could eat anything that was put in front of him.

'It's started again, hasn't it?' Her father didn't look up until he took another sip of his beer.

Of course, he was wrong. Because it made it sound as if, at some period in time, her so-called 'eating problem' had ended. He should have asked whether it was getting worse. She didn't have that answer because she couldn't remember what getting better was like.

'Don't lie, just tell me.' His tone was even, but she knew how easily that could change.

Sophia was resolved on one thing. If he brought up doctors, or started to raise his voice, she would leave.

11

Sophia had experienced only one other Cleaning Day, as it was defined by the Bonhoffs board – *Shitting Day* by coarser members of staff. Twice a year the management formally toured every department making sure that standards were being met at a consistent level throughout the store. The days running up to Cleaning were filled with discreet panic, each department carefully ensuring latest deliveries were received on time, the stock deployed to best advantage, the shelving and display cabinets neat and shining, the look bright and eager.

Cleaning Day also had implications for the windows team. Each window display would be carefully evaluated which meant that Margaret harried the team to carry out their own pre-inspection scrutiny – dusting down merchandise, refreshing props, straightening any round-shouldered mannequins.

Pauline practically disappeared for a week because of the extensive preparatory work in her Cosmetics section. Sophia learnt that there was far more concern over this particular Cleaning Day than previous ones. Initially, this was explained by its being the last before the launch of the seventieth anniversary campaign. However, word started filtering through the informal intelligence network that Herr Claude Von Scheiben himself was putting in a rare appearance.

Herr Claude Von Scheiben, the current chairman's father, had run Bonhoffs like a military camp until his retirement a few years before. His legacy was still palpable across the store in an assortment of rules, traditions and, most profoundly, a vast collection of recycled anecdotes that, with their epic qualities, had achieved a form of canonization. He was most often referred to in the context of contrast, a wicked means of highlighting the failings of Otto, his hapless son. 'Tales of Otto' were almost as prolific, but had a very different hue.

Amidst the general response to the visit of Von Scheiben senior of awed anticipation, Margaret's iconoclasm could always be relied upon. 'I didn't know him, but I knew about him. And that was enough. I only stayed because he was leaving. Then we got son of Frankenstein!'

On Cleaning Day itself, sightings of Claude Von Scheiben were reported across the entire store, including moments when he was alleged to be on two different floors at the same time, as if he was an all pervading spirit. It was only days later that it was disclosed he'd remained at his holiday villa after all, upsetting his many devotees who blamed his absence on a certain inferiority complex of the son lost in his shoes.

Each department received a formal Cleaning Day marking. The window dressing team came through strongly although one window that had mannequins bound together in elaborate chains was judged to be overly provocative, and another dedicated to Household Goods, while complimented on inventiveness, was criticized for ignoring commercial considerations. Margaret surmised this was a comment from an aggrieved buyer who had demanded the inclusion of Peruvian ceramics that Margaret considered 'dreadfully foul'. 'Over my dead body,' had been her collegial reply. Margaret's overall assessment of the report – 'Nothing to worry about from the philistines.'

There was one small comment that did bother Sophia. A mannequin had been accused of having an inappropriately glum expression. It wasn't clear which one was being referred to and Margaret and Sophia argued over this. Margaret was convinced it was Ingrid and was talking about banishing her to the ends of mannequin storage. She had done this before with Sophia's very own Monika, whom Margaret had felt was far too androgynous to be of any appeal, hence her current employ. Sophia was sure that the culprit was actually Luise, although she was fond of both her and Ingrid, and was reluctant to see any further dismissals. Baffled by Sophia's humanity on the subject, Margaret agreed not to blacklist any mannequins, ending the conversation with a look of amused incredulity.

Word speedily filtered through the news network on how other departments had fared. Most had comfortably passed the process with highest praise going to Furnishings, which was apparently traditional because of the last name of its manager – another Von Scheiben. Next was Menswear, which had outperformed Ladieswear for the third time, causing a flurry of consternation amongst the champions of couture. The fact that the management was exclusively male did not go unmentioned.

Pauline's Cosmetics department was satisfied with its ranking somewhere in the upper middle although, as a sign of the times, comment was passed on the regimented clinical appearance of the staff and whether it would be worth experimenting with a softer image. Pauline revealed how institutionalized she had become from the way she expressed her fondness for the starched white 'nurse' uniforms that she had initially so despised.

The biggest criticisms were levelled at the Food Hall, which had experienced the departure of two managers in less than six months. Questions were raised over general levels of hygiene which, given that the Food Hall supplied the staff canteen, created much alarm and far greater seating choice for weeks afterwards.

With the distractions of Cleaning Day now fully over, the windows team returned to the growing fervour of Christmas planning under Margaret's dizzying orchestration. Each member had their display assignments with the essential task of ensuring a trouble-free execution, turning the *mood boards* prepared for each window into design reality. This required the assembling of materials, contact with prop providers, and ongoing liaison with the relevant departments on that most critical component, the merchandise itself. And then, in that momentous first week in November, drawing everything together in one intensive blitz of activity, bringing the immense storefront to life through the compelling drama of Christmas commerce.

Sophia had to play her part while maintaining the momentum of the anniversary project. Margaret was now pressing her on the latter, while frustratingly giving Sophia so little of her time. Sophia was waiting to pounce on Margaret when the message about visitors came through.

Sophia hurried to the main reception desk. As she

approached, a gloved hand started waving wildly in her direction. Frau Bitzel was the very picture of a Lady at Leisure. Frau
Mueller was seated nearby, staring peacefully heavenwards.

12

The Schlosses had gone for an unrepentant modernist look that
Sophia couldn't help but find alarming in its incongruousness.
She had stepped from the heritage of the Coralena hallway into
a brutal world of glass and plastic, curving shapes and bold
colours.

'I get bored so easily,' Frau Schloss explained as she settled
Sophia at the clean glass dining table. Sophia stared through to
her knees beneath, still struggling to take it all in.

The only legacy of an age made ruthlessly bygone appeared
to be the wallpaper. Not that it couldn't also have passed for
avant-garde. The boldness fitted in perfectly with the overall
design, no doubt securing its pardon, for it was of a similar
swirling, weaving pattern that Sophia had discovered beneath
the paintwork in her own apartment, and at the Eckermanns'. It
was formed of the stylish old Coralena.

Herr Schloss emerged from a back room where he had been
busy, on what neither of them seemed prepared to say. Sophia
felt the room visibly shrink as he bounced towards her, warmly
taking her hand. He then kissed his wife on the cheek with careful orchestration that suggested it was done primarily for
Sophia's benefit. Sophia was pleased to see him looking so

sprightly. Her last recollection of Herr Schloss was when he was being assisted off the boat at the conclusion of the Coralena river outing, having become overly enamoured with the delights of the bar.

During the lunch, Sophia found Herr Schloss's overt and uninhibited passion for food, in such stark contrast to her own restraint, a source of utter fascination. There was clearly no mystery as to how he had acquired his ample size and she couldn't stop herself monitoring his pilgrimage of consumption throughout the meal. It was as if they shared an affinity, the very notion of which made her distinctly nauseous.

Sophia enquired if Dieter had successfully fixed their kitchen partition. They seemed surprised that she was aware of it.

'He's such a good boy!' Frau Schloss said.

'No he's not. He's a rascal,' Herr Schloss countered, his tone sharp and endearing in equal measure.

'Did you know he once tried to burn us all down!' Herr Schloss now laughed, exercising his considerable girth.

'Rubbish! Don't listen to him.' The Frau appeared unamused. 'He's talking about a silly prank many years ago.'

Herr Schloss sported a mischievous smile. Sophia was intrigued.

'You must have known Dieter all his life.'

'We certainly have!' Herr Schloss replied.

'Since he was born. During the war.'

Herr Schloss paused, his look rapidly sobering. 'Yes,' he confirmed.

'It must have been so hard for Frau Eckermann.'

Frau Schloss had heard from Frau Eckermann that Sophia was an artist. She made the comment with a glance to her own obtuse works covering her wall. Sophia wasn't sure if she was expecting an assessment, and promptly explained her more conventional style. 'Maybe you'll do one for us. Shall we give her a commission, Willy?' Herr Schloss chortled, professing not to know anything about art. 'I leave anything to do with taste to my wife.'

Taste but not tasting, Sophia thought.

'But you do play cards!' the Frau was keen to presume. Sophia had heard that the Coralena women played every Thursday evening. 'And into Friday mornings,' Herr Schloss wryly noted. Rotating Coralena venues. 'We shoo the men away,' the Frau gleefully noted. Herr Schloss didn't appear too troubled by the exclusion. He smirked and winked at Sophia. 'I do hope you'll join us,' the Frau continued. 'I hate losing.'

Sophia had already established that Herr Schloss had been a dentist before his retirement and was now informed that the Frau had been a dental nurse, originally his, which provided the context of their first meeting. 'A shared love of teeth.' The Herr made the remark in a tired fashion suggesting it had been a long-standing comic observation in which he had completely lost faith. The Frau was still called into her old practice on occasion.

Herr Schloss wanted to find out about her life at Bonhoffs. He first asked her to confirm the veracity of media reports that Herr Von Scheiben had offered half a million Deutchmarks for any information leading to the release of Frank Eggert. Sophia, like every staff member, had received her copy of that particular press release. What she didn't mention was the subsequent joke press release that also made the departmental rounds. It included the 'minutes' of a conversation between Herr Von Scheiben and Herr Voss in which they together explore the great marketing possibilities of the Eggert kidnapping.

The topic momentarily provided Sophia with a striking thought. That the words *RAGE* and *ALONE* haunting her mind were a neat commentary on Frank Eggert's very situation. She dismissed the notion as rapidly as it had surfaced, flummoxed by where it might lead.

Herr Schloss fortunately kept her mind focused on Bonhoffs and she went on to explain about the anniversary project, and her recent Museum visit. She reflected on how she hadn't appreciated the scale of destruction wrought on Kussel by the war.

This prompted the Frau to declare proudly that she had never once left the Altstadt throughout the conflict. 'We were on the front line, just like our men. Whenever the bombs fell, we ran to the shelters. Then we'd come right back up again and get on with our lives! The incendiary bombs were the worst. They knew the war was ending but they never let up. There were nights when the city was one big bonfire. People were jumping into the river but it was also in flames. The scenes were unimaginable – terrible, just terrible.' The recollection had clearly disturbed the Frau. 'Some things are best left in the museums.'

'If it wasn't for the Cathedral, the Altstadt would have gone up in a puff of smoke, just like the rest of the city,' Herr Schloss piped up.

'They wouldn't have dared bomb the Cathedral!' The Frau's

tone was strangely defiant, as if they just still might. It made Sophia ponder her statement. At least it would have been empty of people. To bomb a school, or a hospital, was surely far worse.

'Do you remember a Frau Erica Litmann?' Sophia now enquired, referring to Frau Mayer's friend who had once lived in the Coralena. 'She lived in my apartment before Frau Jodl. During the war?'

They both looked confused.

Sophia touched the exotic wallpaper, sweeping her hand along the wall. 'Why were my walls painted over?'

Sophia returned from the Schlosses confirmed in a new determination. Both they and the Eckermanns had the same remarkable wallpaper. She might be occupying the only flat in the Coralena without its native covering.

Sophia stood on the sofa and searched out the area where the despised white paint was thinning, where she had earlier discovered wallpaper traces. She then jumped down and went in search of her father's toolbox. Returning to the spot armed with a scraper, she started carefully edging away the paint. It lifted easily from the paper beneath.

13

The stone lions at the City Museum entrance were still fortunately napping. Sophia imagined that they had earlier gorged on some scout troop and were now sleeping it off.

Sophia had never visited the library section of the Museum before. It required the ascent of stairs towards the rear of the building, no doubt situated deliberately to deter the insincere visitor. Sophia registered, as instructed by the various signs, and acquired her card that instantly bonded her to her fellow seekers of knowledge arrayed in formidable contemplation around the room. She longed to thud awesome books alongside.

Sophia's mission was to build on her previous project work, translating the principle of period display and her drawing roughs into a series of fully fleshed-out window concepts. 'Energy and Excellence' were Margaret's immortalized words. The visuals must convey an energy that will captivate the eye, the content must demonstrate Bonhoffs' historic commitment to quality.

Margaret had given her a final two-week deadline with the incentive of an unprecedented offer. She wanted Sophia by her side at the board meeting. 'It's your idea and you're doing the work.' Margaret and her protégée would jointly present it. 'Anyway you speak better German,' Margaret added in perfect English.

Sophia recognized that she should feel elated. Instead, she was utterly terrified. She yearned to decline the offer but was struggling to formulate a justification that wouldn't provoke Margaret. She had already made an issue of Sophia's lack of confidence in her intricate yet engaging 'I believe in you, you believe in me, therefore believe in yourself' speech at the time she was handed the assignment. Sophia wondered if this was yet another test. Pauline managed to coax Sophia into holding steady. It was a whole two weeks away. She could postpone the dread.

Sophia needed help finding the reference books and enlisted the librarian's assistance. She was desperate for him to ask her all about her research, even dropping into their conversation tantalizing references to Bonhoffs, but he maintained a frustrating disinterest. He simply led her to the aisle and left her to it.

It was so quiet!

The books she found easiest to digest were the ones that provided plenty of illustration. Those that scored too highly on the Sophia scale of boredom were ruthlessly dispensed with. To her amusement, in one book she found a shopping list once foolishly deployed as a bookmark. Sophia tried to identify the lost meal from the ingredients so meticulously assembled. All far too rich for her taste.

She eventually settled into one perfect book that took the reader visually through a hundred years of couture, from 1870 all the way to 1970. Sophia enjoyed the displays of fine embroidery, outrageous feathers, slinky gowns. Of course, she kept thinking of Frau Mayer and the Evergreen Emporium. She even went in a fruitless search for her special red satin dress in the 1930s section, which was largely devoted to disappointing peasant styles – Tyrolean hats and dirndl skirts. The text made reference to the influence of the Nazi regime, and it suddenly dawned on Sophia that Frau Mayer's dress might well have been a banned costume. Sophia was curious to discover what would turn up in the next section: 1939 to 1945. She studied the romanticized rustic costume, comely young maidens in meadow-flower sundresses. And she pictured the world in flames just beyond the posturing of these innocents.

Margaret had raised with Sophia the handling of material associated with the years 1933 to 1945. Sophia hadn't thought that there was an issue. The window displays were *merely* the presentation of a history of Bonhoffs' commerce. What could be remotely political about that? At the time, Margaret had turned it into a longer conversation. Sophia peered closely at the women, their charming dress, their gushing faces. She resolved to talk again with Margaret.

Sophia arrived for a second day of library investigation to be met by many of the same characters from the day before, largely occupying the very same seats. There was the ever wandering teenager whose books took up most of a table while he barely took up a chair, the elderly man permanently chewing on a pipe, presumably as a protest against being denied the pleasure of actually smoking it. Out of deference, Sophia returned to her own place from the previous day, neatly equidistant from the coffee machine and the ladies' toilets.

Margaret had suggested that Sophia also explore some period magazines and the librarian had recommended a weekly entitled *The World*, because 'it covered so much, she was bound to find something'. She selected the volume January to June 1902, the period that would cover the actual moment of Bonhoffs' inauguration. It prised open like lost treasure.

Sophia's first sensation came from its handling. *The World* was printed on sturdy paper that was built to endure. Sophia surmised that its owners had anticipated her eventual visit. Under its elegantly inscribed title, it proclaimed to be 'the voice of the German-speaking lands'. But the features appeared to cover a wide range of voices. It was more a compendium of life than a focused slice.

Political intrigue, noble weddings, sporting triumph, operatic first nights. Heroes applauded, villains exposed. What Sophia found particularly engrossing was the sense that she was engaging with actual personalities of the times, and in their own language. It was as if the people whose dress and lifestyles she had been resurrecting were now communicating directly with her through this window on their lives.

Sophia managed to locate a mention of the Bonhoffs opening in the mid-February edition, commemorated both in word and image. Sophia scanned the article for the illustrious Von Scheiben name without success, curiously discovering in its place two Herrs Klein, the text of their speeches paraphrased and far outweighed by the attention lavished on the clothing of their respective wives. The photograph was of the building's frontage dressed in garlands, the only faces revealed being the Goddesses of Plenty in pristine infancy.

Sophia delved further into mounting weeks of the intriguing publication, finding herself repeatedly criss-crossing the trail of a serialized story. She decided to sample what proved to be a highly effective mystery concerning a missing colonel, with a dashing detective by the name of Winkel in hot pursuit. The story became the motor that sustained Sophia through several months of *The World* and its world, before she was forced to conclude a shamelessly indulgent day of research.

14

Sophia was by now used to returning home in the evening darkness. More of the trees were surrendering to the demands of autumn, and she watched the winds at play, racing yellowing leaves down the curving alleyways.

Being in the Altstadt reconnected Sophia to her research in the library. The district was the only part of Kussel that *The World* would still recognize. It was the solitary guardian of what once was. It made Sophia contemplate the trauma of ghosts returning to an unfamiliar landscape.

The wheezing sound of the accordion serenaded her as she approached the Coralena. She visualized the motion of Herr Eckermann's moustache, gently rowing in tune with the music. It was such a jolly noise, cajoling the evening out of its gloom. Of course it also signalled that the Frau was somewhere abroad, no doubt on some grand mission soon to be revealed with the next pink envelope deposited in Sophia's letterbox.

At the front door, Sophia glanced up at Coralena in customary salute. She appeared indifferent to the music. Perhaps it was all too familiar. Sophia wondered why her maker hadn't equipped her with sparkling eyes and a beaming smile. She was too young to look so serious, even for a Rhinemaiden. Sophia decided that she and Dieter must take her to their next jive night on the river. After all, it was the three of them who were the only youngsters of the building.

As Sophia made her way up the stairway, she wondered if she would soon be expected to repay the hospitality of her neighbours. Frau Eckermann had been the only visitor since her arrival and Sophia could hardly describe her supervisory sweeps as *entertaining*. She squirmed at the idea of having to tackle any act of cooking. But she could be the newcomer only for so long. She was acquiring obligations towards her fellow residents. It made her feel old.

On reaching the top of the stairs, Sophia discovered the Bruders' door opposite gaping open. Her spontaneous thought was that something untoward had happened and she approached, calling into the flat with growing assertion. Drawn now by the momentum of her actions, she steeled herself and went in.

The apartment was dimly lit and Sophia proceeded slowly, stepping across deep hallway shadows. She was dreading what might be revealed possibly at any moment, and it occurred to her several times that she should simply retreat and alert the Eckermanns. The living room itself was dressed as an Edwardian salon, deep red walls, thick dark curtains, a mantelpiece filled with china, a mass of classical-style paintings consuming the walls.

'What do you want?' suddenly croaked from nowhere.

Frau Bruder was on Sophia's immediate right, sitting with her back to an upright piano. She was in a nightdress, hair matted flat. Inexplicably, Sophia recalled Frau Eckermann's comment about Frau Bruder having all her own teeth.

'The door was open,' Sophia replied. 'I thought I'd better just check if everything was okay.'

'The door is open for Herr Bruder. He's coming.' It sounded almost like a warning.

Why leave the door open? Sophia thought. Frau Bruder was at least speaking coherently even if the content was less so. Her appearance was thankfully as Sophia had previously witnessed. Sophia couldn't think how such a worn face could look any worse, but she assumed she would have recognized it if it were.

Frau Bruder lifted a photograph from the piano top. It was one of three in matching gilded frames. She held it out for Sophia to view. It was the picture of two handsome young men.

'These are my boys. My lovely lovely boys.'

Dieter had told Sophia about the Bruder sons lost in the war.

'I'm going to see them soon. That's why I'm ready to die. I've been waiting for thirty years. They've been waiting as well, my boys.'

The Frau carefully repositioned the photograph on the piano in line with the other two. There was something appealingly child-like in the Frau's movement. Sophia now realized that all three pictures contained the same image.

'You sit outside, on the stair. I've seen you,' the Frau continued, lifting her frail arms in orchestration as she spoke.

'I listen to you. You talk quietly so I can't hear what you say. I know you're talking to Coralena. Does she speak to you?' The Frau now moved to touch Sophia's arm. 'Does she?'

Herr Bruder suddenly came through the doorway carrying a substantial parcel in his arms. He gave Sophia a perfunctory acknowledgement. The Frau became excited as Sophia made to leave. 'No. Don't go!'

Sophia was now experiencing a rising anxiety and the Frau's insistence made her all the more determined to exit as speedily as possible.

Sophia calmed herself and made reference to urgent work she had brought back with her. She added an apology for disturbing them, and began her retreat.

'Why did you come?' the Frau now implored from behind her as Sophia rapidly headed out. 'Why did you come?!' She heard the Frau's repeated question resound as she finally reached beyond the Bruders' front door. The noise it made as she clunked the door firmly shut proved an immense relief.

It took Sophia some minutes to recompose herself. She wondered if the Frau *was* in fact dying, but didn't want to dwell on the proposition. The task to which Sophia had indeed been keen to return provided a welcomed distraction.

Sophia had by now stripped most of the walls of their covering paint, revealing to the world a magnificent wallpaper of swirling blues and yellows that had transformed the appearance of her apartment. It felt like she had been transported to a new home.

Sophia was thrilled with the effect. The wallpaper had similarities to the others she had encountered in the building, yet it was also strikingly different. There was a special energy in the colouring, and a drama to its form that was its very own.

However, she had come up against an unexpected and

bizarre obstacle, which had utterly thrown her brilliant scheme. As she tackled the last and largest remaining wall facing the windows, she found that the wallpaper had been incompletely applied. She had uncovered a rectangle of plain white lining paper from above head height to the floor, about a metre in width. Sophia couldn't comprehend why someone wouldn't have deployed the wallpaper throughout the room. Had they run out of money? Sophia stared and stared at the problem in bewilderment.

It was only later that she made the next discovery.

She had switched on the television supplied by her father. There was a current affairs programme on the continuing crisis of the Eggert kidnapping. Some official was being pressed on whether Krombach could be released while Eggert's life was still in jeopardy. Sophia had ventured into the kitchen to search out a snack, then rushed back out.

At first she started tapping the wall with her hand and then retrieved the hammer from her father's toolbox. The contrast in sound between the wallpapered and lined sections was indisputable.

15

Dieter told her he wasn't going to start hanging out flags to indicate Alex's whereabouts. His flat was as much Alex's, he had apologized to her, and she should consider the incident, such as it was, over. Sophia felt his impatience throughout this latest conversation. She knew he was annoyed that she wasn't joining him in the demonstrations against Krombach outside the prison. What she hadn't revealed was the scope of her decision, extending to all events under Writers Night sponsorship. They were no place for an outsider and, despite his best efforts at *enlightenment*, that was and would remain her status, for the straightforward reason that she had no desire to be an insider. She deeply resented his assumptions, the patronizing. Pauline's incredulous attitude had stiffened her resolve.

Sophia had by now reached the river and was using her progress to Dieter's to draw together all her anxieties over their relationship into one frothy cauldron of frustration. What was his problem with her work that made sustaining a conversation about it such a challenge? Sophia would chatter on about Pauline's manhunt now reaching messianic proportions, Margaret's mind-expanding flamboyance, tales of window display derring-do, and he would listen respectfully then change the topic with his very next words.

And she hated it when she heard, or believed she'd heard, the sounds of a motorbike outside the Coralena. She had learnt not to rely on being the beneficiary of Dieter's visits to the building. When Sophia had such occurrences confirmed, and confronted him, he would invoke his sacred 'other obligations'. Sophia couldn't understand. What were these obligations? And what about obligations to her? 'I can't be expected to call on you every time!' he would say. It infuriated Sophia, because that was precisely what she would do in his position, because that was how she *felt* about him. She wanted Dieter to feel utterly drawn to her, to rush upstairs at every opportunity so that they could talk and laugh and make love, and she would be reassured of their special intimacy. There were times when Sophia was sure she could detect him reining in his emotions, and it all fed that simmering fear, that sense that he was still somehow apprehensive about her, as if she was, as incredible as it sounded, some sort of threat!

Sophia was desperate to avoid succumbing to feelings of possessiveness, and the accompanying guilt made her curse the fact that his parents lived in such close proximity. It made her imagine that they were in direct competition, as if only one claim on Dieter could ultimately succeed.

And a dream had disturbed her. Sophia was running with Dieter, but it was Dieter as a child lifted from one of the photographs on the Eckermann sideboard. They were running away.

It was Marita who answered the door. She looked startled to see Sophia, but not in any hostile way. It was more as if she was expecting someone else. She led Sophia to Dieter in the living room. He was crouched on the floor amidst what Sophia was shocked to discover was a stunning scene of chaos. Books were strewn everywhere, papers lay in forlorn clumps, all the furniture had been pushed haphazardly to one corner. It appeared as if some giant had picked up the room and given it a violent shake.

Dieter took Sophia to a stool in the kitchen and sat her down. She could clearly identify the distress acting on his face, his voice carrying an unprecedented tremble. He explained about the police raid, that Alex had been taken and Bernard was with him, that boxes of material had been crated off. Sophia was in too much of a daze to formulate thoughts, or words.

Dieter began to raise his voice. 'The fucking police are being exposed, so they want to show us they're still in control. They're out to crush the Left just like they did in the '30s. It's starting all over again!' He conveyed an aura of doomed defiance.

Dieter returned to the clearing up and a recomposed Sophia was soon assisting. Marita melted away to her room. While they stacked books, he talked about Alex's arrest being due to his leadership of the demonstrations against Krombach. He had committed nothing illegal and Bernard had already called in with the news that he was being released without charge.

'It's pure intimidation. They want the protest stopped so they can free that fucking murderer Krombach without a fuss. This is the animal who organized the killing of 90,000 – women and children. Can you picture it?'

Sophia couldn't.

Dieter then started describing in detail the moment the police entered – their ferocious banging at the door, how they burst in, screaming orders, how some were brandishing weapons. He seemed strangely determined to relay the full experience, making himself relive the trauma as if he was somehow savouring the very pain it was manifestly causing him. Sophia couldn't understand what he was doing. She witnessed the growing tremor of emotion as he continued his torturous explanation, leading to a final eruption into tears.

Sophia couldn't bear to watch it. Her own emotions

immediately swelled up inside. She went to him and instinctively nestled his head in her arms.

'What is it?' she asked softly. 'What is it?'

'I get scared.' Dieter was now trying to control himself. 'What happens if nothing changes?' There was a fearsome intensity to his voice, as if he was speaking with his whole being, almost despite himself. 'Will you stay with me . . . please?' He seemed to be *pleading* with her.

'I will. Don't worry. Please don't worry,' Sophia whispered. She was stroking his hair, calming him down. He leant into her. Sophia's thoughts were on those solitary figures along the Eckermann sideboard.

Then Dieter looked up at her with an astonishing expression that seared right through. There was such incredible expectation, as if Sophia was some long awaited rescuer of his very soul. How could he see that in her? How could she ever live up to it? And then he spoke in a voice of total assurance.

'I love you.'

16

It was early evening and Sophia had just returned from a trying day of work spent largely trying to skewer Margaret to one spot, long enough to extract her wisdom on a particularly challenging aspect of the anniversary presentation. The first noise she heard was muted. It came from somewhere beyond her front door, from inside the Coralena. She assumed it was someone calling to a neighbour from the stairway, but other sounds followed, a long shuffling noise, then a thud. Next, she heard the ominously escalating clamour of fire engine bells. Sophia went to the window and witnessed the great red beast with its blinking eyes draw to a stop precisely outside.

Sophia weighed up the prospects of this being an actual rescue. She hadn't detected smoke. For a moment she wondered if she should seek out the Coralena rules Frau Eckermann had provided for her, which she recalled included detailed fire drill instruction. She also reflected on whether she could save both Monika and her Snowdrops painting, assuming she could make her exit only once. And which would she abandon if she couldn't.

Against the soundtrack of the fire engine outside, the sight that greeted Sophia when she finally opened her door was quite surreal. Herr Kuhn and Herr Bruder were both clutching the bottom of a set of ladders that were stretched high above the stairwell. At its top teetered Herr Eckermann flailing his hands as he attempted to grasp some sort of net contraption that Herr Schloss was passing up to him.

Looking on from the first-floor landing stood a huddle of distraught Coralena Fraus, the full set except for Frau Bruder, who was also following the spectacle but from closer to the action by her door. Frau Eckermann appeared to be in the greatest distress, which was understandable given the greater risk being assumed by her husband in the unfolding drama. Against the fire engine's clatter, she was calling to him repeatedly to watch his balance. The others joined in with alternating encouragement and gasps.

The analogy of Carnival circus instantly struck Sophia. It wasn't a great leap of imagination to see these four men in colourful clown outfits, each with their distinguishing performance features – Herr Schloss with his great belly, the moustache of Herr Eckermann, the sourness of Herr Bruder, the enthusiasm of Herr Kuhn. The contrasts made a perfect comic composition.

What Sophia still couldn't discern was the cause of such mayhem. Then she heard a rasping sound from above, high into the bay of the glass ceiling. The striking creature suddenly flew into view, a pure white river gull, spinning desperately, helplessly against the impenetrable Coralena sky.

The only repository of calm in the scene was Frau Bruder. Sophia recalled with some sadness that the proposed surprise party for her had been postponed for fear of the adverse impact on the Frau of any form of surprise in her current condition. She appeared not to have noticed Sophia. Her head rested against her doorframe and she was staring wistfully up at the bird, as if their fates were intertwined.

Frau Kuhn guided the firemen up the stairs, and they quickly assumed the role of the Coralena Men at Arms, who were clearly grateful to be relieved. Frau Eckermann waved to Sophia and she headed down to join the sisterhood.

'This hasn't happened in years.' Frau Eckermann sounded distinctly edgy. Sophia was amazed because she hadn't considered the Frau as being anything other than totally secure in her unflappable persona.

'I just opened the door and it flew right in, as if it was waiting for me!' Frau Bitzel added excitedly, ensuring that her critical role in the event's inception received due attention.

The firemen were now extending their own apparatus while the bird careered in obvious alarm, yet also with great beauty. Sophia became enthralled by the grace of its movement, a flurry of white passion against the ceiling darkness.

'He's not coming quietly,' Frau Schloss mused. 'They don't trust us. They still remember the war, when we made pigeon pie. Remember that!' Frau Schloss glanced at Frau Eckermann. 'Even the birds had to make the supreme sacrifice!'

A tense-looking fireman was now drawing close to the creature, extending a hoop of netting, slowly constricting its sphere of movement. The bird responded by flying even more frenetically, then suddenly it made a dash for freedom, plummeting downwards, bypassing the fireman's closing trap, diving across the landing and through Sophia's open door.

Sophia ran up the stairs in hot pursuit. The bird was spinning in the limited expanse of her hallway then swooped over her head into the living room. It circled in the space and, for a brief moment, Sophia felt compelled simply to watch – its speed so swift that it seemed to be moving in slow motion, its magnificent streamlined form effortlessly cruising the air. Sophia finally opened both windows. The bird quickly found its escape route and fled in a great spiralling flight skywards. Sophia followed its ascent until she heard the breaking voice of Frau Eckermann from somewhere behind.

'Oh my God! Oh my . . . What have you done?!'

Sophia turned to behold Frau Eckermann's amazed face as

she surveyed the colourful wallpaper exposed on the walls, and, more specifically, the unfortunate gap of white lining paper.

'You didn't say! Why did you do this? You can't just change everything. What have you done!' The Frau's manner was one of complete panic.

Sophia had already accepted that she had probably broken some Coralena rule. But all she had been endeavouring to do was engage in an act of restoration. Her intentions were entirely honourable. Admittedly, it hadn't quite gone to plan but the force of Frau Eckermann's distress baffled her.

Two firemen now joined them in the apartment. One of them meekly asked if there was any chance of a cup of coffee.

17

Dieter teased Sophia for most of the tram journey. He kept describing how distraught his mother was, how *disappointed* she was in Sophia. Dieter talked about it with the glee of a naughty child finally witnessing the comeuppance of a well-behaved rival. He also claimed to have spoken up for Sophia. 'I told her you did it because you love Coralena, just as much as me!'

Sophia was resolutely *not* sharing in the joke. Frau Eckermann had overreacted. What Sophia had done was eminently sensible, if it hadn't have been for the impediment of the lining paper, which was explained as due to an earlier sealing in of an out-of-use fireplace. Hence the need to paint the walls.

'I warned you about their rules!' Dieter grinned.

Of course, she could equally mock him, and did. Sophia had never seen Dieter present himself so conventionally, wearing a broad-lapelled jacket and shockingly traditional tie that gripped his neck like a noose. 'Won't Daddy miss it?' Sophia brutally enquired. He was also carrying flowers. Sophia couldn't bring herself, yet, to break the news of how her mother despised such ephemeral presents that 'look pretty for a day then die'. Her mother was nothing if not supremely pragmatic.

Sophia was finding Dieter comprehensively exasperating, right from the start of their day, which began with her having to endure the tedium of listening to repeated assurance followed by repeated failure in his attempts to revive his ailing motorbike. And so once again in Sophia's long and troubled family history she was late rendezvousing with her parents. It was her first appearance with Dieter and, uncharacteristically, she had been striving for punctuality.

At one stop, the tram became subject to an invasion by a tribe of noisy youth. An elderly woman got on at the next. Sophia rose to offer her seat and Dieter jerked her back.

'What are you doing?!' Sophia protested. The woman looked daggers at Sophia, then moved past.

'Never offer a person over sixty a seat,' Dieter explained as if stating the obvious.

'Why?'

'They're the Auschwitz generation. We owe them nothing.'

'So they're all automatically criminals!' Sophia punched out her remark, furious at Dieter's relaxed sanctimony.

'Guilty until proven innocent.'

'So what about your parents?' Sophia countered.

'I know all about them. Don't you think I didn't ask? They never voted for Hitler. My father joined the Nazi party in '38 because it was the only way he could get a job as a civil engineer, but he was never a fascist. He just signed a piece of paper. And your parents?'

'My father was wounded in the war.'

'Did he support the war?' Dieter continued.

'He always says the war was a disaster!'

'Because of the way it turned out. Everyone agrees about the end of the war. What about the beginning? What about the years before the war? No one talks so much about that!'

Sophia's mother was at her usual Sunday morning perch on the front steps. Her welcome to Dieter was as gracious as it could be in the circumstances, not eased by his gift of flowers. Her father sped them to church.

The Gospel reading was taken from Luke, which Father Scholtze used to focus the thoughts of the congregation on the plight of the Eggert family, 'local people, committed Catholics'. Father Scholtze spoke with an atypical forcefulness about those who 'abuse the language of justice to preach hate, who talk of liberation and only bring misery. They have made themselves blind to their own oppression.' Sophia's thoughts were on Dieter. He was leaning forward in his seat with a demeanour that suggested he was deriving some sort of satisfaction from the address. 'I guess Judge Eggert's past must have just slipped his mind,' he whispered. 'That doesn't make it right to kidnap his son!' Sophia replied, demonstrably not whispering.

The address ended with a short prayer. Dieter didn't bow his head but then he hadn't throughout the service, and neither had Sophia. When the bells rang out, and the community had gone forward to receive Holy Communion, to kneel before the priest and partake of the body and blood of Christ, they had both been isolated figures of abstention.

Sophia considered her recent proclamation of non-Catholic status and whether being in church felt any different as a result. It didn't, and it made her wonder what the point of labelling was. She had moved out of the family home, established her own self-sufficient life in another part of town – and yet here she was, sitting with her parents in church, feeling as if she'd never left. Would Christ himself have a view? There was a time when Sophia consulted Jesus on everything, to an embarrassing degree. What she must have put him through. Then he left her. He went with Rolf. She was abandoned by them both.

Dieter was gazing at the church's two contrasting images of Christ, the one above them determinedly soaring, the other to their side hopelessly grounded. Sophia wondered if Dieter could formulate an interpretation that would unlock their enigmatic posing. He would no doubt have his radical slant. Indeed, it occurred to Sophia that they could be two dimensions of Dieter himself, the lofty idealist and the rooted cynic. She speculated on what might connect these two qualities and, before she had had time to consider an answer, a word flashed in her mind – fear.

At the conclusion of the service, Sophia felt a few glances of curiosity, but more fell on Dieter at her side. She reminded herself of the bizarre chance of their meeting, and how lucky she felt. Walter had been the last man she had *announced* to the church and she was pleased finally to overlay that particular impression. Her former friend Gerda Hahn stared from afar and Sophia imagined a delicious jealousy. Frau and Herr Stern approached to offer greetings, and Sophia's father introduced Dieter as if an old family friend. Dieter acted accordingly and, in his finely judged jacket and tie, Sophia mused on how chameleon-like he could be.

Her mother knelt before the Virgin, lighting the weekly candle in memory of Rolf.

'What does your mother pray for?' Dieter asked.

'That Rolf is in heaven and not hell.' Sophia paused. 'That she was a good mother.'

Whether it was Sophia's advice not to mention politics or that they were simply hitting it off, her father appeared to latch onto Dieter, leading him out the back to show off his garden while Sophia and her mother completed lunch preparations. When they returned, they were in feverish discussion over Dieter's motorbike and her father revealed his own affair with one, which Sophia confessed not to have known. 'It was in the war.' Dieter then incredibly put some coins in her mother's Sisterhood of the Immaculate Virgin charity box, claiming his yellow crucifix pin prize, smiling at Sophia in triumph. She was feeling outmanoeuvred, but couldn't think over what.

The meal was her mother at her most classic – meaty noodle

soup, liver with apple and onion, fried sausage, stuffed cabbage, potato pancakes. It was solid, of the earth. She was
determined to impress. Dieter was suitably complimentary and
her mother talked of Sophia's own culinary skills. He remarked
that this was something he had yet to experience and her
mother, seemingly embarrassed by such an admission, gave the
brusque reply that Sophia had 'given up'. 'Don't know how she
manages,' was the following murmur easily heard.

As if attempting to make amends, Dieter quickly moved on to
express his admiration of Sophia's artistic talents. She had
recently drawn a 'superb' picture of him. Her father winked at
Sophia as he realized he was already a privileged viewer of the
portrait. She wondered if he recalled his assessment of the
sitter's 'broken hearted' countenance. Her father proudly talked
up Sophia's school art prizes, neatly making her sound like the
very Head Girl she was so remote from being. 'We gave Sophia
her first commission. Her Snowdrops masterpiece. She was a lot
cheaper then!'

Sophia was growing uncomfortable with being the subject
under discussion, thereby inevitably excluded. She was feeling
like the silently observing child sitting with grown-ups. She
turned to the wall location where her Snowdrops painting had
once been gloriously displayed, now given over to the Madonna
and Child figurine. The Madonna looked so benign, as if
unfazed by the weighty significance of her produce. She was first
and foremost a mother.

It was her father who raised Dieter's work. He wanted to
understand the type of law in which he specialized. Sophia

feared that this was where the encounter would begin to unravel, but she needn't have. Dieter deftly handled his reply without bringing up any controversial specifics. Her father tried to dust down the story of an intrepid legal case involving a neighbour's encroaching tree, but Sophia and her mother successfully combined to ambush its telling.

'So, are you looking forward to Carnival?' Her father retreated to another favoured topic.

'Frankly, Herr Krauss, I don't like what it's become,' Dieter replied, sounding almost puritan.

'Well said!' her mother thumped the table in approval.

'Well, Sophia, what about you?' Her father was feeling outnumbered and quickly turned to Sophia lest Dieter elaborate. She thought of the fateful Carnival outing that had ended with Rolf's disappearance, that turned out to be their last. 'You'll be living right in the midst of things this year.'

They liked him. That was Sophia's conclusion. And she decided it *was* a good thing. Her mother put her hand on hers.

Sophia took a bowl of grapes from the table and headed upstairs with Dieter to show him her room. Dieter halted her when she pointed out Rolf's, and asked if they could enter. The request, and the hint of insistence in its tone, surprised Sophia. But it occurred to her that it was after all justified. He had come home with her for a purpose. He deserved to see all that home meant.

Sophia opened the door slowly, entering first. There was nothing extraordinary about the room, except an overwhelming sense of absence. Posters of footballers and comic heroes bestrode the walls, toy soldiers marched along shelves, model planes soared ceilingwards, all in a feeble attempt at cover-up.

'Isn't it a perfect boy's room?' Sophia said. 'I used to come in here all the time. Dress up in his clothes, play his games, read his comics. I was pretending to be him. I wanted to go to my parents and show them, but of course I never did.'

Sophia sat on the bed and Dieter chose the bureau chair.

'Rolf kept his room so tidy. Mine was always such a mess. I think he wanted everything to be absolutely perfect.'

Sophia leant across and revived several soldiers fallen on parade.

'Would it help, if you knew why?' Dieter asked.

'Of course it would help. It would have helped then. Otherwise you blame everything, everyone, especially yourself. My dad was sick for a long time after. We all became a little sick.'

'I'm not Rolf, am I?' Dieter casually continued.

'No, definitely not. I've seen your room!'

Dieter appeared pleased. 'Marita thinks that souls can come back to earth.'

'Like reincarnation?'

He nodded.

'Catholics don't believe in that, do they?'

Dieter wasn't sure. He then stared quizzically at Sophia. 'This is your anger, isn't it?'

'What d'you mean?'

'Rage and alone, remember?'

'Why d'you say that?'

'Well, it's true isn't it? The words in your diary. Rage and alone. It's you. It's your feelings about Rolf.' Dieter paused. 'It's good! It means you still care about him. You're keeping his memory alive. It's his immortality!'

In Sophia's bedroom, they both noticeably relaxed. She quickly explained that the pony prints on the wall were an expression of parental nostalgia. Dieter took off his jacket, loosened his tie, sprawled across her bed.

'I didn't hear them argue once, did you?'

Dieter shook his head.

'Amazing, not even in the car. It's because he's got another trip next week. She's always nicer to him before he goes away. And you're here.'

Sophia knelt on the floor next to Dieter. 'They really liked you.' She put the bowl of grapes on the bedside table. 'You'll have to start coming with me to church.'

Dieter threw Sophia an emphatic sceptical glance. She shifted herself on the floor in order to reposition an arm, and started playing with Dieter's hair.

'How do you describe yourself?' Sophia asked. 'Are you a non-practising, or an ex-Catholic?'

'It's more important what you are, not what you aren't,' Dieter lazily replied.

'I wish I could do that! Sound good. Spontaneously.'

Sophia took a grape from the bowl and force-fed it to Dieter as reward for his cleverness.

'What are your passions, Fräulein Krauss?' Dieter enquired in a mock voice of formality.

'Art?'

'Sorry! That doesn't count. It's a hobby. If it was a passion you'd be an artist.'

'That's not fair!' Sophia pondered the question again.

'Come on! I haven't got all day. What do you believe in? There must be something you can think of!'

Sophia couldn't. Not just like that.

'Then you must have a cold heart,' Dieter concluded cheekily.

Sophia slid onto the bed and sensuously slithered across Dieter's body until their faces were locked opposite.

'I believe in you,' she announced into his face. 'I love you, Dieter Eckermann!'

Dieter rolled from under Sophia, and raised himself on the bed above her. He had assumed an air of exaggerated solemnity. He took the bowl of grapes from the table. He then picked a grape and held it high above her head.

'This is my body,' he intoned.

Sophia gazed up at him. His face was sombre, and beguiling. He placed the grape carefully in her mouth, and she felt the light touch of his fingers on her lips. She slowly chewed and swallowed, all the while keeping her eyes intensely fixed on his expressive gaze.

He picked another grape.

'This is my blood.' He spoke in the same grave, ceremonial voice.

She followed his hand as he placed the second grape in her mouth.

Her mother did so hope that Dieter would visit over Christmas.

18

Sophia sat outside the Bonhoffs boardroom in agonies of terror. She couldn't believe how she had allowed herself to be so willingly trapped. All she could think about were the frightening façades of the dark-suited bosses she was about to encounter – and the delivery of those very first words. Would she simply squeak? Or maybe she would become seized by an all consuming breathlessness and fail to produce a sound. Why didn't she just stride along that corridor, descend in the lift, hurry to the store's entrance, and run, run far away. Think other thoughts! she pleaded with herself.

This was Sophia's first ever visit to the august world of the fifth-floor Executive Suite. In front of her stretched a wall filled with a myriad of distinguished pictures and awards. Immediately across sat an Executive secretary busying at a typewriter, one of a small but feared breed. Treating themselves as appendages of their bosses, they tended to roam the store adopting the same air of self-importance. This made them the least popular and most debated of all the castes that made up Bonhoffs' intricate society.

Sophia urgently focused on a photograph on the wall immediately behind the secretary where the exquisitely proportioned faces of the Von Scheiben family portrayed fabulous bonhomie. The only one she recognized was that of Herr Otto Von Scheiben, whom she regularly encountered gushing from every fragment of company propaganda. She asked the secretary to identify the other people in the picture, and the resultant scowl risked a marking for life. Nevertheless, she did briskly identify the figures, Otto's glamorous wife, the children brimming with teeth and, behind them all, the imposing presence of Otto's father, Herr Claude Von Scheiben himself, the man who had managed Bonhoffs in such legendary fashion until his recent retirement.

Sophia had painstakingly prepared for her role despite Margaret's casualness over the whole matter. She had impressively managed to restrict her word of advice to literally one – the need to be 'up'. Sophia had practised and practised her address for days beforehand, waving her hands before the display boards, making scrupulous notes in large easy-to-follow lettering. She even recruited Pauline to evaluate her capacity for 'upness'. Sophia had selected what she deemed her most businesslike outfit, flimsy armour last tested at the job interview, and had spent an hour beforehand with Pauline camouflaging her hysteria with cosmetics.

Sophia couldn't recall when she'd last prepared so diligently for anything, and Pauline's battery of soothing reassurance – 'career milestone' was one arresting phrase – sparked the occasional insight that she should actually be feeling pleased about her participation. It was at such moments that she also found herself contemplating the thrilling thought that she could yet get to slay a demon or two, the very notion of which had successfully inveigled her into the lift just minutes earlier.

With theatrical flourish, the boardroom doors were finally swept back. Sophia stood up, steeling herself for her entrance. Incredibly, it was Herr Von Scheiben himself who appeared at the door in an immaculate suit that shone authority. She had never beheld him so closely before and the impact of the company icon made flesh was immediate. Sophia caught herself simultaneously inhaling and exhaling. She presumed that he had emerged from the meeting to welcome her personally, and felt quite overwhelmed by the gesture. He approached, gave her a cursory glance, and sailed past. Soon, other board members followed, trooping out in their uniformly austere personas, all paying her the same courtesy, as if she was a curiously misplaced mannequin.

It was Herr Voss who fortunately recognized her and broke the news, both dramatic and utterly tragic, that Margaret had been fired. For what he wouldn't reveal. It had transpired the previous afternoon. He would only add what was another piece of calamitous news, that the anniversary windows project had been 'put on hold'. He threw in an unconvincing 'for now', no doubt in an effort to temper Sophia's devastated expression.

'I will be explaining the full situation to the team later,' he said curtly before excusing himself. The secretary added her own 'I told you so' glare, as if Sophia had pretensions far above her Bonhoffs station. Sophia imagined in all sorts of creative ways where she might lodge her clacking typewriter.

Sophia stumbled along the corridor in the board's wake, feeling completely shell-shocked. What she now wanted most of all was simply the opportunity to make her presentation, to insist to Herr Von Scheiben and his grey underlings that they come back and hear her out. She was sure she would have pulled it off, even persuaded them of its merits. How could they dismiss all her work? Instead, she mindlessly passed the procession of colourful awards and old photographs decorating the corridor walls.

Sophia glanced up at one of the pictures, portraying the post-war rebuilding of Bonhoffs, with Claude Von Scheiben in heroic pose thrusting a spade as the Goddesses of Plenty were being hoisted into position at the entrance. Sophia started examining some of the other depictions. She sensed that the secretary was watching, which only encouraged her. She was suddenly drawn to a photograph which leapt out at her through the sheer power of the image. It was an extraordinary shot of Bonhoffs in flames – a great sea of fire surging across the roof, bursting through the upper windows. Fire-fighters the size of ants were engaged in a futile struggle from below.

Sophia continued down the corridor. The material appeared to be displayed in rough chronological order, and she soon arrived at what appeared to be the oldest photograph. A small gold inscription confirmed its subject – the inauguration of Bonhoffs in 1902. It was a picture of the building impressively garlanded, and Sophia could just about identify a cluster of couples standing to its fore. Sophia called on the secretary to verify if this was indeed the Klein brothers, the store's original owners, whose acquaintance she had made in the library. The secretary waved Sophia away, brusquely telling her to take all her enquiries to the Public Relations office. Sophia was convinced it was them. They were such a distinguished grouping.

Sophia took the lift down to the ground floor, still in a daze, now focusing her anxieties on the fate of her mentor.

'Creative differences,' was the indecipherable explanation

Herr Voss proposed at the staff meeting later that day. Margaret was not someone one could ever accuse of having creative similarities! He didn't take questions. He finished with a few cold words of tribute to the woman with whom he had been conducting a passionate affair over several years. It felt like a funeral. Sophia would await the more authoritative pronouncements of the intelligence network.

What offended most was how Margaret had been treated. She had been a senior member of staff for some years, and yet had been summarily dismissed with a notice period of mere hours. None of the team had been given the opportunity to say goodbye. One day she was there, the next – gone!

Sophia had lost her inspiration. Someone who believed in her abilities. A mother to her. The anniversary project was in limbo. She felt abandoned, betrayed. At that moment, she would have walked out herself at the slightest provocation. Was that indeed what she should now do?

19

Dieter was collecting Sophia from work. He too was having a stressful time at work and they had agreed to a relaxed evening in at the Coralena. Dieter had graciously offered to transport her home on his bike, a relationship first, and Sophia was looking forward to the novelty. She stood with the doormen, Hans Friedrich and Alphonse, who were expressing their commiserations over Margaret. The only insight so far gleaned was that there had been an 'incident', and it involved Herr Von Scheiben himself. 'I'm sure he's not her type,' Alphonse muttered, echoing the scenario on which most staff had settled.

Dieter soon burst onto the horizon, weaving impressively through dense traffic towards her. The raucous sound of the bike seemed far louder than Sophia had ever experienced, causing her much embarrassment as it drew up in front of a rotating gallery of intrigued departing staff. Alphonse assisted Sophia onto the rear of the beast while reconfirming that she was not going to be persuaded out of her proposed mode of travel. The Goddesses of Plenty, with their beckoning arms, also seemed reluctant to see Sophia leave by such means.

As if to prove their point, Dieter drove the bike as though he was being chased by phantoms, zigzagging in and out of traffic lanes, driving at considerable speed round the tightest of corners. Sophia finally managed to convince him that her screams were not out of pleasure.

She came to realize that they had bypassed the Altstadt – Dieter had other plans for their journey. They were soon travelling by the river, racing the boats and tugs meandering along, unruffled by their noisy competitor. One hooted its farewell as Dieter veered off, proceeding into countryside now slowly submitting to the evening darkness. Sophia witnessed cattle being harried homewards across a vast meadow, a distant village sprout lights as if dusted with glitter. The roads were emptying of custom, the engine's hum their constant commentary, the great beam of the bike's headlight slicing a pathway through the dusk.

Sophia assumed Dieter had somewhere special he wanted to take her. She didn't have an inkling where they were headed. All she felt was an overwhelming excitement. They could have been anywhere in the world. They could be anyone.

Dieter turned up a road that slipped into a forest. Trees formed around them as they went, like overgrown pedestrians. Huge branches criss-crossed above, melding into a triumphal arch. And then, sudden release from the forest, a rush of light and, in front, a stunning silvery lake, a fallen moon. Sophia had never imagined such breathtaking beauty, that such beauty could exist.

And they continued, around the side of the lake and on. To have stopped would have broken the spell. For this was a journey that had its own unique destination. Sophia felt she was encountering something from deep inside Dieter. He was showing her a very private place – that beauty was his soul.

They got back to the Coralena mid-evening. It had been so exhilarating. Sophia hugged Dieter when they dismounted, and kissed and hugged him again.

She had her own surprise for Dieter upstairs. He was by now only too familiar with the scope of Sophia's fare and had goaded her about looking forward to the bird food. But Sophia had resolved to rekindle a skill. She was going to cook for him, real cooking. She had telephoned her mother for the details of a favoured recipe, sparking much curiosity, and had even paid a visit to Frau Eckermann's anointed greengrocer to requisition ingredients. The previous night had been one of fevered activity.

There would be soup and meat and potatoes and bread. She had even bought wine and candles. The fridge had never looked so bountiful.

Sophia was putting on a show for Dieter, and in so doing, imparting a message. They had expressed their love for each other, they had made love on countless occasions. Sophia wanted to underscore that she was fully committed to him, whatever that might mean, now, or in the future. She was going to honour their journey. She would use that night to tell him everything.

As they came through the Coralena doorway, Dieter talked about how he had never shaken off the sensation of homecoming. Sophia reflected on how the Coralena had been their matchmaker, the 'mother' of their affair. Dieter kissed her as they made their way up the stairs with Sophia attempting to keep him at bay in feigned heroic resistance. She was trying to go forward but he kept pulling her back. He was insistent, powerful, holding her down, kissing and touching her as if he was willing someone to catch them, as if this was a demonstration for Coralena herself. Sophia was giggling, revelling in his game, intoxicated by it.

She handed her apartment keys over to Dieter and he opened the door. He entered first, heading into the living room with Sophia behind, relieved to be finally inside, excited to be alone with him. The curtains were open, and the moonlight bathed the room in gentle illumination, lifting Dieter's profile against the darkness.

Sophia considered leaving the lights off, but she wanted

Dieter to experience her controversial alteration to the room. She was hoping he would approve, defend her against her critics. She switched on the light and the drama of the enveloping blue and yellow wallpaper instantly sprung to life.

Dieter remained with his back to her, then he turned.

Sophia was shocked by how he looked. His face was contorted into an expression of complete and utter terror. She could see he was shaking, almost *crying*.

Sophia went to hold him but Dieter pushed her away, hard.

'Get away. Get away from me.' His voice was a low rasping growl, thick with fierce conviction, a strange inhuman sound that Sophia had never previously encountered.

Dieter swung away from her and careered from the room, out of the apartment.

PART 3

WINTER 1971

1

Sophia hadn't expected to find sleep that night. But she must have, because of the dream.

The shock of his departure, its manner, had left her stunned. She felt, and wanted to be sick. She thought that if she could empty out her insides she might be able to expel what had just occurred, and the deluge of grief she was now experiencing. But she was too numb to motivate herself.

Slowly, methodically, she had cleared out her fridge, gathered the slabs of bloodied meat, the bundles of vegetables, all the materials she had marshalled for their special meal, their special evening, and discarded them in the bin.

Something incredible had happened, something unbelievable.

Sophia sat on the stairway that night. The building was at its most subdued. The hallway lights were off and she wasn't inclined to put them on again. In the darkness of the Coralena, in her company, Sophia reflected.

What came to mind was a time with Rolf. When he had once summarily decided not to speak to her. She had spent interminable days in the purgatory of his silence, the nature of her crime undisclosed. She recalled banging and banging on his unyielding bedroom door. 'I'm sorry. Please let me in. I'm very sorry!' She could hear her little girl's voice still, shed the tears she had shed then. She had endured the very same emotions when he died, beating her hands against that door, profuse with apology, a door now sealed forever.

So what was it now, with Dieter? Someone must know? What terrible offence had Sophia committed? Didn't she deserve to know? It was the silence she couldn't take, not again, that awful silence.

The alarm rang and rang, and Sophia left it to expend its energy. She lay on her bed, absorbing the strange imagery of her waking dream. Frau Mayer had been there, and Sophia was wearing her red satin dress. It was a special occasion, like a wedding. She was holding a baby. It was baby Jesus. The one she had held in her church nativity play, except that the doll was alive, wriggling in her arms. Her parents were there, so was Frau Eckermann. She couldn't see Dieter but he was somewhere around. She moved to an open window. She saw right across the Altstadt, all the way to the river. She gazed down at baby Jesus clinging to her. And she jumped.

If only she could dismiss the previous night as part of some mad dream.

Sophia was so glad to turn to Monika's comforting face. It was a beautiful pointed look that Sophia aspired for herself. They were soulmates from their very first meeting, which was why Sophia had been determined to rescue her from Margaret's banishment. Monika was the only witness to her intimate life. If only they could talk. What had Sophia done? Maybe Monika could explain. She was so sorry, so very very sorry.

Sophia contemplated spending the day in bed. Her body felt so drained. She studied for a while a curious wobbling streak of light that had eluded the curtains to add its graffiti to the wallpaper. She realized she needed to escape the apartment, and the Altstadt. It was that quest that finally stirred her into raising herself. She got to her feet, still in the now crumpled clothing of the evening before, and carried herself slowly into the kitchen.

It was when she came back to the living room that she saw the open diary on the table. The new word was neatly written out for her, by her – *LOST*. For the first time, its appearance left Sophia unperturbed. *LOST*. She considered this her other self's abrupt summary of the evening's events. The conciseness of the conclusion impressed her. Was everything indeed now lost?

Sophia wrote a word in her careful hand to the correct magnitude and flow. She inscribed it in the diary below the original *LOST*. She might as well add this further one to the growing collection of mysteries – *DIETER*.

2

Sophia was hardly in a mood for the chaos of Christmas window preparations. A whole two days had passed since Dieter had stormed out of her flat, and his absurd verbal assault was still their last communication. She was beginning to fear that it would remain so for some time.

She had had the unsettling experience of passing Frau Eckermann that very morning. She had been efficiently polite, raising the wallpaper issue yet again with the dubious reassurance that she would 'pop by' to discuss it. Sophia had tried to read into the inflections of her voice what she might know, what Dieter might have disclosed of that fateful night. But she was inscrutable. For a fleeting moment, Sophia had considered asking how he was.

While the waltz of commerce played on, behind Bonhoffs' window partitions the display team was engaged in the most elaborate and most demanding of all its seasonal transformations. Tinsel, fake snow, Christmas trees and piles of infuriating needles, garish green and red, goblins and sleighs. The absent Margaret had excelled herself with the intricacies of her concoctions, which required feats of substantial engineering, all under the uncertain supervision of her lover, now believed to be ex, Herr Voss.

He had apparently witnessed Margaret's dismissal. Von Scheiben had insisted on viewing the anniversary project on the eve of the board meeting, and had bizarrely snapped when he learnt of its nature. Margaret had mounted a defence in her typical emphatic way and he had flown into a rage, prompting Margaret's retaliatory own. But there could be only one winner. Margaret had ended the altercation by calling him a Nazi, and her fate was swiftly sealed.

The veracity of the account was strengthened when Sophia had the promised conversation with Herr Voss, his 'updating' on the standing of the anniversary project which confirmed its demise. He mumbled something about changes in policy and left hastily, as if he had already indulged Sophia far more than the situation, and her status, required. Sophia had tried contacting Margaret without success. The speculation was that she had returned to America for an extended holiday.

And that wasn't all that was being said. Like a feeding frenzy on a carcass, Margaret's departure unleashed a whole host of eccentric and fanciful rumours, including one claim that Pauline had brought to Sophia's attention, that she was a Jew.

'Why would she hide that?' Pauline had asked Sophia.

'Did she need to say?' Sophia had replied.

The buzz at work did help to suppress those other relentless noises in Sophia's head. She hadn't brought up the Dieter incident with Pauline but, from her uncharacteristic silence, Sophia presumed she had sensed some catastrophe. Sophia was prepared to raise it. In fact, she was desperate to unburden herself. Her reticence was the challenge of composition. She simply couldn't formulate what to say. They had spent a magical evening in the countryside outside Kussel. They had returned to her flat for a romantic meal and . . . and what? He had cursed her and left. Sophia could hear Pauline's line of questioning. What did you say? Nothing. What had you done? Nothing. She had switched on a light. And? And nothing else! Sophia thought about inventing an argument just to make the debacle more credible. He had accused her of being *too* something, fat or ugly.

What Sophia did reveal to Pauline was the manifestation of the new word. Sophia had now torn out the inscribed diary pages and clipped them together neatly in alphabetical order – *ALONE, LOST, RAGE.*

Pauline inspected them carefully, as if fragments of a forgotten civilization. She asked Sophia to copy out the words and she performed the weary party trick verifying her complicity.

'You're a celebrity!' Pauline cheerily declared. Sophia was unimpressed. She wondered how truly wretched she appeared.

Pauline had several suggestions. The first entailed her engaging in an all night vigil to effect an encounter with Sophia's doppelganger. 'I'll sit with Monika.' However, the infrequency of the visitations swiftly quashed that particular proposal. She then ventured an equally preposterous idea involving a camera.

'Do you think they're your own feelings?' Pauline asked.

It was a question Sophia had mulled over many times. Her father's first thoughts were those, and Dieter himself had also proposed it. She could own the terms so easily. The loneliness and isolation she had suffered after Rolf's death – being with friends whose *normal* lives seemed to grow beyond her, teachers who failed to grasp her pain. How lost she became – watching the family she had known disintegrate around her, suddenly challenging everything she had believed. And of course the rage, lots of rage, for the grief she was forced to endure, for the grotesque stain of shame, but most of all for the role she had felt compelled to assume – that of family saviour.

But, despite its aptness, the premise refused to work. The more she had dwelt on it, the more convinced she became of its inadequacy. It just didn't feel true.

'Don't you have any idea?'

Sophia did. Brother Rolf – not as object, but subject. She

explained to Pauline what had happened to him. What he did. And his silence.

3

Frau Eckermann was prepared to make a concession. Sophia could select the new colour for the walls.

She was nevertheless adamant that the 'mess to the room' had to be promptly addressed. The flat looked 'hideous' and Sophia had been a 'silly girl'. She had gone on to inform her that it had been decided to deduct half of her original deposit to cover the decoration's cost. Sophia noted how she deployed the term 'it', as if the Frau could hide behind a supposed neutral overseer, perhaps Coralena herself, to whom even she was made to account. Sophia stilled a seething indignation.

Announced by her singular tap-tap at the door, Frau Eckermann ascended at least three or four times in order to re-examine the walls and re-express her disappointment. Following each departure, Sophia would use Monika as the recipient of a volley of invective she could only then set loose. The sudden frequency of such visits did inevitably lead Sophia to speculate on their true purpose, and she assumed the most straightforward.

Sophia expected that Dieter would have by now relayed something of their last evening together. The Frau had to be monitoring its aftermath. She never referred directly to Dieter, nor did Sophia. But the Frau made enough general enquiries after her wellbeing, each followed by the trap of a gaping pause, to suggest Sophia could rely upon her maternal empathy should any admissions be forthcoming.

Of course, Sophia resisted giving her any such satisfaction. She simply sat out the silence, using the time afforded to evaluate the Frau's general behaviour over her relationship with Dieter. The Frau had never addressed the subject directly, which in itself was peculiar. And when she had spoken of Dieter, Sophia recalled only too clearly her exclusively negative sentiment, expounding on Dieter's failings, warning her off him. Sophia also remembered Dieter's odd remark about the Frau accusing him of 'taking advantage' of her. It made her ponder what other insights he had been subjected to. She drew what seemed the obvious conclusion, that the Frau actually had to be satisfied with the turn of events. Could she have in some way engineered them?

Sophia reflected on the generosity and kindness that Frau Eckermann had lavished on her, and the shock of what she was now entertaining – that the Frau was her adversary.

Sophia hadn't heard from Dieter and it was now well over a week. She had resisted the overwhelming temptation to contact him. Which had not however stopped her from strolling down by the river, past the moorings of the dance club, staring up at his apartment block. She was sure that she just needed to see him, just to look into his face again, and she would somehow know whatever it was she needed to know. And it would mean that she could finally overlay in her mind that tortured last expression of his that had itself become her own torture.

That weekend began with Sophia wandering aimlessly in town. Pauline was visiting relatives. It was raining and she had allowed herself to soak and chill, letting physical discomfort complement her emotional state. Her thoughts drifted back to long lonely weekends of the past, recalling those sick desperate feelings of her teenage self, when she would catch the delicious class whispers on a big school party – the clothing being worn, what girls were chasing which boys – and she hadn't been invited.

Carnival clothing was starting to make its appearance on the streets and Sophia passed a group of high-spirited youngsters ghoulishly composed. In Thomastrasse, she lingered outside her favourite art gallery, staring in through the window like a beggar. She loved this world because it defied the realms of knowledge. Art was an instinct, derived from one's very being. This was the world she had once fantasized for herself before art college taught her to think realistically. Margaret had revived something of that feeling, that she had something uniquely her own to contribute, and Margaret was gone.

At a café on Neumarkt she vaporized an impressive quantity of cigarettes while observing office workers scurry in a landscape of glass and steel – structures, totems of a modern era that could claim to represent today's Kussel more faithfully than any other. Sophia wondered if these people had any awareness of what lay trampled beneath their freshly laid carpets. The scene owed its very existence to a past being denied, and it made her consider if there were two types of heritage, looking forwards and backwards respectively, each on the hinge of the present. And you could only look one way.

Sophia caught a tram home, disembarking at the Cathedral stop shivering with cold. Ahead of her, she had a weekend long vision of bleak television and vacuous Monika. She had recently received an invitation to a Coralena card evening that had deflated her even further. 'We shoo the men out!' Sophia brought to mind Frau Schloss's exultant words. Maybe she'd do more drawings. She'd promised Monika a portrait. And one day she might yet return to that art gallery on Thomastrasse. What would Dieter be doing? What was he doing!

All kinds of noises competed for ascendancy as Sophia climbed the Coralena stairway. Herr Eckermann's accordion played in marked disharmony with a rising orchestral piece contributed by the Schlosses. The merry widows had their television on at a volume that suggested they were entertaining the street. Sophia was curious how Frau Bruder was faring, but not sufficiently as to want to enquire, their disturbing exchange in the Frau's flat too fresh in her mind.

She wondered if all the Coralena was now aware of what had transpired with Dieter. From oblique comments, she presumed that they were. She had happened upon Frau Kuhn with such large consoling eyes through her spectacles that it drove Sophia to spend some minutes in front of the mirror trying to assess how extensively feeble she now appeared. She even deliberated on wearing more make-up, with thoughts of the Cosmetics glamour women and their magical powers of illusion. She had still to open Pauline's house-warming gifts.

One of the great curiosities of their relationship was how it had never directly arisen as a topic with any neighbour. Sophia recognized how ironic it was to complain that no one pried into her affairs, and yet the silence seemed to convey its own message, as if the building had been holding its collective breath. It made Sophia reflect on how hard Dieter had worked at their relationship's concealment, and she castigated herself for so willingly colluding. She had never understood this timidity, with the only clue she could think of being the bizarre way he referred to his Coralena links, his deep sense of obligation, as if the neighbours all somehow *owned* him.

But she was not prepared to damn Dieter. To do so felt like another form of collusion. She had decided to hold steadfast to one primary image, his expression when he had looked at her in that incredible way, when he had said he loved her. She was not prepared to abandon what she saw in that look. *What he saw in her*. And there was no ambivalence.

Now delivered to her flat, Sophia quickly dried herself off and changed her clothes. She was still shivering. She put on a second sweater and poured steaming coffee into herself, all the while exhorting the heating onwards to even greater heights.

The television was as dismal as she predicted. A cartoon character chased another with a sizzling stick of dynamite. She managed to plunge the off switch before the explosion. Her next companion was a women's magazine that had completed its circulation of several Bonhoffs departments before its remains were passed to her by Pauline. She flicked and put it down. She considered going home to her parents but it felt like some sort of defeat. She surveyed the walls, her infamous walls, and pondered what colour of paint she should select that would once again consign the extraordinary wallpaper of blue/yellow allure to the past. Sophia also wondered about the nature of the fireplace buried beneath the tragic white panel. Another Altstadt feature lost to posterity. She had broken the house rules in reviving the house style.

The more she stewed on what was being demanded of her, the angrier she became, stirring a whirlpool of all her many frustrations. Beyond Frau Eckermann she could add so much more, Dieter, her parents, Bonhoffs, and back and back, to art college, the fractious friendships of her hated school days, of course Rolf. She always kept arriving at that familiar destination – what *she* had done wrong, what *she* must do to make amends. It was the cause of so much of her cynicism, and her deepest pain. Why did she feel so unworthy? And she had long ago come to recognize how her fear of confrontation had become the tool of her own destruction. She was so tired of the post-event rehearsal, lacerating herself over what she wanted to say, should have said. She seemed to be forever locked into the self-imposed role of victim. When would it change? Wasn't she angry enough?!

There was another perfectly obvious way to deal with the 'problem' of the walls.

Sophia brought out her father's toolbox from under the kitchen sink. It had proved such an invaluable ally right from the beginning of her Coralena move, giving Sophia a tangible sense of her own power.

She glided her hand across the blight of smooth white lining paper. With a knife, she tore off a strip from its side, revealing a covering of plaster beneath. Sophia considered that Frau Eckermann's aim was to return the room to its condition before her arrival, and it occurred to her that that perfectly paralleled what had been achieved with herself and Dieter, in all probability also at the Frau's instigation.

Sophia located a hammer. She swung it in the air feeling its strength pull at her shoulder. She then found a chisel. She placed it at the side of the rectangle of white and proceeded to tap at it firmly with small rhythmic hammer swings.

Flakes of plaster were soon falling. Sophia took out an old sheet, which she spread on the floor. She didn't have to strike too deeply before she reached some sort of wooden board beneath the surface plasterwork. Sophia knocked away the plaster in a series of blows down the side of the lining paper, confirming the continuing presence of the wood which she could now confidently predict was applied to the precise area of the fireplace alcove.

Sophia set to work. She secured a precarious balance on a chair and began a systematic journey across the top of the rectangle, carefully chipping off the plaster, which was rapidly decorating her hair and clothes. She opened a window to clear the air, and also switched on the radio as she realized her fiendish scheme necessitated careful disguise. The cheering twangs of Country and Western provided rousing encouragement.

By the time Sophia permitted herself her first serious break, the rough wooden board had been exposed all the way to her knees. The plaster had fallen easily and lay in soft piles. She was not unfamiliar with the delights of swinging away with a hammer. It regularly featured in her Bonhoffs window work. Nevertheless, she was tiring and her right arm in particular was signalling its suffering. If only Monika would finally relinquish her onlooker role and give her a hand!

It was early evening and Sophia was pleased with her progress. She also noted that the work had been an effective diversion from thoughts of Dieter. She was beginning to anticipate the revelation of the fireplace, conjuring up in her mind elegantly proportioned features that she presumed would have a similar impact as the distinguished wallpaper. The room's appearance would be restored to its original harmonious form, on the basis of which she would argue a forthright case with Empress Eckermann.

Sophia re-engaged for the final assault, bending to crumble the remaining plasterwork, her sense of drama heightened by a musical background now of soaring operatic arias. Before her soon stood a slab of plain wood lodged in the wall like an upright coffin. She had hoped that, following its exhumation, it would simply keel over, but it remained obstinately to attention despite Sophia's diligent prodding. She returned to her co-conspirators – the hammer and chisel.

Sophia was able to slot the chisel into a slither of space between the wooden panel's left edge and the wall. The first whack of the hammer caused her to reel back as the reverberations shot up her arm. The chisel had made little progress and she could see that she had hit the wall as much as the chisel itself. She swung again, this time trading energy for accuracy, and the chisel managed to foray inwards, creating a small but definite bridgehead. A cracking sound followed a further blow, which she feared might have travelled. To bolster the screen of noise, Sophia switched on the television, and solemn detective dialogue now partnered the opera raging on the radio.

Another strike produced a screech of tearing, yet the panel remained stubbornly intact. Sophia needed to regroup her strength. She sat on the sofa, nursing her raw hands, and a throbbing arm. She watched a heroic policeman's unconventionally operatic wrestle with villains on television. She reassured herself that this would be the final onslaught. She went to the wardrobe and found thick winter gloves.

Sophia decided to reverse the direction of attack. She attempted to lodge the chisel into the wood's right flank, but it proved difficult to secure. It felt as if the wounded board sensed Sophia's resolve and was now fighting for its life. Several times the chisel fell to the floor before Sophia was able to gain sufficient foothold. The next swing produced a piercing sound, like a shout. With another, she felt the wood lift. She swung again, and again. The panel suddenly burst open in glorious surrender, coinciding with a musical crescendo, which Sophia prayed would have covered the shocking noise.

She stepped away from the wall. There was no going back. She peered into the breach but all she could observe was darkness beyond. She made final loose swipes with the hammer to force remnants of humbled wood to fall to her feet. Before her lay the blackness of a raggedly outlined hole. What she was failing to register was evidence of a fireplace.

Sophia lifted a torch from the toolbox. She was able to highlight odd bits of wood and grime on the floor, and confirm conclusively the absence of the promised fireplace; nor could she make out signs of a chimney flue. But there was something at the rear of the hole. Cautiously, she placed one foot inside. The torch traced the full form of a door.

Sophia was baffled. She switched off the radio. Local news was on the television. She was looking at ugly scenes, anti- and pro-Krombach supporters clashing outside his prison, baton-wielding police charging a crowd. Sophia speculated on whether this would become her next encounter with Dieter, but he failed to materialize. The story cut to the serenity of a single image. The youthful face of Frank Eggert was now before her. Positioned below was the caption '62 days', signifying the tortuous count that was consuming the nation. Sophia immediately felt something oddly recognizable in the picture, which she couldn't properly process before it disappeared. Her attention was now requested for the subject of Roman excavations, and she switched the set off.

Sophia sat on the sofa pondering this unexpected, bizarre scenario. There never was a fireplace. Why had Frau Eckermann indicated there was? She thought about heading down to the Frau to demand an answer, but then realized the stupidity of doing so. Sophia surveyed the formidable mess created by her own fair hand, the grotesque breach in the wall, the debris of plaster and wood across the floor. And all for what? Once again the building had confounded her scheming. She wanted to scream at Coralena for so misleading her. Instead she laughed. It was such a disaster! There was no way she could repair what she had so expertly undone. No pot of paint could cover up the enormity of her enterprise. What now? Shit! Shit!!

A driving voice tried to sway her on the question she was now weighing up. It told her in an unambiguous warning *not* to venture through the newly revealed door.

The kettle was put on. Crackers and cheese consumed. Sophia cleared flakes of plaster off Monika's wig. It was getting late, soon it would be too late. She picked up the torch and entered the hole.

The air was thick with dust. The light from the main room cut some way in, but only to the foot of the door. Sophia flashed her torch along its edge. It seemed straightforward enough. She tried the handle, which turned, but the door itself resisted opening. She attempted both pushing and pulling. In frustration, she finally launched her shoulder at it, causing the door to jolt forward, issuing a shower of dust that sent her spluttering in retreat.

Sophia soon confirmed that the door had moved a short way, but it wouldn't budge further despite the application of her full weight. She decided to test if she could nevertheless squeeze through the conceded gap. She put her left side through first, scraping herself uncomfortably against the door's edge. She then began to ease the rest of her body round leaning in against the door, pressing it back. As she managed to swivel herself into the darkness, she dropped the torch. Sophia was suddenly frozen in absolute terror, adrenaline in riot round her body. For the longest of seconds, she scrambled to pick up the torch, its beam askew somewhere below. She finally retrieved it, swinging it furiously upwards, swooping it around her, using it as a sword to fend off encroaching demons.

Sophia took some moments to compose herself. She then carefully took in the surroundings, fanning the torch around her in systematic strokes. She was at the bottom of a small flight of stairs. She kicked away rubbish impeding the door, enabling it to prise fully open, re-establishing her link with home in the living room beyond. She regulated her breathing.

The stairway ascent was taken slowly. With each step, Sophia resecured her position, shining the torch in every direction before advancing to the next. She likened herself to a deep-sea diver in unchartered waters. The stairs themselves were bare sturdy floorboards, the walls unadorned, crusty with inattention. Odd remnants of unidentified clutter languished on the floor. And above loomed a second door.

Sophia tapped at this new door, confirming its constitution. Cautiously, she proceeded to turn the handle anticipating a second epic struggle. To her surprise, the door simply swung open as if, having passed some vital test, she was now expected.

Sophia quickly deployed the torch to sketch out her new surroundings. She presumed she had reached the uppermost level of the Coralena. She was in a space, some sort of room, or loft. She located a light switch on a wall, which she fiddled with to no avail. She then realized that the crude light-bulb socket dropping from the ceiling had no bulb. She slowly circled the room, each step carefully measured, the torchbeam reviving the sparse contents. In a corner there was what appeared to be a mattress, with pillows. A simple wooden table stood against another wall supporting a stack of crockery. A chair was toppled on its side. A couple of roughly positioned pictures were stuck to one wall. Old newspapers lay under the table.

She had discovered a tomb.

4

Some of the apartment blocks coyly refused to identify themselves. Adersstrasse was a long street and Sophia was having trouble locating Ludwig Towers. She had to ask a boy kicking a ball against a kerb. He didn't know but stopped a man who did.

The building had a plain appearance, walls of grey alleviated by broad lines of cream over windows and doors, in a grudging attempt at adornment. Sophia had visualized Frau Mayer in more splendid surroundings, but then couldn't think why.

'Come in. Come in.' Frau Mayer greeted Sophia warmly. She was dressed in a modest housecoat in marked contrast to her more exuberant business attire that Sophia had come to expect. 'Is everything okay?' She glanced uncertainly at Sophia as she closed the door.

Sophia nodded vaguely.

'Good. You didn't give me much notice. You'll have to excuse the mess. When you live alone . . .!'

There was too much of everything in Frau Mayer's living room to know what might be the referenced mess. The room reflected her profession, brimming with a vast array of *objets*.

Every available space seemed to be crammed with glass ornaments, antique vases, ornately framed photographs, pewter pots, clocks, ceramic figurines in exaggerated poses. A cluster of gaily coloured ornamental shoes faced in on each other by the fireplace as if their invisible owners were in conversation above. Sophia wondered if this was a stockroom.

Frau Mayer retreated to her kitchen shouting through an enquiry on Sophia's progress with the Bonhoffs anniversary project.

'It's going well,' Sophia replied into space. 'It'll be launched early next year. I hope you'll visit.' She couldn't bring herself to negate the Frau's efforts.

On one wall was a striking painting of an ancient ship in storm-tossed seas, faces of the frenzied crew grappling with rigging. Sophia pictured the contrasting scene below the waters as expectant Rhinemaidens calmly assembled. Her father was the next topic announced from the kitchen but Sophia lost the bulk of the transmission.

'I'm still keeping the red dress for you.' Frau Mayer returned clutching a tray with a plate of pastries poised at one end.

'Will I yet convince you?' Frau Mayer looked at Sophia with her familiar mischievous twinkle. 'Maybe I will!'

'When would I wear it?'

'All the time, my dear, all the time!'

Frau Mayer poured coffee for them both and presented Sophia with the fait accompli of an exotically shaped pastry.

'You'll still get into the dress, don't worry. Would you believe I was once as thin as you?' Frau Mayer carefully selected photographic evidence from a collection on the mantelpiece. Sophia struggled to recognize her features. Frau Mayer was in the spring of life, bedecked in some sort of feathered costume.

'It was fancy dress. For Carnival.'

Sophia looked closely at the photograph. It was a whimsical birdlike dress, noticeably low cut.

'Don't look too close!' Frau Mayer laughed causing a small fragment of pastry indelicately to splutter free of her mouth.

Frau Mayer was soon guiding Sophia along a row of prized photographic memories. 'That one! Yes.'

Sophia picked up the picture. It was of three fräuleins, one of whom she could now confidently identify as a *plucked* younger Frau Mayer. The two other young women had similarly buoyant faces, as if they were all vying for the photographer's exclusive attentions. They were seated at a table and the bustling background suggested a restaurant. Frau Mayer was wearing a flower-patterned dress, the one in the middle a blouse and cardigan adorned with a brooch, the third some sort of tunic with a headband battening down her hair. There was a refreshing naivety about all three. They were just girls. Sophia fleetingly considered the tragedy of ageing.

Frau Mayer leant forward and pointed out the woman at the centre. 'That's her,' she announced, then leant back to maximize Sophia's space of manoeuvre around the photograph. She concentrated on the face.

'Erica Litmann,' Frau Mayer clearly enunciated the name as if effecting an introduction. 'My oldest dearest friend.'

It was a round delicate face, framed by dark curls in ringlets to the shoulders. The features were dominated by a striking smile, wide and generous – a seduction.

'I hated her,' Frau Mayer continued, ensuring Sophia's attention.

'She was the prettiest. Look at her! I paid eighty Reichmarks for that dress. A fortune in those days! How could I compete?'

Sophia returned to the picture sensing that their competition was not yet fully played out.

There were things about Frau Litmann that Frau Mayer couldn't tell her. For example, she wasn't sure if she had been born in Kussel. She believed she'd moved to the city as a child but couldn't say from where. Nor could she remember much in the way of detail about her family, except that her maiden name was Lebrecht. She'd met Erica in the 1930s when they were both in their teens. They were members of the same youth club, meeting on the games court through a shared passion for netball. 'I was defence, she was attack. I couldn't say who was better.' Sophia sensed she probably could.

Frau Litmann married when she was twenty. 'We all married so young in those days. You take your time. You've got lots of time.' To a man called Philip Litmann, a chemist. And they lived in the Coralena.

'When?' Sophia asked.

'Let's think. In '38, or early '39, definitely before the war.'

Frau Mayer appeared to be enjoying such an attentive audience for she left to find more pictures. 'I know I've got more, with both of them. I was maid of honour at their wedding!'

Sophia re-examined the picture of Frau Litmann while she

waited. She was certainly attractive, her demeanour girlish but there was an undoubted confidence to her character. She was strong. Frau Mayer returned clutching a greying folder. 'Here they are!'

Frau Mayer held out the image of a young couple. Frau Litmann was now presenting herself as a paradigm of responsible young womanhood. She sat on a chair facing the viewer squarely, a purposeful posture yet softened by the same alluring smile as before. Behind her stood her husband, Herr Litmann, a young man prematurely encased in a stiff suit.

'I've got one of them with the baby,' Frau Mayer added.

'They had a baby?' Sophia was taken aback.

'That's what people did in those days. They got married and had babies!' The next picture revealed the Litmanns quaintly seated with a tiny baby nestling between them. Sophia noticed how Frau Litmann was focused intently on the child, her face mutated once more, this time to express a fierce pride.

'A boy, called Oliver. Do you know when that was taken – 1940! They were taking photographs in 1940! Look at them. You'd think they didn't have a care in the world.'

Sophia took hold of the picture. She was dumbfounded. It was all becoming so very real. What had been vague notions in her head were now made flesh and blood. And they had a baby. Oh my God! A beautiful baby. It was becoming too real. Sophia fixed on Frau Litmann, her expression. The way she appeared completely absorbed by the baby. Motherhood was an instinct.

'What happened to them?' Sophia now asked what had always been her first question.

'What happened to them?' Frau Mayer stared at Sophia with an air of disappointment, as if this *first* question had indeed already been answered. 'Ask him!' She tipped her head ceiling-ward. 'Ask God what happened.'

Frau Mayer's face suddenly darkened. 'What time is it?'

Sophia glanced at her watch. 'It's just after five.'

Frau Mayer gasped, then rushed out of the living room with Sophia meekly following.

Soon the television was switched on in an adjoining room, and they were watching the popular quiz programme – *Right Now!*

'I got four answers last week,' the Frau boasted.

Sophia looked on as Frau Mayer now settled her attentions on the screen ahead.

5

Rain engulfed the Altstadt as Sophia made her way back from Frau Mayer's. It was the cold rain of an encroaching winter season. Sophia observed how the worsening weather had the power to transform even the most brightly adorned buildings into sombre hues. It made her long for the return of the despised tourist hordes with their cameras and T-shirts, indicative of an Altstadt basking in the glories of summer.

Emerging from a road ahead of her, slowly marching up its centre, Sophia suddenly noticed an eccentric-looking man. He was dressed exclusively in black, including top hat and plume.

His pace was deliberate, his gaze fixed rigidly ahead. The hearse soon came into view behind, just as the man turned in Sophia's direction.

As she approached the procession, Sophia considered the deliberate theatricality of the leading man, his face so effectively conveying his grim announcement. Could there be death without Carnival? It was the living that demanded death have its ceremony, that through such formalities, the living can go on. Sophia had been denied her own participation in the *occasion* of Rolf's death. Her parents had sent her away to her grand-mother's 'for her own good', on the premise that she would escape the trauma, and the shame. Suicide meant shame, Sophia learnt. Father Hubner had refused Rolf a Catholic burial. Not because he was cruel. He was simply applying the rules. What they all believed was the price to pay for mortal sin. Rolf had killed his soul, killed his soul!, and was buried somewhere far, in a cemetery marked for hell.

And Sophia was sent away to her father's mother, to face trauma and shame alone.

The first car accompanying the hearse soon passed. Without thinking, Sophia stared in. The grieving faces of the unknown bereaved looked out at her in mirrored curiosity. Sophia rapidly averted her gaze confused by her own intrusiveness, realizing she was trying to locate herself inside.

The scene had unsettled Sophia and she was keen to get back to the sanctuary of the Coralena. She was travelling hurriedly through a familiar landscape yet, in the darkening conditions, in the wind and the wet, the streets had acquired a strange ambience that Sophia was finding disquieting. The stately façades of the neighbourhood buildings seemed to take on a new appearance. She saw buttresses jutting from upper floors, forbidding doorways, roofs crowned with fencing, walls re-enforced with sturdy metal studs. The Altstadt was a prison.

Sophia was so relieved finally to reach the Coralena. She rapidly negotiated the stairs, anxious to avoid meeting any neighbours. She hadn't begun to think how she would approach them. An envelope under the door greeted her arrival. It was a letter of complaint from Frau Bitzel regarding excessive noise from the previous evening. Sophia was pleased to note the absence of her usual affectionate doodlings suggesting a longed-for sobering of this particular merry widow. The Frau specifically, and only, referred to an 'extraordinary operatic far-rago', which Sophia understood as indicative of the central disturbance going fortuitously undetected.

Prior to visiting Frau Mayer, Sophia had spent that morning clearing the apartment. She used the blessed interlude of her neighbours' attendance at Sunday Mass to carry down some of the larger items of debris, generously distributed to the rubbish bins of the nearby streets. Like Santa Claus, she had slung on her back the plaster remains wrapped in the floor sheet, which was disposed of in one of the large commercial containers behind Marienplatz.

Sophia sat on the sofa and once again contemplated her per-plexing situation. She had succeeded in re-establishing the integrity of the original wallpaper. She had restored to the flat its attic. And, most profoundly of all, she had uncovered the remnants of lost lives. What surprised her was how calmly she was taking the find. She would have expected herself to flee the flat in panic with all sorts of ghostly imaginings harrowing her mind. Instead, she was feeling almost a reassurance, as if her endeavours could yet be vindicated.

It was only after her visit to Frau Mayer that Sophia reacquainted herself with the attic. She carried up with her two species of light bulb and, to her delight, not only was one amenable to securing, but the light switch also responded to duty's call. An additional light source was added when she pulled away a rag crudely blocking a skylight.

Sophia methodically scanned the newly illuminated surroundings. The crookedly positioned pictures on the wall were magazine cut-outs. One was a glorious vista of the River Rhine against the rugged backdrop of the Forty Hills, the second a group of flamboyant models showing off a long-lost season's fashions. Sophia noticed someone had pencilled in flowery moustaches to each face and, with a fingertip, she traced the flow of their lines, checking for any legacy of pencil on her finger.

Sophia picked up the chair from the floor, discovering that its odd angle of projection was due to a clump of ragged towels beneath. She studied the dishes on the table speculating on the nature of their final meal.

The newspapers on the floor were from the early 1940s. Sophia slid them across to the mattress and, using the musty pillows to prop herself up, began flicking through. The dominant topic was progress in the war with front-page articles proclaiming triumph after triumph for the German army. One headline announced 'German Mastery over Europe!' Sophia contemplated the exclamation mark at its end, transforming the statement into a shriek. A photograph showed lines of troops marching through the Arc de Triomphe. But there were other stories – Carnival highlights, the arrests of black-marketeers, holidaying in Bavaria, a goodwill visit by Dutch fascists, theatre reviews.

Sophia was intrigued by one feature on women dedicating themselves to a knitting campaign for the soldiers of the Russian front. 'We are with our men!' read the caption, the affirmation of a large Kussel matron. It made her think of her own father, whether he had been a beneficiary. Sophia knew hardly anything about her father's war experiences. It made her realize how little her parents' backgrounds had ever been of interest to her, perhaps because the subject would so often arise in the form of accusation. How Sophia should be *because of what they went through*.

Anyway, she had sensed in her father a definite reticence concerning the war. She had witnessed him switch off enough television programmes to know his silence was a decision. Sophia would have linked this with the stirring of painful memories relating to his injuries. She remembered absorbing the sentiment that his illness that followed Rolf's death was some sort of recurrence from the war. Yet, on that very topic, the story of his wounding that necessitated his transfer back to Germany, he was remarkably forthcoming. In church, Sophia had once debated with him the purpose of prayer. She couldn't understand the point of communication so relentlessly one-way. He argued that prayer could be purely an expression of emotion, like giving thanks to God for what you have, like his deepest gratitude for receiving the Russian bullets that brought him home.

Sophia reflected on how her father's attitude mirrored her mother's. What they both seemed most prepared to talk about was the war's conclusion, the tragedy of Germany's collapse, their struggle to establish themselves in its aftermath, the harshness of the winters, the cold and hunger, how faith gave them the resolve to start a family, daring to bring new life into such a fragile world. Sophia knew these stories inside out. They were the defining family legends. But what were their perceptions *during* the war? How did they view their world when these very newspapers Sophia was now reading were freshly off the presses? When Germany was marching to proud exclamation marks in Paris. When the Litmann family was only streets away, cowering in an attic.

Sophia surveyed the room trying to visualize their presence. She had been introduced to their images. She knew who they were. A young couple in fear of their lives, hoping for hopeless redemption, terrified of every sound, especially their own. And they had a baby! She was resting on their bed. Touching their things. She looked again at the newspaper, at the women in the article knitting her father's sweater. She imagined herself transported back to that time. Where would she be?

Sophia put her hands on the mattress to ease herself off. As she pressed down, she felt her hand connect with something firm. She prodded the mattress, confirming an object's presence, and lifted a corner. The pistol was shiny and black. She got to her feet and swung the weapon around her as if readying herself. It felt too light to be real.

Sophia now turned her attention to the table, having identified a slim set of drawers positioned underneath its surface. She opened the first, which revealed bleached paper shreds covering several clinging patches of material. They were crude, flimsy in her hands, their yellow so luminous, like discarded Carnival fragments. She knew their import. She had even worn one as part of dress code for the Writers Night exhibition. Sophia put one of the stars against her chest, and then drew it away. Death, and life.

In the adjoining drawer, she extracted some sort of mechanical toy, a colourful clown whose protruding arms clutched tiny bright cymbals. Sophia duly wound up the creature, fascinated to discover if it would be amenable to an act of resuscitation. To her amazement, the clown proceeded to stomp gaily around the room, rhythmically clashing its cymbals, issuing forth a considerable piercing noise of dubious musical merit.

Sophia was full of admiration for her plucky discovery. She realized that she was deriving some sort of macabre pleasure from the sense that she had managed to find an attic survivor. She then grew worried that the sound might carry below. And, for the briefest of moments, she didn't know if she was concerned for herself, or for the inhabitants of thirty years before.

6

Sophia could picture meeting Dieter and being the perfect model of civility. Containing her emotions was after all Sophia at her most characteristic! She assumed he was continuing his Coralena duties and, while she hadn't actually caught sight of him yet, she had taken refuge in the belief that some form of future meeting had to be inevitable. And the onus would be on him. He could talk, or he could walk away. Anyway, she would see it all in his face, in the way he would look at her. That was what she had missed the most. She thought it should have been other things – his fun, his noise, their moments of physical intimacy. It was all that, and it wasn't. It was how she felt when he gazed at her with that extraordinary wistful expression. As if she held his very soul. It made her feel so incredibly *worthy*.

Yet, for the moment, all she could allow herself was the agony of abandonment.

The next time Dieter's name came up, it was with Frau Eckermann herself.

Sophia was rapidly acquiring outlaw status. The Frau had begun their conversation on the Coralena steps with a report of a loud disturbance over the weekend. Sophia apologized, confessing to an overzealous passion for opera. 'Consideration' was the Frau's watchword. With no adjustment in tone, she then enquired if Sophia had encountered the infamous dog accused of defiling the steps on which they stood. Sophia felt that it was being inferred that she herself was the true culprit, perhaps being caught in the very act. Next, the Frau raised the matter of the paint colour for her apartment walls. Why had you lied about the fireplace! Sophia wanted to thrust back in her sanctimonious face.

The Frau then did an astonishing thing. She somehow somersaulted her demeanour to ask with sudden and unselfconscious affability if Sophia was planning to attend Carnival launch. Sophia realized that she hadn't replied to this most recent pink diktat inviting her to join the Coralena's very own Carnival excursion, and quickly parried with vague references to other arrangements. 'Well, you absolutely must make a point of seeing our costumes.'

Sophia began to contemplate if Dieter himself would be participating. She was mulling over the merits of their first meeting being in front of the neighbours, pleasantly reflecting on how excruciating it would surely prove for him, when she heard the Frau emit his name, as if she had unnervingly just plundered her mind. The Frau was being ostentatiously casual.

'He's so busy now with some case. Don't know what it's about!' The Frau then reconstructed her face once again to form a countenance of pious pity, skilfully accentuated by her clutching of the crucifix around her neck. It was a look Sophia knew well from her own mother, that other sister of the Sisterhood of the Immaculate Virgin. 'I'm so sorry that your . . . special friendship with Dieter came to an end. But don't feel sad. He's a difficult boy. I should know! There are plenty of other men out there who are just looking for a pretty young thing like you.'

Frau Eckermann had assumed the role of commentator on events, and was declaring the verdict. Sophia hadn't been informed by Dieter or anyone that their relationship was over. Was the Frau his messenger, or herself the author of the message? Sophia considered her fawning face and, for the first time, appreciated its potential for real menace.

Sophia was now wrestling with a churning fury. She craved to expose her knowledge of the terrible secret that must haunt them all. But she knew it was too significant a matter to raise without careful calculation. The confrontation would come. It had to. A massive hole in Sophia's wall guaranteed it. And, surprisingly, she didn't feel apprehensive. It was as if the anger that had galvanized her into tackling the walls was now emboldening her with the Frau.

She asked if Sophia was feeling all right, then leant forward and kissed her forehead. Sophia's face flared red.

Pauline obviously understood Sophia's current mood from the conscientious way she sought to 'make plans' with her. But Sophia declined Pauline's offer to imbibe Carnival with her. Sophia was actually dreading the event, launching as it did months of intermittent manufactured frivolity all the way to Ash Wednesday.

On the holiday itself, Sophia remained resolutely Coralena-bound until lunchtime. She moped at her window, watching the mass of people marauding through the Altstadt streets, convinced in her resolve to thwart Carnival's suspect charms. What eventually persuaded her onto the streets she could claim was simply the opportunity to view Carnival from the unprecedented perspective of an indigenous Altstadter. More authoritatively, it was the lengthening day, and the allure of diversion.

The Rheingasse was filled with people, a bloodstream of colourful movement pumping towards Marienplatz at the Altstadt's heart. It reminded Sophia of the height of the tourist season, yet the ambience couldn't have been in greater contrast. The tourists came in respectful camera-clicking awe. The Carnival crowd had a boisterous proprietorial swagger that Sophia found herself resenting. She wanted to shoo them along. Instead, she allowed herself to become swept up by the irresistible tide.

The children were the most impressively turned out – jaunty hats, clown painted faces, bright uniforms, whistles and drums. Sophia measured them against the recollection of her own outfits, carefully concocted with her mother before dispatch with father and Rolf. Her mother's preference was to assemble Sophia in traditional princess or fairy guise. She, of course, wanted a more masculine image to match her brother. Sophia's favourite was undoubtedly the silvery Wizard costume, with a fearsome wand that increased Kussel's frog population manyfold. She remembered Rolf as a policeman, and a Roman soldier. And once he had covered himself in a sheet, cutting two uneven holes which regularly slipped, inducing in him far greater panic than any intended victim. Father simply wore the same gold coronet each year, his one meagre concession to the event he so deeply loved.

Sophia's most profound Carnival memory was the infamous occasion of Rolf's drunkenness. She could still vividly recall the alarm on her father's face as their search for him turned frantic. And how the car had to be intermittently stopped for Rolf on the journey home. Sophia didn't witness what occurred when they returned, she and Rolf being quickly dispatched to bedrooms, but she heard it, they both did, standing by their respective doors. Her mother blamed her father, levelling a host of accusations that mushroomed far beyond the immediate incident. Something must have really scared her. Father didn't sleep at home that night, but was back the next, and they both tried to pretend he'd been there all along. Rolf received various punishments, including the confiscation of his beloved bicycle. Sophia's reaction to it all was to commit to a whole host of vows that promised best behaviour. In retrospect, it was the fact of her father leaving that was probably the biggest shock. It was the first time Sophia became less certain about things. Up until then, she had assumed that they were locked into some sort of permanent cycle of living. She had never entertained the possibility that this might be a fragile construct. It was a realization that came to fill her with dread.

As Sophia approached Marienplatz, she started to identify clusters of trampled leaflets at her feet. Sophia had heard of the campaign to link this year's celebrations with remembrance of the Eggert family's plight. But she also made out other scattered notices, calling for Krombach's release.

Sophia soon encountered a group of Eggert leafleters who appeared too caught up in the exuberance of the occasion to be delivering so sombre an announcement. Sophia now read of the incident that saw Frank Eggert bundled into a car after university class, Herr Von Scheiben's generous reward for information, and an emotional appeal from his parents.

Sophia scrutinized his reproduced picture. Eggert had the appearance of a typical doleful teenager. She considered how his face had somehow registered when she had been confronted with it on the television screen, but the sensation wasn't revived. She couldn't help. She then studied the heartfelt plea of the parents, which she weighed against Dieter's contempt for Judge Eggert and his SS past. Was Dieter commenting, or condoning? She had never managed to clarify where he stood on the kidnapping. What Sophia found so outlandish was the very idea of being equivocal.

Marienplatz was awash with people. The harassed staff of the cafés and bars were courageously endeavouring to satisfy the huge swell of custom. Great-bellied men in bright clashing Ruritanian uniforms, hat plumes and breeches, guffawed and clunked tankards of beer. Highwaymen teased Bishops. Rhinemaidens flirted with pirates. Children chased between legs. Babies paraded on shoulders. Balloon traders stalked, jugglers juggled, shimmering brass bands thumped out their repertoires in a contest for domination from every corner of the square.

It had been many years since she had been in Marienplatz for Carnival and the ever burgeoning mêlée of people persuasively restored Sophia to her original stance of abstention. The crowds were awaiting the arrival of the Mayor, making his grand entrance encased in a golden carriage straight out of Cinderella. He would then perform the traditional speech laced with as much humour as he could muster, end with the consumption of a metre of ale which was known to be watered down for the sake of any remaining dignity, and finally see off the parade to the Cathedral.

Sophia began wriggling her way to the rear of the square using a vast banner demanding 'FREE FRANK EGGERT' as her target. She was weaving in the wake of a simpering child being pulled behind a marching mother.

Sophia knew immediately it was Dieter. Despite his having his back to her, she recognized the manner of the slouch, the way his hair fell. And he was in the bosom of the family. Sophia identified the Kuhns, the Schlosses, the widows and, of course, Herr Eckermann and the ever circling Frau. To her amazement, Frau Bruder was also present, demonstrating a remarkable resilience, or perhaps wantonness, being carefully cosseted by her husband. One could easily acknowledge from their costumes that these were seasoned Carnival attendees. All the men sported the identical, ridiculous curved red jackets with silver epaulettes. It was plainly the uniform of the Coralena corps. The women were less regimented but no less distinctive in colourful bonnets and frocks. Frau Eckermann looked the very picture of a milkmaid – somewhat overripe, Sophia mused.

Sophia quickly realized that she had also been spotted. Frau Schloss waved. Herr Kuhn called on her to join them. Sophia realized that she had declined the original invitation on the basis of the deceit of other plans, and was now shamelessly caught out. No doubt Frau Eckermann would add this to Sophia's growing tally of grim Coralena crimes. Dieter must have sensed the commotion, because he himself now turned in her direction. His outfit set him apart from the others. It appeared to have a nautical theme, and he was wearing a sailor's mask complete with protruding mock pipe. He stared at her from the safety of its cover and Sophia raged inside. She wanted to run across and rip it from his face.

Instead, she backed away. She spun round and began pushing through the throng towards the square's nearest exit. She was furious with herself for deciding to venture out. A nearby brass band was thumping an unbearable noise. Manic crowds were jostling and surging round her, eccentric, gruesome faces lunging from every angle. She was in a whirlpool being dragged by its flow.

Somehow she managed to locate a side alley and started manoeuvring down it, competing against a massive counter-flow of people still entering the square. Suddenly, she felt something grip her arm. She looked round to see she was being held by a man in a bright blue costume. He was wearing a Prince's mask, topped by a crown, marked by a grotesque slash-ing grin. Sophia couldn't identify much of the face beneath. All she could make out through the mask were eyes, that they were large. He moved to kiss her. Sophia attempted to jerk herself free but he pulled her against the wall. She could smell a suffocating stench of alcohol. Hordes of people were crushing past – fami-lies, women with children – and she was centimetres from them, being assaulted by a stranger. She wanted to scream but all her energies were focused on what was now a life and death strug-gle to push away this heinous invader. After terrifying seconds,

Sophia finally succeeded in sliding from under him. She fled down the lane, careering into bodies, hearing a barrage of curses as she forced her way through. All she could think about was the man's eyes, the indifference in his eyes.

7

The freezing winds were blasting across the steps as Sophia fought her way up. She was overtaken by a group of yelping teenagers, outperforming her in their enthusiasm to escape the conditions. Sophia once again marvelled at the exaggerated serenity of the Museum lions, their all weather constancy, their complacent smugness.

Sophia had no reason to be at the Museum, in terms of work that is. Her anniversary project had been killed off as surely as Margaret herself. There was a growing atmosphere of hysteria at Bonhoffs with the Christmas season now in full swing. Shoppers were appearing in vast hunting packs, creating a relentless momentum that Sophia was finding oppressive. Anyway, Herr Voss had little time for the windows team. While they awaited the appointment of Margaret's successor, they were effectively rudderless. Sophia had used the accepted rationale of competitor espionage as the ruse to facilitate her flight.

She enjoyed re-experiencing the pleasure of flashing her library card at the Museum front desk. She was a member, she was serious.

Her first mission was to reacquaint herself with the turn of the century magazine, *The World*, which she had found so engaging on her last visit. The dashing detective Winkel had failed to unmask the Colonel's killer in the story serialization, certainly by June 1902, and Sophia was determined to skim every subsequent edition until she had established the terrible truth. It was either his wife or his best friend. Sophia was convinced it was the former, Winkel thought it was the latter. In the end, it proved to be a conspiracy involving both.

Sophia also turned back to the February coverage of Bonhoffs' inauguration that she had discovered previously, and this time made notes.

She then approached the librarian on a very different subject. He appeared baffled by her request. After all, Sophia had been previously exploring the intricacies of period design and haute couture, and this new interest must have seemed totally incongruous. He was nevertheless helpful and Sophia was invited to wander into a whole new section of the library. She passed titles such as *The Industrialization of the Ruhr* and *Bismarck and the Making of Germany*. She had her references but was finding it difficult to follow the sequencing.

It wasn't that Sophia didn't know what had happened to the Jews in the war. She was aware of it in the broadest of terms, the headlines. But it wasn't the sort of topic one ever discussed. How would it arise? Sophia compared her understanding to the way that she was familiar with her father's war experiences, more through what was left unsaid. She hadn't studied the subject in school and, even if she had of done, she would have found it all deeply dull, as she did history in general. But this was different. She had motive, and it was personal.

The librarian had advised that there weren't studies exclusively devoted to the Jews of Kussel, but there were books with a wider focus. She located the first, which was a general history text on the Jews of Germany, but it finished its coverage in 1933. All she gleaned was brief testimony to the Jewish presence in Germany from Roman times, and that there was a community of 10,000 in Kussel at the book's precipitous end. She picked out the next, one with a disturbingly straightforward title – *The Extermination of Rhineland Jewry: 1933–1945*.

It was a book written by a Belgian academic and Sophia found its style quite technical and hard to follow. As she continued reading she wasn't sure if she was struggling with the style of the writing, or the actions being described. It was the way the two somehow didn't connect, the juxtaposition of the cold matter-of-factness of the language, and the horror of the events.

There were 10,000 Jews in Kussel in 1933. Some 423 souls returned from the death camps in 1945.

Sophia sort of knew, but hadn't really known. Not its scale, the methodology. The utter perversion, the stunning evil. She could now understand the silence. Who couldn't look away? Who couldn't? It was all explained in the images glimpsed in the spaces between the words.

Sophia had brought a pad of paper with her and she felt a compulsion to draw. She began by sketching a single naked form, head shaved, gaunt, lifeless and thin. She then added another of the same starkness, and another, and another, repeating the exercise rhythmically until the figures were forced to interlock and tangle. The lines of individual bodies started to blur in the growing mêlée of torsos and limbs, turning the page into a grotesque montage.

Sophia had planned to return to Bonhoffs by lunchtime, but remained in the library for the day.

What she couldn't penetrate was what the people *believed in*. It was something that became an obsession as Sophia endured the awful material before her. Where was faith, what was their faith? And then she realized it wasn't addressed because it wasn't there. How could it have been? Faith had died! It had been extinguished along with the Jews. It had to have been. It surely couldn't exist alongside such wickedness. Wasn't that also in the silence?

Sophia found herself needing to break away, and she ended up in the small Museum canteen. There were children and families, the bustling noise of play and shouting. She was amazed how all this had been able to carry on. She wanted to stop them, gather them around her, bring down her books and explain.

On her way back to the library she made a detour, returning to the Museum's twentieth-century room. She re-examined the display from the war – the individual portraits of anti-Nazi martyrs, the adjoining images of vast Nazi rallies. Good and evil had been given the very same coverage, as if this was an outrageous attempt to portray some kind of equilibrium. Yet it was through the pictures themselves that this folly was exposed, the incredible imbalance of numbers.

Sophia moved on to that breathtaking photograph behind the display, the one of Kussel as a bomb-ravaged city. It had been such a distressing picture. Now she wasn't so sure.

8

'Lord, how we yearn for you, in our hearts, please renew. Through your word, we banish strife, so we can live a righteous life.' Hymn 163 rang out across the assembly. Sophia focused on the text. It was not something she generally did, listen to the actual words. She examined around her the earnest, dedicated congregants lost in the throes of song, hymn books carefully positioned in upright hands – the synchronicity, the relish, the passion. They were good faces, the very best. But were they masks?

Sophia thought about all the churches at prayer that Sunday – the same sacred songs, the same holy scriptures. And she thought about back then. The same faces, the same songs, the same scriptures. And she considered all the Sundays in all the years of the extermination of Rhineland Jewry – 1933 to 1945. How many Sundays would that be? She started to calculate. If there were 52 weeks in a year, and it was roughly 12 years. That made 624 Sundays. And one should include the feast and festival days. Easters and Christmases. The saints' days. Hundreds and hundreds of church days. All those prayers, all those words. And then they went outside.

All life is precious, God given. That's how her mother had tried to justify it, why Rolf wasn't buried in consecrated ground. Rolf was a murderer! Every ounce of life is given such vehement veneration. No contraception, no abortion. That was the teaching. All the rules so zealously upheld. What happened to their rules? What happened to their rules?

Sophia looked to the church's twin icons of Christ. She wanted to accuse, condemn them for what this people had done. But she saw something. Jesus above the altar was fleeing skywards. His earthbound other self, draped in his mother's arms, was hopelessly vanquished. Flight and Despair – the divine response to such a faithless following. That was it! In a dazzling instant, the enigmatic demeanours that had provided Sophia with endless speculation all her churchgoing life were finally unravelling. And to have merited this wisdom filled Sophia with a strange elation.

She dreamt of Christ that very night. She was returned to her church nativity play. Her parents were standing admiringly by her, as was Frau Mayer, and Herr Litmann. She was holding up the baby Jesus, a gorgeous wriggling baby with passionate eyes. Outside could be heard a clamour of shouting. There was banging at a door.

Sophia anticipated it when she awoke, the new word awaiting her scrutiny on the table. It was trimly entered in her diary as the ritual prescribed, yet was of a very different order. Sophia read the entry, and became immediately excited. She nursed her thoughts on the sofa, taking time to comprehend fully what had been her instinctive inference, the sheer magnitude of it. The more she dwelt on the word, and played on linkages with the others, the more persuaded she became of her conclusion. It was extraordinary, awful. But what Sophia derived most of all was a sensation of tremendous gratitude. It was what she had merited, because she couldn't look away.

'Of course I can keep a secret. Are you some sort of agent?!' Sophia's telephone call easily secured Frau Mayer's visit to the Coralena. 'You wouldn't believe when I was last there.'

Sophia waited for her at the corner of Rheingasse. The temperature had dropped dramatically, further exacerbated by menacing river winds. Sophia welcomed the chill's embrace, cooling a bubbling agitation. Frau Mayer arrived, her head peeping from a smothering winter coat.

'What an evening!' Frau Mayer complained. 'How can you be outside in this dressed like that?'

Sophia thanked her for venturing out in such weather and apologized for the short notice. No, she wasn't a secret agent, she repeated.

'But you're a woman on a mission. I like it!' remarked the Frau.

When Sophia opened the Coralena's front door, Frau Eckermann was descending the stairway, almost at the bottom. She stopped on the final step, elevating her stature for the encounter. Initially, she didn't recognize Frau Mayer but Sophia knew precisely when she did. Her face momentarily crumpled, but then just as rapidly sprung back to its familiar urbanity, like a spongy toy.

'How are you?' Frau Eckermann enquired of them both. 'Terrible night, isn't it.' Sophia couldn't discern if she was acknowledging she had already made Frau Mayer's acquaintance. Sophia recalled its previous denial.

'Sophia, are you keeping well?' Frau Eckermann squinted exclusively in Sophia's direction. 'You've not been your usual self lately. Your neighbours are all commenting. We're all keeping a special eye out for you. You must look after yourself.'

There was something in the Frau's manner that suggested her remarks were being made more for Frau Mayer's benefit. Sophia wondered if she had been the target of Frau Eckermann's sojourn upstairs.

'I'm feeling fine, Frau Eckermann. Really. But I do have something to report.'

The Frau's frown eased.

'I was coming back yesterday and I saw *two dogs* by the Coralena. Two of them. Big! Don't worry, Frau Eckermann. I chased them away just like you said.' Sophia beamed.

Frau Eckermann quickly repaired to her apartment, departing with an affecting, firmly executed tug at Sophia's arm. She felt its cautionary import. She was pleased.

'She looks just the same,' Frau Mayer sighed.

As they made their way up the stairs, Frau Mayer breathlessly asked if they'd added more floors. Her spirits dramatically revived on entering Sophia's flat.

'Of course, I remember it! Very well, very well.'

Frau Mayer sat herself on the sofa eagerly taking in the surroundings while Sophia procured a glass of water for her.

'It's not the same as it was, but this was definitely their home.' The Frau scoured the room in apparent search for features she could acknowledge.

'The wallpaper?' Sophia tried to assist. Frau Mayer shrugged indifferently. Her face suddenly darkened into melancholy.

'This is where they really died,' the Frau declared in a heavy tone. 'In the town they loved. Not up some chimney in Poland.'

Sophia was soon escorting Frau Mayer to the attic stairs. They ascended carefully, with Sophia leading. The Frau gasped when she entered the room covering her face with her hands. Sophia moved the chair across and eased the Frau onto it. She stood above, gently rubbing her back. They remained in silence for some time.

'You know I can almost feel her here. My good good friend Erica Litmann.' The Frau shook her head.

She started to relate a dramatic narrative that was the story of her own wartime flight to Sweden. 'They chose to stay,' were the Frau's concluding words, expressed in a way that conveyed the weighty significance of such a decision.

'And they were definitely taken?' Sophia blurted out the essential question behind the Frau's Coralena summons.

'Of course,' the Frau replied.

'All three, Frau and Herr Litmann, and the baby.' Sophia couldn't disguise tenseness in her voice. 'Was it confirmed?' Her tone was inquisitorial, almost aggressive. 'Do we know for sure?!' As if she thought the Frau might be holding something back.

Frau Mayer was perplexed, staring hard at her edgy

interrogator. 'Of course we know for sure.' And upset. 'They didn't come back! What else does anyone need to know? What are you asking?!'

Sophia didn't know herself. All she had was the new word delivered to her in the morning, and the sensation of what she had to do. But she couldn't tell that to the Frau. Who could she tell?!

She wanted to press Frau Mayer further but realized the pointlessness. What else could Sophia expect her to say? If there had been only a handful of victims, the world would have known of them in appalling detail. Sensationalized coverage would have filled the media. Dedicated journalists would have expended interminable hours in research. This was all just too too vast, too overwhelming. There was no room for the indulgence that was merely one small story.

Frau Mayer stood up, signalling the end of the conversation. She examined the dishes on the table, which she thought she recognized. Sophia showed her the toy clown, which she clearly didn't.

'I have something for you.'

The Frau gave Sophia an envelope. It contained the photographs of the Litmann family.

'I have enough, too many, believe me. It interests you. Take them.'

Sophia once again studied her Coralena predecessors whose lives she was re-establishing. She held up the family portrait, concentrating first on the child, bearing such a sublime expression whose acquisition she presumed would have chiefly preoccupied the photographer. It was the face of every beautiful baby, too immature to reveal conclusive features that might have predicted future appearance. Herr Litmann's resolutely dignified air made Sophia wonder if he had had any intimation that this would be his last record, his final opportunity to exhibit his existence in the world. Frau Litmann was immersed in her baby. She still portrayed that defiant maternal pride, a marked seriousness in contrast to the exuberance of the earlier photographs, her younger self. Yet, Sophia found this countenance far less intimidating. It was to this very look that Sophia was now committing herself.

Sophia guided Frau Mayer down the attic stairs to the living room. She made coffee while the Frau enquired about the other Coralena residents. They agreed that the Frau's description of a certain ogle-eyed customer had to be Frau Kuhn. Frau Mayer couldn't recall Frau Eckermann ever visiting her store.

Frau Mayer queried the secrecy surrounding the attic's existence. Sophia referred to its recent excavation, 'it had been blocked up,' and how she hadn't yet 'got round to' announcing its discovery. The Frau looked suitably suspicious and warned her to be careful. 'For you it's just history. For those of us who went through it, it lives on.' Sophia was learning that.

They followed the worsening weather from the window. Sophia offered to walk Frau Mayer home, which she emphatically declined. 'I'm not one of these old ladies!' The Frau thanked Sophia for helping her revive memories of a 'dear dear friend'. 'That was also part of the tragedy. The people who would have remembered were also lost.'

9

Pauline was excited because she was finding Sophia's unusually spirited behaviour contagious.

Sophia had insisted that they meet away from their usual position in the canteen, secreting themselves in a remote corner. Pauline braced herself for juicy revelation.

Sophia began by confiding in Pauline about the attic. It was not the sort of subject matter Pauline had been counting on, but she could muster a degree of interest. Sophia started to explain what she had learnt of the Litmann family, and presented their photographs. Pauline studied them.

'Pretty family,' Pauline said.

'They died in Auschwitz.'

Pauline put the pictures down.

Sophia placed on the table the collection of words from each of the morning visitations, the clandestine work of her sleep-walking other.

ALONE, LOST, RAGE stared up at them.

Sophia paused, playing up the moment of drama, then placed alongside the new word from that week's beginning – *BABY.*

'Baby?' Pauline examined it. Sophia commented in the style of a researcher that it was clearly of a different nature to the rest. The others were more descriptive emotions of some sort. But what was *BABY*?

With Pauline following curiously, Sophia now turned card player, shuffling with the ranking of the words, inserting the word *BABY* between *LOST* and *ALONE*, creating space between the two sets of words.

LOST BABY   ALONE RAGE

Sophia lifted the picture of the Litmann family – Frau and Herr Litmann, with baby Oliver.

Pauline stood up anxiously.

'Are you trying to freak me out?'

'The baby in the picture. He's called Oliver. Oliver Litmann.'

'Don't say it,' Pauline warned. 'Please don't!'

'Pauline, he's still alive! I know it like I know myself. He's the lost baby!' Sophia's face relaxed into an expression of tired exhilaration. Just hearing herself openly declare her extraordinary conclusion punctured the strain of it all. It was what she had so hoped.

'Now you are freaking me out!' Pauline demonstrably bit her lip, peering down at Sophia with withering incredulity. 'Are you telling me that you . . . No. You're not saying that you're somehow getting some sort of message . . . Wow! Sophia, you need to calm down!'

'It all makes absolute sense!'

'But you just said that that woman friend of theirs told you they were killed, all of them.'

'She doesn't know for sure. How could she? All she knows is they didn't return. But the baby wasn't taken. I'm certain of it.'

'You didn't tell her about this?'

'No. I haven't told anyone. Only you.'

'Thank God!' Pauline evidently viewed this as some sort of reprieve. She drew herself up, and in a slow and deliberate manner 'advised' Sophia to destroy the notes, dismiss the whole affair, and start to plan her move out of that 'weird geriatric home'.

The force of Pauline's conclusion did succeed in making Sophia appreciate the full significance of what she was proposing. That the words were not self-generated. That some sort of 'other voice' was communicating through her, with her. It inspired in Sophia a welter of puzzling emotions, but not fear. That was part of her defence. What she didn't reveal to Pauline was the overwhelming sensation of power. Sophia was somehow changing, could change. Margaret had once explained to her that if you believe in someone who believes in you, you can believe in yourself. Sophia was now grasping its truth, and its import. Faith was an encounter that was predicated on reciprocity of belief, each side being justified in the other – mankind and God, child and parent, friends, neighbours, lovers. It was the very essence of life. It was what Sophia had known as a child. Faith had been the mainstay of her world – faith in family, in God, in community. It was the Eden from which she was so tragically cast out. And now she was being afforded another chance. She was being *believed in* again. That was how she understood what was happening to her. It was that wonderful.

'And if it's true. What are you going to do?' Pauline challenged.

'Find him,' Sophia answered without hesitation. It was the sacred mission with which she was being entrusted. 'Bring him back.' Pauline was aghast.

*

Sophia walked with Pauline back to Cosmetics, through the clamour of Christmas custom. On the way, Sophia divulged another discovery, what she had learnt about Bonhoffs' past in the Museum library.

'Herr Claude Von Scheiben bought Bonhoffs from the original owners, two brothers called Klein, in the late 1930s. It was when all businesses were being forced to *aryanize*, which meant the eradication of all Jews. The great Von Scheiben family paid practically nothing. They stole Bonhoffs!'

Pauline suddenly pulled Sophia to one side, looking round to check that they hadn't been overheard.

'That was why the anniversary project was cancelled!' Sophia continued into Pauline's face. 'Heritage, tradition, continuity. Von Scheiben couldn't face it!'

'Stop it!' Pauline rasped. 'Just stop it!'

Pauline now began a speech, talking to Sophia in what she appeared to regard as the gravest of terms – 'as a friend'. Her tone could best be described as one of straining wrath, the delivery enhanced by her white clinician's uniform as if her words represented in some way an official pronouncement. Pauline was growing very concerned, very. Sophia had to break with eccentric and unhealthy obsessions. She was becoming absurdly morose. And, most seriously of all, she was harming herself. That was obvious from her appearance. Sophia was far too thin for her own good and was looking positively ill. If it wasn't for the speed with which Pauline was once again on demand at the service counter, Sophia would have blasted her with a furious rebuttal.

In truth, Sophia had already reluctantly acknowledged to herself that her health was deteriorating. She was experiencing moments of queasiness that were novel and worrying. Earlier in the week, she had been in the windows reviving a flagging display when she was overcome by a strange dizziness. She had staggered down the ladder and squatted on the floor in the company of picnicking mannequins for some minutes before she felt strong enough to continue. And she was anxious about the nausea becoming noticeable, because she wasn't going to start with doctors again. Her parents had ensured that she had had her fill of them. She just prayed it would somehow resolve itself.

Sophia was brooding on this as she journeyed back through Kitchens. Out of the corner of her eye, she caught sight of an unusual hat. She had carried on for a few paces before its distinctiveness fully registered as familiar. Sophia turned to watch the cowboy hat disappear into a scrum of shoppers heading up an escalator, with Dieter's flatmate Alex, she was certain, ensconced underneath.

Sophia's curiosity turned to apprehension, then alarm. She had learnt from Alphonse that Bonhoffs' security had recently been stepped up. Herr Von Scheiben was a prominent figure in the campaign to release Eggert. Krombach's own release was expected any day, as was the feared backlash. Sophia remembered all too vividly Alex's cheerfully positive disposition towards the torching of department stores, or 'dens of commerce', as he preferred. Her heart began to race. She was convinced he was carrying a bag.

Sophia set out in hot pursuit. The crowds made her passage

more difficult but she was sure she was tracking him through Travel Goods. She walked at as rapid a pace as she could manage without attracting undue attention. Fortunately, the cowboy hat served as a useful beacon and she finally caught up with its plumage parading in Bedrooms and Bedding. Alex had flopped himself onto a bed while being attended to by a bemused member of staff. He was not alone. It became evident that he was performing before a long-legged woman whom Sophia quickly recognized as Marita. She was laughing as he bounced, and was soon persuaded to join him while the salesman shifted uncomfortably above them.

The couple moved on to Furnishings with Sophia following at a discreet distance. Alex was carrying a large holdall, which became her central fascination, and dread. He started opening drawers, swinging cupboard doors. Sophia's eyes remained rooted to the bag, daring Alex to reveal his true intentions while he acted out his contrived comic role. She stayed with them through Office Supplies, and on to Jewellery where Alex, ever the expansive consumer, selected the most extravagant items for Marita to model.

After some minutes, Alex turned precisely in her direction and signalled her to approach. Sophia was immediately embarrassed at being caught out, heightened by the casualness of his behaviour which suggested that he had known of her presence for some time. She nervously advanced, giving a firm 'stay with me' look to the perplexed saleswoman behind the counter.

'You know, these are all just things,' Alex explained to Sophia, while gazing in mock admiration at the display case of glittering jewellery. He undid the bracelet round Marita's wrist and returned it to the saleswoman.

'Vanity, vanity, all is vanity.' Alex smiled sweetly at Sophia.

He put two clenched fists together in front of his face, puffed his cheeks and let out a growling 'exploding' sound as he thrust open his fingers.

As Sophia absorbed the menace of this final gesture, Alex took Marita's arm and they headed for the down escalator, Alex gaily swinging his bag.

10

Over the past days, Sophia had watched the Coralena receiving subtle Christmas embellishments – a small plastic tree on the ground-floor landing, strands of tinsel twisting down the stairway banisters, a Three Wise Men card stuck to the inside of the front door. All invisibly executed as if Coralena herself had been busily at work.

Before joining her parents for the St Nicholas Day holiday, Sophia had resolved to make some drawings of the Coralena's striking interior, captured from her favourite perspective.

As she sat at the top of the stairs completing her sketches, she heard the distinctive roar of a motorbike, setting off a parallel buzzing in her head. Soon, she was leaning over the banister listening hard for any cast-up fragments of hallway greeting. The irrepressible music of Herr Eckermann's accordion soon struck up, firmly drowning any vestige of hope.

Sophia had received her latest pink-attired invitation, this time to a Coralena tea on Christmas Day. Frau Eckermann had added a request in her delicate hand that they meet 'as soon as possible'. Sophia now felt precisely the same. Indeed, she contemplated bursting in on the cosy Eckermann family scene that very moment. But Sophia recognized that she still had to complete one final act of confirmation. And then she would bring the house of Coralena tumbling down.

Her parents had evidently been hard at work. Sophia was impressed with the Christmas decorations coating the outside of the house, which demonstrated what she had long suspected, the superfluousness of her role in past preparations. The front door had been adorned with colourful holiday symbols, appropriately complemented by her father's dress. He met her at the door in his green and gold St Nicholas bishop's outfit enjoying its annual airing. Only in the privacy of his home would her father fully indulge his love of pantomime. The mitre on his head was playfully askew and Sophia straightened it. She admired how he still tucked cotton wool under the hat to age hair that had long ago turned entirely grey on its own.

Everything was laid out for the Advent celebration. The decorations externally announced, thematically continued in blasts of colour throughout the house. The windows had been edged white, red and green streamers hung strategically, and at the centre of the window bay stood the majestic Christmas tree dotted with every shade of bauble. At its top, the Virgin Mary looked down with her hands expressively open, as if unashamedly claiming credit for the work. Sophia surmised that this spectacular annual display must have been the original inspiration for her current employment.

Sophia had broken the news about Dieter. Her mother had asked too many times whether he would be joining them for Christmas. Sophia had now ensured his name would no longer be dangled in front of her, loaded with all their expectations. She was also guaranteed a warm family welcome, returning as she was in a condition that her parents could neatly fashion into the wounded bird in need of their compassion. It was Sophia's classic role, the fragile daughter myth that she thought she might finally escape. The role her parents were still too scared to relinquish.

The candle lighting was conducted by her mother. She began with the Advent candle, positioned on its traditional wreath bed by the window. She then kindled a second candle alongside, which households throughout Germany had been requested to display in the campaign for the safe return of Frank Eggert. Her mother paused for a moment of silence and Sophia contemplated that latest number – '83'. It was branded on every newspaper in the land, it called forth from radio and television – the agonizing march of days that marked his incarceration.

The coming of Christ was then proclaimed in familiar song, her father's booming voice largely drowning out the women's. Sophia's own favourite was 'The Lord awaiteth in the Night', requiring harmonies of some intricacy. Family parts were well established, and they stared at each other in quiet challenge as each performed their particular thread in the interweave of the tune. A piece of cotton wool dropped from her father's head in the course of the last verse, finally sabotaging Sophia's effort as she became quickly lost to a fit of giggles.

Sophia had the honour of opening the door of the Advent calendar, that glorious countdown to Christmas, discovering inside the traditional foiled chocolates, which she would once have wrestled over with Rolf. Her father then conducted the sombre ritual, which he still insisted upon, of asking Sophia if she had been a good girl.

For children, this was the awful climax to St Nicholas Day. When she was young, the fathers of the neighbourhood had a custom that they would play the part of a disguised St Nicholas for another's children. It meant that a mysterious man would enter Sophia's bedroom in the evening, sack slung over his shoulder. He would proceed to read out a balance sheet on her behaviour over that past year, achievements and failings – when she had helped mother in the kitchen, when she had failed to tidy her room. The young Sophia was amazed that St Nicholas knew so much about her. She would then be required to apologize for any misdemeanours and promise to do better next year, with sweets and fruit her reward.

The legend held that irredeemably naughty children were whisked away by St Nicholas, and the clearly conscientious neighbour had a mock leg of an errant child protruding from his sack. Its manifestation each year terrified her.

Sophia thought about her father's question. Had she been a good girl? Over recent years, she had used up most of her stock replies of humour and cheek. Rolf had been a good boy, yet he had chosen to go with St Nicholas, and his family had never considered themselves good again. It had to be the worst form of transgression to live with – an unspecified indictment, a missing central witness. The trial could never come to court, and the accusation festers.

Sophia looked at her father's expectant face, and at her mother's, who was willing the ceremonies to end so she could rescue her baking apples from the oven. Goodness was at the heart of faith. It was the right enquiry. And at Christmas, God was a mere babe in his mother's arms. It was a question posed in the name of a pure child, and it made Sophia suddenly realize that the ritual was stunningly flawed. It should be the young quizzing the old. It had to make more sense. The ones who had lived their lives being called to account by those who had yet to follow – into the very world of their making. She considered her father's face, and she now asked herself if *he* had been good or bad. It was a frightening question for the simple reason that she didn't have the answer. She didn't know her father, what he did when confronted with that choice. All she knew was his silence. He had never revealed his wartime past. Why the silence, Father? What lay behind the silence?

Sophia couldn't face eating. That morning, she had awoken to a tenacious nausea and the idea of allowing food to enter her body was utterly repellent. She made no pretence of this, firmly declining the various inducements placed before her, watching the growing frustration of her parents turn to dismay. That's who she was. She wasn't a good girl, St Nicholas. She'd told you that.

Sophia just felt an overwhelming need to rest. She excused herself and went up to her bedroom.

Lying on the bed, staring up at the pony prints, Sophia recalled when she had introduced Dieter to her bedroom sanctuary. She had declared her love for him, and he had performed an act of priestly communion that Sophia had found disturbing, yet also strangely moving. He had confronted her on her lack of beliefs, and she felt proud that soon he would no longer be able to accuse her of being a bystander.

Sophia smelt the sheets in search of any lingering legacy of his aroma. Would he be thinking about her? Sophia was certain of it. They were broken fragments of the same whole. That was how it felt. The most torturous aspect of their situation was their being apart, with Sophia all the while so aware of how much Dieter was depending on her. She just had to be with him again – to explain, reassure him. And it would all be over.

She wondered if Dieter had been forced to stand before Judge Eckermann that day to have his own worthiness appraised. Having witnessed the way the Frau so freely pronounced on Dieter's failings, Sophia assumed it was a custom applied with great relish down the years. She reflected on the Frau's mastery of manipulation, and what must have been the considerable burden of growing up under such dominion. Sophia began thinking of Dieter as an abused child, and a deep sadness started to shudder through her. Her only consolation was the knowledge that it was the Frau who would now be called to account. And it was Sophia herself who would act as her holy St Nicholas.

11

It could have been described as a pre-emptive strike. Sophia enjoyed deploying the same mode of gentle tapping at the door that was Frau Eckermann's own signature.

The Frau displayed her usual inflated pleasure on greeting Sophia, ever so cordially inviting her in. Sophia displayed a complementary disguise, suppressing her feelings to project an air of studied naivety.

'Are you keeping well?' the Frau enquired, escorting Sophia into the living room.

'Yes, thank you.' Sophia took off her jacket while the Frau circled, ushering her to what Sophia had come to appreciate was the designated visitor's armchair beneath the wall crucifix, next to the endlessly cornering goldfish.

'Are you well?' The Frau repeated the same question as if she hadn't heard Sophia's reply, or perhaps she had given an incorrect answer.

At the far side of the room now stood an imposing Christmas tree, topped by a teetering angelic form. Sophia couldn't think how it could have been transported indoors.

'And you?' Sophia asked. Maybe she had simply failed to respond with her own courtesies.

'Oh, can't complain. I'm a soldier!' The Frau replied with an ever so slight emphasis, suggesting Sophia might not be. Sophia slung her jacket across the arm of the chair.

'Can you believe it! Almost two weeks to go now.' The Frau gushed over her extensive Christmas plans, which included a senior citizens lunch being organized by the Sisterhood of the Immaculate Virgin. She then enquired of Sophia's. 'You'll enjoy spending time with your family, I'm sure. But I do hope you'll join our Christmas tea here at the Coralena.'

The Frau offered Sophia coffee and she readily accepted. The Frau disappeared into the kitchen giving Sophia her opportunity to scan the photographs along the sideboard. She quickly pounced on one, tucking it into a jacket pocket. Christ maintained his indifferent watch from the wall above. The fish sailed on.

'It hasn't been easy for you, I know.' The Frau returned with cups on a tray. 'Moving into a place with all us old people, with our funny habits. Away from home for the first time. Not easy at all.'

The Frau handed Sophia her cup and sat in the armchair opposite. Sophia perched uncomfortably, half listening to the Frau but more preoccupied with calculating whether the photo's absence would prove noticeable from where the Frau sat.

'We wanted someone young. I said that to Herr Eckermann right from when we first advertised. Let's brighten the place by getting a young person in. It would do us all so much good.'

Sophia now just needed to placate the Frau on whatever the latest business was, and then extricate herself as speedily as possible. Sophia decided to anticipate the process.

'Yellow! I was thinking about yellow for the walls. A pale yellow. Or magnolia. Maybe. But I prefer yellow. What do you think?' Sophia looked to the Frau expecting forthright views. She appeared surprised.

'It's too late for that, my dear. This way is best for all of us. We're a community here, a family. We so much wanted you to feel part of it. Everyone made such an effort. But it never really . . . suited, I'm sure you agree.'

For the first time, Sophia was registering the gist of the Frau's remarks.

'We had such high hopes when you first arrived. We really did!'

Sophia now fully realized what was afoot, the true nature of the Frau's business. Sophia was listening to her own obituary. She surveyed the suitably regretful, steadfastly resolved Frau and was reminded once again how extraordinary she was – her exquisite diction, her ladylike poise, her formidable form. She could deliver in triumph or tragedy.

'We have old-fashioned ways here. It's not about right or wrong, just different. 1972. A new year's approaching. Time for a fresh start. You'll find somewhere with people your own age. You'll enjoy it a lot more, I'm sure of it.'

The Frau leant across and put her hand on Sophia's. She felt its coolness.

'You'll still come to Christmas tea I hope. It'll be a chance for all of us to say our goodbyes properly.'

Sophia walked slowly up the stairs. Her head was spinning as she tried to assimilate the shock of her dismissal. She had been given to the end of December to remove her things. The Frau had graciously extended what was a strict two-week notice period because of the holidays. Sophia wondered if she'd consulted Dieter on tenants' rights. The headmistress had expelled her from school.

Sophia came out of her thoughts as she identified an apparition dressed in white at the top of the stairway. Frau Bruder was waiting for her, holding onto the banister for support.

'I'm so upset!' Frau Bruder appeared upset. She spoke in a feverish way.

Sophia noticed that the Frau was barefoot, and quickly tried to ease her towards her apartment, but she resisted.

'I voted against her at the meeting. I spoke up for you, I did!'

Sophia tried to look appreciative but was far more concerned to see the Frau safely returned to her flat. Sophia took her arm and managed to begin slowly shifting her towards the door. The Frau was gripping her shoulder like a clamp.

'Forgive us,' she moaned. 'We did our best for them. Forgive us!'

Sophia suddenly stopped.

'You know what happened. Coralena told you, didn't she? You know!'

12

Sophia knew he was at the jive class, because she had followed him there.

She had waited by Dieter's apartment to find out if he would emerge for his regular Monday night session and hadn't been disappointed. Dieter was keeping up with his passions.

She was standing outside the boat club at a careful distance. This discretion was being aided by a river fog slowly enveloping the evening. Sophia had been warned about the infamous Altstadt 'soups' that plagued the winter months and was now undergoing her first experience at what she joked to herself was an inspired moment. She also considered descending fog an ideal analogy for what had occurred between herself and Dieter. She watched the boat lights struggle for attention in the murky haze.

Sophia waited until she was certain the first dance session had begun before she ventured down the gangplank and onto the boat. She had ensured she was wearing the correct uniform, dispensing with her jeans to wear that 'pretty' dress. She had even decided finally to engage with Pauline's gift of cosmetic potions, enlivening her face with mascara and rouge. That night she was a lady, maybe even a discreet prowling Rhinemaiden.

Inside, the venue was festooned with all manner of Christmas decor. She hung back in the bar area watching the dancers go through their paces. She quickly located Dieter towards the rear of a row of couples. She again admired the ease with which he twirled and twisted, a master of this singular world. She was excited to be in his presence. She even allowed herself the vaguest feelings of hope.

The session broke up on the hour. The dancers headed to the bar. Dieter ordered a beer. Sophia approached as he paid.

'Dieter!'

His relaxed manner was instantly lost. He took Sophia firmly by the arm and led her through an exit door onto the boat's fogbound deck. Loud horns could be heard blaring from nowhere. Sophia felt something deeply surreal in the context of their encounter, the two of them wrapped in a mist, as if the very first beings on earth.

Sophia considered his face, recalling the moment when he had first come through her door, when he had offered her his help, and help had turned to love. She knew that face was still there, concealed behind an inexplicable *anger*.

'Okay, what do you want?' His tone was businesslike, urgent, cold.

'What d'you mean, what do I want? I want to know what's happening. What happened to you?' Sophia replied indignantly.

'What happened to me! What happened to you? You know what they call you in the Coralena now, your neighbours, they call you the crazy one!'

'Do you think I care?' Sophia felt herself break into a defensive smile. 'Do you want to know what they called me at my fine Catholic school? Because my brother committed a mortal sin and was going to hell? Because I couldn't cope with his death and fell apart? My parents transferred me to a new school and I wasn't allowed to talk about him to anyone. Do you know what that felt like? Having a brother who killed himself, then having to deny he ever existed? You want to call me names? Go ahead. I'll give you ones if you want!'

Dieter appeared to compose himself. 'Whatever we did is over.' He was speaking softly. 'You've got to let it go.'

'You need to know something. Something very important. Do you know the name Oliver? Oliver Litmann?'

Dieter looked at her blankly. Shook his head.

'Think! He lived in the Coralena. During the war. In my apartment. He was your age!'

Sophia paused in a moment of final preparation. And the pause lingered. Suddenly, she didn't know if she could go through with it. Sophia felt her whole body melting, as if the momentous nature of her next words were beyond her every capacity. She studied his face, its expression. He was so remote from her now. They were strangers, opponents even. Could she do it? Could she really do it?

Sophia stiffened her resolve by reviving the images encountered in the Museum library. The conviction she had burnt into her brain then. Whatever else, she wouldn't look away. Not now. That was her responsibility, and her power. She stared hard at Dieter, using his blue blue eyes as a channel through to another face buried behind this bleak façade. The one that had once pleaded that she stay. And the words came. They spilled out gently.

'He's you. Dieter, he's you.' It was over with. She had said it.

'What! What did you say?'

'You're not Dieter Eckermann. You're Oliver Litmann. Your parents were Jews!'

Dieter's face froze in disbelief. Then cracked in rage. 'I can't believe what you're saying! What are you trying to do? Is this to get back at me? Is that your game? You're sick! You *are* mad. You stole the photograph of me from my parents, didn't you? They told me they thought you had taken it but I didn't believe it until now. Sophia, you need help. Look at yourself!

Have you seen how you look? Just . . . stay away. Stay away from me!'

Dieter spun on his heels, as neatly as he had been spinning moments earlier on the dance floor, and stomped down the deck, into the fog.

'I believe in you, Oliver Litmann!' Sophia screamed into nothingness. 'I believe in you!'

Sophia grabbed hold of the boat's railing. She couldn't digest all that had just occurred. It went by too fast. His words felt like a beating. She was aching, dizzy.

There was a time after Rolf had died when Sophia was in tears every day. Sometimes she thought they might never end. Then she suddenly understood that she wasn't crying over Rolf, but for her parents. They had become so desolate, despite all their pretence. Her father was in the house for a while after Rolf died. He was ill with some sort of breakdown she heard linked to the war. Then, when he got back to work, he was hardly ever around. Her mother retreated into an intense domesticity. Sophia had not only been abandoned by Rolf, but also by her parents. That was what led her to the stunning realization – it was all down to her. Only she could repair the family. She would somehow have to fill the void left by Rolf's loss. She would dedicate herself to being the good daughter, *and the good son*. The key was discipline. What came out of her, and what went in. She would make this sacrifice. If they would only be happy again, stay together and be happy.

Sophia looked out into the bleakness beyond the boat and burst into tears. It felt so so good. Sophia was crying over

Dieter, and Rolf, two absent sons, two lost souls. And she was crying over the girl she had once said goodbye to, that other lost soul, her own.

Sophia started to follow the progress of her teardrops as they slipped from her face and fell rhythmically into the blackness of the Rhine below. The fog had curtained the river into a pond. It was an atmosphere of intimacy, and peace. She stared down at the river, wondering if the Rhinemaidens were looking up in mirrored curiosity. Rolf so loved the outdoors. He had simply returned himself to nature. It couldn't be a sin, to want to escape life's pain, to ease oneself into the waters, into the maidens' waiting arms.

Sophia spent the evening in the club, basking in the sensation of Dieter's presence through his very absence. She had spoilt his evening. She became engrossed in the way even the most unattractive of men seemed to acquire a certain grace through the magic of movement. Some bought drinks for her and she drank. She was even enticed onto the dance floor, twisting and spinning with strangers until her world was a blur.

A man loud on car ownership persisted in offering Sophia a ride home but she managed to shake him off. A concerned doorman proposed finding her a taxi but she really did want to walk. After the noise and sweat of the club, fortified by light-headed bravado, she welcomed the bracing cold air on her cheeks and the dramatic stillness of the Altstadt surrendered to fog.

She headed in the vague direction of the Coralena. To her

amazement, she couldn't use the Cathedral as her trusted guide because it had simply been consumed. The fog's engulfing of the surrounding space had given the neighbourhood an extraordinary ambience. It felt like the Altstadt was now roofed in, a giant's palace with its buildings grand doorways off corridors of road.

As she travelled, the occasional figure would sweep in and out of view in sudden and startling fashion. Sophia savoured the knowledge that she was reciprocating the effect. On that night, everyone in the Altstadt had become apparitions. It made her imagine that she had entered a parallel universe, where the souls of the dead were being revived, switching places with the living.

Sophia decided to break into a run. She wanted to discover if, by so doing, she could become completely uninhibited by vision, completely absorbed by this ethereal world. She began by jogging, picking up pace as her confidence grew. She was using the pavement as her route map. Passing cars growled and died. She was listening to the methodical thudding of her feet, following their acceleration, hearing their echo in her heart's pounding rhythm. She felt hidden by the fog, yet at the same time vulnerable to it. She conceived that she was being chased. That they were coming for her and she had to flee. Sophia was now running at full speed, hurtling herself forwards, lifting herself from the ground, flying, soaring, desperate, desperate to escape.

Exhaustion finally forced her to a halt. She fell against a wall. Her head was exploding. She felt the insides of her body converge into a great spasm. She crouched down and retched, expelling a spew of watery vomit, heaving repeatedly. Her body was drained, but the protest of convulsions continued again and again before she was finally granted reprieve, allowed to slump to the ground.

Sophia somehow limped her way back to the Coralena. She wished there had been a way to transport herself inside that would have avoided confronting the gaze from above the door. Sophia was so sorry. She asked Coralena to pass on to everyone her profound apologies for the embarrassments she had caused, right from the very beginning of her life, to all the people she had ever known she was so very sorry. No one was more disappointed than herself. There was just too much to live up to. She deserved their scorn.

Sophia roused herself to negotiate the lock. With slow and measured steps, she made her way through the hallway, past the puny Christmas tree, and started her stairway ascent. Soon, she found herself engaged in an epic struggle. All her energy seemed completely drained away. She thought of herself as the attic clown in its final throes. Every step seemed to take on mountainous proportions. She kept repeating over and over the mantra not to be sick on the stair. She lowered herself to the floor and began to crawl. She considered how much easier it was to journey on all fours, and couldn't understand why she didn't do so normally. She accomplished another step, then paused to prepare herself for the next. They had to be taken one at a time, one careful step at a time.

At some point, Sophia woke to find she was being assisted up the remaining stairway. There were gentle woman's hands around her. She was being laid out on her living room sofa.

13

Sophia phoned into work sick the next day. It was just about all she could manage when she first dallied with consciousness, still dressed in the stained clothing of the previous evening, her body a profusion of aches. She had staggered to the kitchen to make some tea, which she proceeded to consume and throw up in a perfect demonstration of cause and effect.

Sophia slept again until mid-afternoon and arose in more reassured condition. She opened the curtains to expose a bright, clear winter's day. The Cathedral had been restored to its rightful place after its obliteration in the fog. The contrast with the night before couldn't have been more stark, which made Sophia wonder if she had indeed travelled to another world.

Sophia downed great gulps from a container of milk in the fridge, and then went on to luxuriate in a steaming bath. As she lay in its healing waters, she recalled the memory of her stairway rescuer, but confusingly not her identity. She wondered if Coralena herself had taken pity on her wretched state.

Sophia dried off her body in front of the wardrobe mirror, inspecting the tired rubbery face before her – pasty white skin, lips sallow, eyes wounded and sore. She could plainly make out the lines advancing across her forehead whose ultimate form she could foretell from her mother's severe creases. The evening's pretence of fulsome make-up had swiftly evaporated.

She dropped the towel and summoned Monika to the mirror, again comparing their dramatically thin shapes. Sophia wasn't disturbed by the thought of her withdrawal from their competition. It had been her solace for far too long. She had controlled her body, thinking she was controlling her fate. And now fate was taking control. She was being forced to grow up.

Did she really look like the pictures out of the war as her mother claimed – the emaciated bodies of the starving, and the starved? Sophia considered the notion that she herself was a survivor. And how she had to make herself strong.

Sophia slid her hands down her body. She felt the falling folds of her tiny breasts, the taut fit of skin across her ribcage. She settled her hands on her stomach searching out any emerging roundness in its form. Sophia had missed periods before. At the height of her 'problems', they'd completely seized up for months. But she sensed this was different. She had stopped taking the contraception pills because they were making her so unwell. She hadn't told Dieter because she didn't want to lose the intensity of their lovemaking.

Sophia turned herself sideways to the mirror. She tried to extend her stomach as far as she was able, puffing it out. She was imagining what pregnancy would in time demand, how her body would grow misshapen and large, to carry a baby, a whole life inside! Monika couldn't understand. Sophia was a woman, therefore equipped with that staggering potentiality – to be a mother.

A sudden tapping at her door made Sophia jump. She picked up clothing and scurried to the attic, maximizing the distance between herself and the lurking Frau. She was the last person Sophia wanted to meet.

Safely upstairs, Sophia dressed herself, sat herself down at the attic table, and began what she had so far managed to put off, her revisit to the events of the previous night. She cringed at the insufficiently blurred picture of her cavorting on the dance floor, the alcohol consumed with extravagant abandon, the madness of her fogbound journey home. But she reflected most of all on her exchange with Dieter.

The photographs were on the table in front of her. She picked up the Litmann family with baby Oliver poised in the nook of his parents' arms, a gentle, cheerful face. She then lifted the picture of baby Dieter taken from the Eckermanns' sideboard. This one was obviously older, the face more defined, the character of a boy emerging from the blandness of babyhood. But the similarities were magnificently present – the colour of the hair, the shape of the eyes, a certain twist at the corners of the mouth. It was the selfsame baby. She was convinced of it.

Sophia would soon be banished from the Coralena, and a final purging of her apartment's past would inevitably ensue. Time was running out. That was why she had felt compelled to confront Dieter directly, and had hoped the revelation of his true nature would have instantly resurrected some dormant memory. Instead, she had received the cruellest rebuff.

Dieter's behaviour had devastated Sophia. She considered it yet another manifestation in the revolving carousel that was

Dieter's character. She began speculating on what might be the impact of his situation, having in effect two identities compressed into the one being. She had lost Dieter. Could she yet win Oliver?

Sophia heard another muffled sound from somewhere below. What would the Frau have wanted with her? Sophia had disclosed her hand to Dieter, which would have undoubtedly been transmitted back. She also supposed that whichever neighbour had assisted her on the stair the previous night would have conveyed something of her state and, even more damningly, the state of the apartment. Coralena had to be buzzing with latest news on the crazy woman in their midst.

Sophia tried to imagine how the Frau might react. She was certain of one thing, that she must be in some sort of jeopardy. Sophia opened the drawer and took out the sleek black pistol she had found under the mattress. She raised the gun perpendicular to her face picturing herself back to back with Frau Eckermann in a dawn duel, with Dieter their prize.

Sophia finished her gunplay and turned to the more congenial toy clown, its face admirably fixed in an irrepressible grin despite enduring decades-long neglect. She noted the fact that it had to be the only legacy of baby Oliver still in existence, more formidable an adversary of Frau Eckermann than anyone. She gave its winding mechanism several firm twists and once again set it loose on the floor. It spun forward, thrashing its cymbals in a frenzy of clatter. Sophia longed for its noisy lament to shudder throughout the Coralena, across the Altstadt.

14

Sophia had an unusual encounter or, more accurately, non-encounter with Herr Kuhn.

Occasionally their departures for work would coincide on the stair, and he would escort her to the tram stop, expounding on a range of topics in a way that Sophia invariably found far too vigorous for so early in the day. As she came down the stairway on this occasion, catching Herr Kuhn ahead of her, instead of waiting, he skipped down the remaining steps and, by the time Sophia had emerged onto the street, he was beyond every horizon.

Pauline's reaction on first sighting Sophia was to drag her immediately off to the toilets. She described her frenetic cosmetic applications as an emergency fix. Sophia looked 'absolutely gruesome!'

More potions were applied at lunchtime and Pauline demanded an explanation as to why Sophia had come into work if she was still feeling, and indisputably appeared, so awful. Sophia wasn't sure herself, except for the need to get away from the Coralena. And the need to talk.

Sophia knew how disapproving Pauline was of the whole matter but she simply couldn't carry its burden alone. Sophia also needed someone to hear out what she was doing, so she could understand herself. And Pauline was the only person in whom Sophia could confide. That was Pauline's burden.

She listened to Sophia's update on events with an expression that placed her firmly in the camp of Sophia's neighbours. It was only after Sophia pre-empted her response by producing both baby photographs that Pauline indicated she was 'prepared to entertain' a discussion, but only on a strictly hypothetical basis.

'*If* the babies were the same, you still don't know what actually happened. Maybe the Eckermanns saved the child from certain death. Maybe his mother gave him to the Eckermanns, and they're the heroes for taking him in!'

'So why conceal it if that was true?' Sophia replied.

'Maybe it's best not to know, best for Dieter.'

'Who can make that decision? His real parents? Don't we all have a right to know where we came from? Who we are?'

Sophia brought up the Eggert abduction. 'The police, the army, the whole country's involved. Prayers are being said in every church. It's being debated daily in the Bundestag. All for one lost boy. This is another kidnapping!'

And Pauline was determined to match Sophia tone for tone. 'You're playing with people's lives. A child and his parents. This is big stuff. Big stuff! He's spent practically all his life with the two adults he believes are his parents. Do you really think you have a right to interfere? You'll end up ruining all their lives!'

'I've been with Dieter. I know him! He's so . . . sad inside. I can't explain. I just feel what I feel. If he could know who he really is, it will change him. Make him better.'

'Is this about Dieter, or is it more about you?' Pauline paused, then decided to complete the sentiment. 'Aren't you just trying to get back at him for how he treated you?'

'He's dead!' Sophia finally declared with an intense sincerity that shocked Pauline. 'Don't you understand? He's dead!'

The exchange clearly stayed with Pauline, distressed her, because she wanted to see Sophia later that afternoon.

In the toilets, Pauline exploded into a withering tirade of accusation that totally dumbfounded Sophia – there was no evidence to support what Sophia was doing; she had become obsessed with her ridiculous diary words as a way of dealing with her own frustrations; she was putting other people's lives and happiness in jeopardy because of her own selfishness. Then Pauline arrived at her conclusion.

'So what if he was once a Jew. Will it really help him to know? I wouldn't want to be told that news! Would you?'

The presentation of Pauline's final point in the form of a question had a stunning impact on Sophia. It drew out of her the realization that she had the instinctive capacity to agree. That it was *within her*, whatever thought process might have formed her actual response. Sophia focused hard on what Pauline had just said, that it was preferable not to be a Jew. Was it really such a terrible remark? Yet Sophia couldn't get out of her mind that astonishing title in the library – *The Extermination of Rhineland Jewry: 1933–1945*. What was in the air they breathed that could make Pauline sound so reasonable – still, today?

Sophia had wanted to be furious with Pauline, but now didn't much care. Her only feelings were of overwhelming sorrow, for Pauline, and for them both. And her thoughts turned to what could be done. It was a reaction that suddenly cheered her. She was pleased with herself. In fact, the more she considered it, the more contented she became, and proud.

15

Her father said they were worried about her. He would come by.

Sophia thought about persuading him to meet her in the city centre after work. She was concerned about the attic. And then she decided it would be far better if he saw it. And then she wanted him to see it.

Sophia was able to decode her father's every tick and inflection and she appreciated the constrained way he surveyed the reformed room.

'Why haven't you told Frau Eckermann?'

'She's asked me to leave.'

'Why?' Her father appeared a little less constrained.

'I broke their rules.'

'Is this what's been making you ill?'

Sophia laughed. 'No, this is what's been making me better!'

Whatever indignation he may have harboured seemed to wash from him when he entered the attic itself. He sat on the chair just as its only other visitor Frau Mayer had done, and in the same respectful silence.

Sophia started recounting the story of the attic residents, showing her father their photographs as she unveiled their lives. She ended the narrative as Frau Mayer would have done, with all of them in Poland. Her father's response throughout was hard to gauge. He maintained a look that suggested he was surprised by Sophia, but not in any critical way.

Sophia ended with the question that she had never asked. She still couldn't pose it, because this was an inquiry that could only emanate from the Litmanns, as her father stood before them. So she asked *their* question. He needed to explain it to them.

Her father sat silently for some moments. Sophia began to wonder if he would speak. 'I could say lots of things. I could tell you all the things they write in books. How insecure people felt. The draw of men with easy solutions. The way they controlled everything, every aspect of life. The real answer is, looking back from the world we're in now, I don't know what happened. I honestly don't know.'

Her father stood up. He looked as grave as Sophia had ever seen him.

'It's like feeling you were drugged, or poisoned, or something. And you did terrible things under its influence. And then you recover, and you have these frightening memories of what happened to you, of what you did. Except you can't believe it was really you. You can almost convince yourself, as long as you don't think too hard.'

Her father talked about being a member of the Hitler Youth because his friends were, because they went hiking together, sang songs, built campfires in the woods. He was only eighteen when he joined the army. 'You know what we were? Loyal. That's all. That's what they used. They were evil men, and we gave them our loyalty.'

He started to describe faces he had seen in Russia. Faces of the elderly, young faces, faces of children, lines and lines of faces being marched from a village, being escorted, he was escorting, to their death. He could remember the faces because he saw them every day. And then he met one again, one made flesh. When he was called in to identify his dead son.

Her father sat down again, his eyes were tired and red, and he started sobbing. Parallel tears were soon streaming down Sophia's face. In her mind, she was spinning back to the last time they had shared tears, the day her father had brought her the horrendous news about Rolf. And she now finally understood the guilt that had scored his face. The guilt that Sophia had absorbed. Her father believed it was what he deserved.

Sophia moved to hold him. He was only eighteen. Just a boy! It wasn't his generation at all. She would stand with him before the Litmanns. They would stand together. And it occurred to Sophia that anyway the Litmanns had more pressing concerns. Their focus was on the present. What now? they demanded. What now?

When her father had composed himself and they had returned to the living room, he related another story, of a freezing miserable Christmas outside Moscow. When the shifting snows were a river of white. He had conceived that he was admiring the Rhine of his youth. Warming thoughts of summer swimming and the way the water sparkled in the sunshine. And he had longed to stride out into that river, into the Rhinemaidens' welcoming embrace.

Later, Sophia was thinking about her words. *LOST*,

ALONE, BABY. Those three could be easily linked. But *RAGE*? Who was experiencing the rage? Sophia realized it was herself.

16

Sophia's route to the shop was consciously prolonged to take her past Dieter's block. She noted the motorbike's absence and so felt comfortable sauntering right up to the door, and around the side to where the bike was normally parked. She was defying his edict to stay away.

On reaching Berger Allee, Sophia casually perused windows as she passed along the row of antique stores. One exhibited a stuffed white river bird poised to take off in flight. Sophia considered the paradox of the image, how the means of capturing such beauty had fundamentally defiled it. She scanned the rest of the goods on display, a vast accumulation of eccentric objects of every description, each once assigned a proud owner, decorating a mantelpiece, adorning a table. It made her wonder what had happened to the rest of the Litmanns' belongings. There must have been far more than the paltry attic remains. Sophia supposed some discreet, judicious dispersal to the benefit of every neighbour. Perhaps she had unknowingly already encountered them – drunk from one of their cups, gazed up at one of their paintings. Her thoughts turned to all those who were transported off, who didn't come back. What became of their things, so many things? Was she looking at them in this very window? The stuffed river bird peered out at her. Sophia hurried along.

The Evergreen Emporium had several customers in noisy debate when Sophia entered. One man was immodestly topless, struggling to enclose himself inside some sort of African safari jacket. A pith helmet languished on the counter.

Frau Mayer at first ignored Sophia, which made her feel oddly comfortable, as if she was family. Sophia identified some new items of characterful clothing on display. A mannequin at the store's rear had adopted an equestrian theme that gave it an unprecedented distinction.

Frau Mayer soon chased out a final customer and flipped the door sign to *closed*.

The offer of refreshment was gently refused – twice. Frau Mayer settled in beside Sophia and enquired about her Christmas plans. Sophia answered curtly.

'You're here on business,' Frau Mayer concluded, nodding knowingly. Sophia sensed she was still anticipating her confessions of a secret agent.

Sophia sat for a moment lost to a tussle with language, appearing to have forgotten the very purpose of her visit.

'Is it about the attic?' The Frau tried to help.

Sophia finally managed to establish a formulation of words and began. 'What if I could save someone, someone who is a victim of the Nazis?'

Frau Mayer considered the question, and promptly grew baffled. 'But the Nazis aren't with us any more, thank God.'

Sophia drew back to evaluate the Frau's response, then

re-engaged with what she hoped was just sufficient clarification. 'Someone who was a victim, at the time.'

The Frau pondered. She had the concentrated look of a chess player. 'Are you bringing back the dead?'

Sophia paused for a moment, intrigued by the response. 'Yes. I suppose that's right!'

'Then you must be the messiah!'

Sophia was taken aback. Her necessarily impeded articulation of the issue wasn't working. She found another approach. 'What about someone who is a survivor, but doesn't know he is?'

'A survivor who . . .' Frau Mayer got to her feet. 'Is this some sort of puzzle? Are we playing a game?' The Frau's expression was sharpening. Sophia just hoped her utter sincerity was being imparted.

'Do you mean like, someone who has lost his memory?' Frau Mayer began touching a military tunic hanging from a rail.

'Yes, I suppose . . . yes!' Sophia was relieved to have finally latched onto something sufficiently analogous without revealing too much of her hand.

'Maybe it's best to have forgotten such things! I can think of survivors who would feel blessed if they could only forget.'

Her response roused Sophia. 'You're a survivor! Do you want to forget?'

Frau Mayer stared hard at Sophia. It was an affronted quizzical look. For the first time there was palpable tension between them.

The Frau answered with roused emotion. 'To forget would be

to deny what happened, to shame the memory of those who died. We can't forget. Mustn't!'

'Everyone has a right to their past, don't they?' Sophia stood up, staring into the well-constructed frown titling Frau Mayer's face. 'If you don't know, you're still a victim. I can bring back one more life!' Sophia gripped the Frau's arms. 'It's not much, I know. But I'm the only one who can do it. I don't know why it's me. I really don't!'

Sophia was close to tears, and then they came. Her face was soon awash with them. Frau Mayer located a handkerchief and put her arms around her.

'I don't know what's got into that amazing head of yours. Look after *yourself*, Sophia. That's the most important thing of all.'

Sophia wiped her face.

'I have a Christmas present for you and you're not allowed to refuse. Promise me.'

Sophia duly committed herself and Frau Mayer emerged from the back holding up the red satin dress.

'I can't take that!'

'Ah now!' the Frau cautioned.

Sophia was astonished by the gesture.

'Show it to all your friends at Bonhoffs.'

Sophia held the dress to herself. It was as captivating as when they had first been introduced. She hugged Frau Mayer.

'And you'll look after yourself.'

17

Apart from her commute to and from work, Sophia tended to remain in her apartment during those last days before Christmas. The weather had turned sufficiently cold to inspire the usual speculation on whether this year's would prove to be a white one. Pauline wanted her to join an excursion to the traditional Christmas market in Marienplatz but Sophia didn't feel inclined to brave conditions in the evenings. She would turn up her heating and follow events in the Altstadt from the panorama of her windows. In truth, Sophia wasn't feeling too well. Monika had started joining her in bed. She woke to swells of queasiness most mornings, not that she minded. At some point she supposed she would have to pay a visit to a dreaded medical personage, but it would only be for a succinct act of confirmation. Sophia was convinced she was pregnant. She was carrying Dieter's child!

Sophia hardly came across her neighbours during those final days. When she did it was the briefest of encounters. Frau Kuhn asked about the timing of Bonhoffs' winter sales. Herr Schloss was sorry to hear she was leaving. There was no longer the tap-tapping of an intrepid Frau. It was clear they were done with her.

The atmosphere at Bonhoffs reached a crescendo of shopping mayhem. Goods with the great Bonhoffs imprimatur were being transported to the four corners of Kussel and beyond. Enthusiasts streamed through the doors right up to the very seconds before closing on Christmas Eve. Herr Von Scheiben sent a note of congratulation to every department, declaring it the most lucrative Christmas season in the store's history. Sophia had heard that Bonhoffs' seventieth anniversary was being dedicated to an Olympic theme, exploiting the country's pride in hosting the 1972 event. With the windows team still in leaderless disarray, Sophia could easily slip away. She returned on several more occasions to the Museum library.

Herr Claude Von Scheiben had been an early funder of the Nazi party. He was included in the privileged honour guard when Hitler visited Kussel in 1937. Bonhoffs was handed to him as his reward. Sophia also discovered that the Goddesses of Plenty, Fidelity and Integrity, had been modelled on the wives of the original owners, the Klein brothers. The eldest, Oscar Klein, made it to New York by the outbreak of war. His brother Heinz, with his wife and three children, made it to Treblinka.

Sophia considered how Bonhoffs had been meticulously reconstructed as a faithful replica of its pre-war look. They used the exact stonework, the precise glass. They brought it all back to life, careful brick by careful brick. Did anyone notice what was missing? Would they dare to? Wouldn't anyone dare to? The seventieth anniversary celebrations were about to pervade the store. No. No! It was a fabrication. As much a lie as that other deceitful invention – Dieter Eckermann.

Sophia also accessed the library's archive of film. She tracked down newsreel footage from the war, and followed shocking imagery of bombing raids on Kussel. Because they served propaganda purposes, the horrors of the havoc wrought were fully portrayed. Sophia watched spellbound through raging firestorms, the crash of buildings. And there was one sequence of fleeting seconds that enthralled her. She ran it over and over. A figure stepped from a blazing building, completely engulfed in flame. It stood, formidably erect, then stretched out fiery arms at either side. And Sophia saw manifest in that astonishing form nothing less than the awesome judgement of Christ.

Bonhoffs closed early on Christmas Eve. Many of the staff were repairing to a local bar for end of season drinks before joining the great holiday diaspora. Sophia resisted its allure despite Pauline's insistence. Anyway, she had decided to fast that day, reviving the Christmas Eve tradition, cleansing herself for the days ahead.

Pauline walked Sophia to her tram stop. They exchanged gifts, with Pauline declaring that hers wasn't more cosmetics. Her parting words were delivered as a prescription. Sophia must 'get drunk and have fun'. 'I want to see the old Sophia back again in the new year.' Sophia couldn't bring herself to tell her that the old Sophia was going forever, Pauline dearest. She wouldn't be coming back.

The tram taking Sophia to her parents was crowded with homebound workers intoxicated, at the very least, on the anticipation of the celebrations ahead. Some were bedecked in party hats and streamers, bellowing across distances that could comfortably carry a whisper. Sophia discouraged their eager glances, engrossing herself in the more sedate company of a humble cigarette.

Sophia used the journey to reflect on moving back in with her parents. She wasn't going to remain for long. She had had only the briefest taste of freedom, but had discovered how well it suited. They would be relieved to have their daughter returned, with the result that Sophia would be expected to resume her customary role – the source of continual attention, providing all the noise and controversy that her parents themselves would foster in order to validate this family. If only they could face each other, instead of feasting on her. Sophia no longer feared that consequence. She had long ago recognized that their sense of individual loneliness was most acutely apparent in each other's company. Of course, for her mother, any notion of separation would immediately mobilize the demons of shame. Sophia was establishing a new rapport with her own demons. She had learnt that in the Coralena.

Her father met her off the tram. But it was more how her Mother received her. Sophia was finding the topic of her health so tiresome. She felt victim of a great conspiracy with the same stale script at its core.

Her father installed Frank Sinatra on the record player, mother schemed in the kitchen, Sophia admired the Christmas tree in the living room brooding over its stash of presents to which she now contributed her own. The Madonna at the tree's summit with her open, expressive hands conveyed her gratitude.

As Sophia reconnected with memories of Christmas past, she couldn't help but succumb to a wave of delicious expectation. She recalled how she and Rolf would be banned from the living room for the immediate days before Christmas. They would suffer the excruciating thrill of exile for the final Advent count-down until Christmas Eve itself, when mother would run through the house ringing a bell, making her gleeful proclamation, 'I've seen the Christ child! I've seen the Christ child!' This would be the signal for Sophia and Rolf to rush into the living room to gawp at the gifts baby Jesus himself had provided for them.

Her father carefully lit the candles on the Christmas tree. Sophia glowed before this fairytale image. The final Advent candle was kindled by her mother, and she asked Sophia to light the additional one for Frank Eggert, as for each Advent week. There had been much speculation on whether Eggert would be set free for Christmas. His parents had made just such an appeal with high emotion on television. In the end it was his nemesis Krombach, in a discreet midnight release, who became the beneficiary of the season of goodwill.

After collective song came individual performance. Her mother gave her usual poetry rendition, this time selecting a Schiller piece – 'O tender yearning sweet hoping, the golden time of first love, the eye sees the open heaven, the heart is intoxicated with bliss, O that the beautiful time of young love, could remain green forever.' Sophia heard the perfectly judged melancholy weaved into the recitation. Her mother was speaking up.

Father brought out a set of playing cards, protesting with faltering conviction that he had acquired new tricks. Sophia was impressed how, after a series of convoluted manoeuvres, he eventually did produce her four of diamonds, but was annoyed by his refusal to divulge his discreet workings, citing such previous confessions as the cause of his dwindling repertoire.

Sophia brought to mind Rolf's final Christmas performance. He had wanted to present a play and Sophia was made to suffer an uncontested yet arduous casting process before her own part in the production was assured. Rolf was aching to wear again his latest Carnival outfit, the Roman centurion, which necessitated, so he claimed, Sophia's role as his captured tribal slave. As a true nascent thespian, he had prepared a detailed script, which left it in no doubt who warranted star billing. Of the play itself, all Sophia could recall was Rolf's frustration with her for forgetting lines, and a deep gratitude to her mother for negotiating her ransom.

For her turn this Christmas Eve, Sophia opened her parents' New Testament.

Blessed are they which do hunger and thirst after righteousness, for they shall be filled; blessed are the merciful, for they shall obtain mercy; blessed are the pure in heart, for they shall see God; blessed are the peacemakers, for they shall be called the people of God; blessed are they which are persecuted for righteousness sake, for theirs is the kingdom of heaven; blessed are you, when men shall revile you, and persecute you, and shall say all manner of evil against you falsely, for my sake.

The exchange of gifts was executed equitably. Sophia was satisfied with the response to her presents – the cap became permanently secured to her father's head, her mother filled the house with the perfume. Sophia herself was grateful for the nightdress, the sizing and shade of which she had already been consulted on, and the assorted toiletries in colourful packaging.

At the festive table, her mother started contemplating 'plans' for Sophia's return, proudly declaring how she was encouraging her father to arrange for the installation of a telephone in her room. In less than subtle response, Sophia sought their opinion on the attractiveness of various city-centre neighbourhoods. Anyway, she could totally subvert the conversation by breaking some news – her decision to leave Bonhoffs.

'Why?' It was her father who asked but her mother looked the gravest. He couldn't understand why she wouldn't remain in situ at least until she had resolved her next employment. Sophia announced bluntly that she 'just couldn't'.

'Because that would be too sensible,' her mother smirked.

'It would be immoral to continue working there.'

Her mother laughed in the way she had made her own. 'Please *do* explain!' A great guffaw that emphatically resisted any notion of humorous intent. In an instant, Sophia was thrust back to silly child, which she took as also part of her mother's 'plans' for her.

So Sophia did explain. Or at least she started to. She referred first to the illustrious past of Herr Claude Von Scheiben, and had just introduced the Klein brothers when her mother interrupted.

'I'm not having this discussion.'

Sophia acted confused. 'Why not? I thought you just asked

me to explain.' Her mother never wanted actual discussions. She wanted her points agreed, her disapprovals noted.

'Because it's Christmas, that's why! I'm sitting down with my family on the holiest night of the year and I don't need to have it upset by you bringing up . . . history lessons.'

'About what happened to the Jews? Is that what you mean?'

'That's not what I mean.'

'So we can only talk about the past when it suits you!' Sophia's anger was pulsating through her. 'The edited bits you can enjoy. When it's all about you and what you went through. Is that it? Don't you know what Christmas is all about? It's about the birth of a Jew. Does that upset your Christmas?!'

Her father tried to calm the situation but it was too late, too late for Sophia. It was a discussion she now craved. She finished *explaining* about Bonhoffs. She explained about the Litmanns. She explained about factories carefully constructed that put living people in at one end and manufactured dead ones out the other.

'The guilty were punished,' Sophia heard. The Von Scheibens hadn't been punished, nor had the Eckermanns, nor Krombach, nor Judge Eggert, nor the tens of thousands pictured at the Nazi rallies, nor the millions who had voted them into power. And what about those who looked away? What about them?

Sophia picked up the New Testament. 'Blessed are they which do hunger and thirst after righteousness, for they shall be filled; blessed are the merciful, for they shall obtain mercy; blessed are the pure in heart, for they shall see God.'

Sophia pointed to the Madonna and Child on the wall. The

piled yellow crosses of the Sisterhood of the Immaculate Virgin charity box. The crucifix around her mother's neck.

'It's a murdered Jew. A murdered Jew, don't you see! He's in our homes. We wear him around our necks. It's our shame! *It's our shame!*'

Sophia couldn't remember when her father had last struck her. Maybe it was when she had poured glue down the old settee. It was more like a smack then. This was a slap. It was delivered hard. Sophia ran up to her room.

When her mother came to find her later Sophia was in Rolf's room, reading one of his old comics. She was following mild-mannered Bruce Banner who, compelled by his outrage at injustice, transforms into the rampaging Incredible Hulk.

Her mother seemed startled that Sophia was wearing one of Rolf's sweaters. She joined Sophia on the bed, started stroking her hair.

'I often wonder what it would have been like if my mother had lived longer. Would I have been like you, arguing with her all the time? I'm sure I would.'

Sophia put the comic down. 'What do you remember about her?'

'Big big hands on a hospital bed. I was too young.' Her mother paused. 'Sometimes I get so jealous of you. That you had a mother and I didn't. I know it's wrong.'

'Maybe you shouldn't have given me her name.'

Her mother looked confused, then worried.

'Rolf once told me he wanted to be a cat in his next life,'

Sophia said. 'Because they lived their lives out of doors. Do you think that souls can come back to earth? Maybe if they're in special pain?'

'Rolf's at peace,' her mother replied, with a certainty that suggested it was a long held belief. 'No one took his life from him. It wasn't illness, or a car crash. He did what he felt he had to, to find his peace.'

Sophia contemplated her own reincarnation. She wouldn't be earthbound. She would be a great bird sailing the skies. Sophia had never liked cats. It made her wonder how she had ever thought she could be like Rolf. She had just been trying to fill his space. And what she had been really doing was making herself as small as possible, hiding herself away.

Her mother squeezed Sophia's cheeks. It was her special message. The way she would hold Sophia when she wanted to express affection.

'We're both very very sorry. We really are. Let's not fight. Please come down and eat something. It's Christmas!'

Sophia considered how she would be as a mother. It was such a scary, exhilarating thought. She was convinced of one thing. She would never abandon her child. Following Rolf's death, she recalled her mother packing her belongings before her dispatch to Grandmother's. Sophia had imagined her parents were leaving her forever, just like Rolf. And when she came back, she found it was true. The people who had once cared for and loved her had somehow tragically been replaced.

But Sophia also understood that her anger was an expression of potency. A mother and child. Sophia was about to attach herself to this great chain of life. The bonds were God given, enigmatic, eternal. So Sophia simply hugged her mother, hugged her so tightly she could hear the converging thump of hearts. And she thought of her mother's mother, and herself as a mother, and that ultimate mother, the Madonna lording over Christmas, giving birth to her blessed boy.

Before leaving for midnight Mass, Sophia searched out the prize she had won for good behaviour at Sunday school, the beaded cross she had once worn every day. She repositioned it carefully around her neck.

The church was bustling in expectant festive mood. Children thrilling to the lateness of the hour roamed the grounds in marauding packs. The sanctuary itself was illuminated by an army of candles creating an ambience of awe and mystery. Obscure families never encountered the rest of the year swelled pews.

Father Scholtze stood at the church's entrance, as was his custom for the occasion, basking in the communal ingathering at its most replete. Sophia let her parents continue on ahead, while she took the opportunity to engage him. She had an enquiry.

'If you consciously rob someone of his identity, so that he doesn't know who he is, even his name, it would be like killing his soul, like a mortal sin.'

Father Scholtze was tackling a multitude of outstretched hands and appeared startled by the statement.

'Yes, that sounds about right!'

'One more, please Father. What would it mean if you were to undo a mortal sin?'

Father Scholtze now smiled, 'Why, it's an act of grace, of godliness itself.' He paused, looking at Sophia with a penetrating curiosity as if the full magnitude of the subject matter was only just sinking in. 'Good luck!' he added uncertainly.

Sophia was delighted. Father Scholtze seemed so much more humane than his fierce predecessor.

Friends of her parents had saved seats for them. An elaborate manger scene almost the breadth of one wall was being guarded by haughty-looking members of the Church youth group. Sophia concentrated on her two anguished Christs above the altar and to its side. On her last visit, she had finally succeeded in decoding their demeanours – Flight and Despair. Their message was stark, damning. Sophia wondered if she was alone in recognizing their meaning. She looked around her and latched onto the only other face that appeared to be sharing her frustration – the Virgin holding out her wretched son. Her defiant expression was Sophia's own. Look! she was pleading. A murdered Jew! Look everyone! Sophia felt compelled to join her demonstration. She had to *do* something. Flight and Despair. What supreme act could mitigate such a terrifying judgement?

The noise quietened to a silence. Father Scholtze made his processional entrance in his most prestigious priestly robes. The hymns and prayers were sung with a special energy that reflected the occasion. Father Scholtze began his homily, 'I live not now with my own life, but with the life of Christ who lives in me.' He spoke of the significance of Jesus's birth for the future of mankind. 'We were damaged, but we can be healed. We must believe in Jesus, as he believes in us. Love Jesus, as he loves us. Unite with Jesus, as he unites with us. A baby was born. His life is in your hands.'

Sophia was stunned. She now knew what she had to do.

The bells rang out for the climax of the Eucharist. Father Scholtze held up the wafer, and then the chalice of wine.

The chamber soon resonated with sombre chanting. 'Lamb of God, you take away the sins of the world, have mercy on us. Lamb of God, you take away the sins of the world, have mercy on us. Lamb of God, you take away the sins of the world, grant us peace.'

Sophia joined the stream of congregants making their way forward to receive Communion. She knelt before the altar, genuflected and carefully prepared herself. She glanced again at the two images of Jesus, then closed her eyes. Father Scholtze placed the sanctified wafer on her tongue, intoning 'the body of Christ'. She focused intensely on the feel and texture of the host as it dissolved in her mouth. Then the chalice was held before her, announced as 'the blood of Christ'. She conscientiously consumed.

Slowly, she raised herself and turned. She was now a Jew.

After the service, her mother lit the candle for the soul of her lost son Rolf. Sophia mirrored the act, lighting one next to Rolf's for the soul of Oliver Litmann. She took her vow then, to reverse one mortal sin for the forgiveness of another.

'Blessed are they which do hunger and thirst after righteousness, for they shall be filled; blessed are the merciful, for they shall obtain mercy; blessed are the pure in heart, for they shall see God.'

Her father drove her back to the Altstadt. He wanted to talk, filled with sad apology. Sophia didn't need that from him. It was well into the early hours of Christmas Day and she was exhausted. They would speak about such things, but not now.

It felt strange walking into the Coralena at so late an hour, and on so auspicious a day. She could detect in the air above the stairway the lingering aroma of celebration. Fragments of tinsel littering the floor provided more blatant testimony. Sophia tried to picture what mischief her neighbours would have got up to – Herr Eckermann manning the accordion, Herr Kuhn's everlasting stories, Frau Bitzel's *joie de vivre*, Herr Schloss's copious consumption, all neatly orchestrated by their leader, the indomitable Frau Eckermann. Sophia had landed herself with an extraordinary band of fellows.

18

Baby Jesus was Oliver in her dream. Sophia was with him in the manger, singing songs, caressing him. She released the toy clown and its clamour turned to a wail of sirens and banging. She heard a door crashing open and heavy footsteps running up attic stairs. Sophia was now sobbing, and Oliver started to cry. Men in uniform snatched him from her. They forced Sophia down the Coralena stairway. She was struggling with them but was too weak to resist. All she could hear were the screams of her baby. The neighbours were lining her route, each positioned in front of their respective doorways, each face with the same expression of benign indifference. 'Why did you betray me?!' Sophia shouted to them. 'Why?' She glanced behind her, following the stairway to its summit, catching sight of a mysterious floating figure, a young woman with Coralena's face. She was crying. As Sophia was shuffled through the doorway, she turned to see a policeman hand over baby Oliver to an impassive Frau Eckermann.

No. No! No-o-o! Sophia jolted awake. She got up from the attic mattress, went down to the living room and quickly dressed.

While the kettle boiled, Sophia found the black bread she had purchased the previous day. Firstly, she held it to her face and inhaled its aroma. She then proceeded to pull away great chunks, playing with the meaty texture in her hands. There was something so primitive, elemental in the bread's constitution. It felt as if she was touching something of life itself. Finally, she folded each piece carefully into her mouth, disciplining her anxieties, letting her mouth fill, embracing the sensation. She would have to give herself time, but it would come. She would no longer deny herself.

Sophia left her flat carrying a holdall she had previously prepared. She slipped down the stairs, and joined the crisp quiet of the Altstadt early on sacred Christmas Day. Before starting on her journey, she turned to bow before Coralena. Coralena had won her over on their very first meeting. She had united her with Dieter. Sophia followed the route of the thin watery tear stain travelling down the building's façade. Coralena had borne witness, and couldn't look away.

It felt the coldest day Sophia had yet experienced in the Altstadt. An icy film was soon coating her face, and she walked briskly in an effort to generate heat. She was passing along deserted streets, through a desolate Marienplatz, heading towards Frau Mayer's flat. It would have been too cruel to disturb her at such an hour. Anyway, her presence was uncertain. Recalling their last meeting, Sophia realized that she had been so selfishly lost to her own emotions, she had failed to make the simple enquiry about the Frau's holiday plans. Sophia drew the Christmas present from her bag, the quiz book of the Frau's favourite television show, and let it clank through her letterbox.

Sophia was now making her way in the direction of the Cathedral, that great hulking beast across the landscape ahead of her, its pre-eminence unquestioned on such a day. Sophia's attention was drawn to its towers spotlit by a sharp early sun. She watched as the light shimmered down them, and grew intrigued. It suddenly occurred to her that the great spires were not about the earth soaring skywards in tribute to man's greatness, but were rather the heavens being channelled downwards, to teach his humbleness. And Sophia imagined the thousands of Kussel's citizenry who had packed the building just hours before, all come to pay pious homage. They didn't know Jesus wasn't there. He had gone into hiding during the war but was found, transported to Poland and crucified. But Jesus could return. Sophia had discovered that route to atonement. *If they would only embrace the totality of Christ.* It made her reflect on how many Catholics there were in Germany. Could six million have achieved true Holy Communion on Christmas Eve?

Sophia joined one of the first trams into the city centre. The driver wore a colourful Christmas hat with a bobble, receiving her warmly as if an anxiously awaited guest. He cheekily asked if she had a present for him in the bag, which became the precursor of a lengthy conversation, exclusively one-way, until the next stop when thankfully more *guests* arrived and his interests roamed free. Sophia focused on the neighbourhood life slowly reviving beyond the window. She saw a group of children at a street corner eagerly comparing Christmas booty, one holding her nose as if therein lay a guarantee of warmth; an elderly couple being gingerly moved along by their dog; a wearied group of young people in dress long drained of party flamboyance on their return from too long a night of celebration. The old terraced tenements of the Altstadt soon gave up their escort, making way for the new city, and Sophia was again struck by the abrupt contrast between these two worlds. And she reflected on how it wasn't after all about making a choice. There was so much to remember, and so much to forget. It was knowing which was which.

When the Bonhoffs' caretaker arrived, he was clearly astonished to see Sophia waiting for him. He seemed to take this as some sort of rebuke, grumbling an indecipherable greeting that remarkably managed to avoid reference to the occasion of the day. He rattled open the various door locks and scurried through.

Sophia had experienced Bonhoffs out of hours a good many times by now. It was one of the unfortunate privileges of her job. However, the sensation of walking in the stunning stillness through the vast chandeliered halls continued to fill her with awe. It was like being on a massive glittering cruise liner in dry dock.

Sophia fantasized that she was now visiting the store on its very first day. She was in the distinguished company of the Klein brothers, both dressed in immaculately tailored morning coats. As they travelled through the various departments, the brothers dispensed flattering attention and earnest advice. Sophia draped herself in an elegant lady's cloak and sought their assurance that it was the most recent Parisian fashion. 'Would the Fraus Klein wear such a garment?' She had to check. She tried on soft felt hats but they couldn't achieve consensus on a colour. The leather handbags won collective approval.

Sophia requested that the Herrs Klein accompany her to the fifth-floor Executive Suite. She pointed out the photographs on the walls, the post-war rebuilding, the dramatic image of Bonhoffs in flames that was its cause, and then took them all the way back to the picture of the store's launch, with their barely discernible faces at its foot. The brothers were quietly joined by their wives, which felt to Sophia as if the Goddesses of Plenty had sprung to life, for they were indeed exact images of 'Fidelity' and 'Integrity' who had welcomed her to the store each morning. They were all so very grateful to Sophia for remembering them. She could only apologize that it had taken so long.

Before leaving, Sophia decided to enter the hallowed

Bonhoffs boardroom, an experience that had eluded her just weeks before. The chamber was wooden panelled, with a dignified, serious ambience that lived up to expectations. The table at its centre dominated the room with heraldic designs along the walls that made Sophia picture a gathering of medieval knights. It was obvious which chair was assigned to the Chairman. It presided at the table's head and was the only one awarded arms. Behind, lay a hugely proportioned portrait of an enthroned Herr Claude Von Scheiben. Sophia approached and studied the face. It was one of great character, the courageous crusader. That was no defence, Sophia thought.

She now took the lift from the heights of Bonhoffs' fifth floor all the way down to its humble basement.

Sophia left the lights off when she entered the mannequin storage area. She allowed herself simply to wander in the darkness, encountering one after another of hazy human shapes, faces peering out at her with the same blank expressions. It reminded her of her journey through the Altstadt fog, when shadow figures emerged and faded before her, when the neighbourhood had become the refuge of lost souls. She was soon surrounded by these stark naked forms. They were crowding around. She stumbled into torsos strewn on the floor. Bodies were lying across each other in tortured entanglement, twisted limbs thrusting out at her at strange fantastic angles. She saw hands reaching up, penetrating pleading stares. There was so much agony. She fell back, leaning against a side table. Slowly, she moved her hands across its surface, identifying the bizarre clumps as an assembly of hairpiece scalps.

She collected herself, opened her bag, and heaved out the large petrol can, followed by a second.

19

As Sophia made her way to the river, Frank Eggert was preparing the release of his Christmas statement from a Berlin hideaway. It was pages and pages of a jargon-infested diatribe, lambasting the crimes of his father's generation, the hypocrisy of a 'dying society'. 'I call upon the great German people, West and East, to unite and mobilize in support of the forces of progress everywhere. I call out for justice on behalf of the world's oppressed, for those who have no voice.' It had all been a stunt.

Nothing was moving on the Rhine. Even the very waters in their tranquillity had evidently ground to a halt in deference to the specialness of the day. Sophia ambled down a riverboat gangway to its end, took off her glove and knelt to wave a hand in the river, playing with its icy texture. She watched her breath manifest into puffs of white cloud. The stillness made her consider if the Rhinemaidens themselves had repented their ways. She couldn't believe she had the whole expanse to herself, as if her own private lake. It was the same proprietorial sensation she had experienced when she had first observed the Rhine from the windows of the Coralena. It made her think about when the river was always just as it appeared now, and she tried to imagine the wonder of the first Romans stumbling across this massive brooding bulwark of the German lands.

Sophia took out from a pocket one of the photographs she had been given by Frau Mayer, of Herr and Frau Litmann. Their pose of exaggerated formality accentuated the impression that they were still adjusting to adulthood, joining an adult world that would quickly consume them. She was carrying their grandchild! That was why God wasn't angry with her for becoming pregnant. He understood what she was doing. She was bringing another Litmann into the world. It was a righteous act. And this baby would be allowed to live and grow. Sophia would dedicate herself to that. It was the instinct with which she had been blessed, as a mother.

Sophia had missed Rolf's funeral, and it had occurred to her that the Litmanns had never received one. They were now relations. Sophia was entitled to conduct such a service. And so, before God and man, Sophia fixed on the portrait of the Litmanns, paying her last respects, then committed them to the waters, letting the photograph fall gently from her hand. And she asked the Rhinemaidens to pray for them, and for Oliver their victimized son, and for herself, the bearer of their legacy.

Sophia began her journey back to the Coralena. She was certain that the severity of the cold was intimation that the Altstadt would yet have its white Christmas. As she walked, she reflected on her days in the neighbourhood, all that had transpired since her summer arrival – Frau Eckermann, Dieter, the diary words, the Evergreen Emporium and Frau Mayer, the attic. And she thought about how this was all about to reach its culmination that very day. Looking back, it all seemed to form one complete whole, one inevitable process.

Sophia switched her thoughts to the year ahead. She would find a new job. If only it could be something that exploited her love of art. She and Dieter would look for somewhere to live, preferably with as much character as the Coralena, but not in the Altstadt. Coralena understood.

Sophia felt so full of hope, filled to bursting with it. She and Dieter were so different, yet also the same. He had once accused her of having a cold heart. It had just been concealed. They had passions to share. It would be like starting all over again, and like they'd been together all their lives. The baby would look the image of Dieter, she was convinced of it. She could cry all the time now.

20

Sophia could hear the growing clamour from below, the Coralena family gathering at the Kuhns for their next affair. At their final meeting, Frau Eckermann had insisted Sophia join the Christmas tea to deliver a proper farewell. She wasn't going to disappoint.

She only wished she was more practised in the skills of make-up application. She was now regretting that she hadn't taken advantage of Pauline's advice. She was finally beginning to appreciate it for what it undoubtedly was – the workings of an art form. A face was an empty canvas on which to invent. Make-up was Carnival.

The foundation powder went on first, darkening her face,

creating a somewhat tanned look that she certainly never achieved naturally. Her suntans, such as they ever were, covered the complete range from pink to a bright bright red.

She applied black eyeliner followed by thick mascara, enjoying how her eyes swelled with the effect. The eye shadow turned them seductive and smoky. The blusher exaggerated her cheekbones and built a fuller face. The dark red lipstick made her mouth pronounced and generous.

Sophia was excited by the results. She studied the picture again and reappraised her appearance in the mirror.

The red satin dress, Frau Mayer's present, was wriggled down her body and Sophia enjoyed re-experiencing the embrace of its fit. She twisted to admire the daring V-neck plunge, which conveyed the impression that she was almost growing out of it.

The biggest challenge remained the hair. The dye's application, its setting and drying, had blackened most of the apartment in the process. And now curling tongs were failing to provide the 'bounce' faithfully promised across the effusive packaging. The locks for which Sophia had forever dreamed were still eluding her. She nevertheless persisted until a passable effect was achieved.

As her final accessory, Sophia went up to the attic, to the drawers under the table. She returned to the wardrobe mirror and used pins to affix to the dress the yellow star patch.

Outside Sophia noticed it had started to snow. She went to the window and watched the steady white stream, like an invading army of tiny parachutists. The snowdrops of her most cherished painting. With the Cathedral dominating the scene, it was the perfect Altstadt Christmas image. It made her contemplate how souls travelled back to earth. Do they fall from the sky as brightly imagined snowflakes, fluttering homewards?

Sophia examined the photograph of Frau Litmann one last time, then twirled in front of Monika.

Heads certainly turned when Sophia entered the Kuhns' apartment. Herr Eckermann lowered his accordion, Frau Kuhn's eyes spun like laundry in a washing machine, Herr Bruder fixed her with a glare. 'What have you done to your hair?' asked a deeply confused Herr Schloss, while he focused more on the dress. Sophia surveyed their faces, her Coralena neighbours, and it occurred to her that she was the only one without a mask.

Frau Bitzel approached and offered her a drink as if they had been in each other's company for hours. Frau Eckermann and Dieter were by an elaborate Christmas tree and she watched the Frau take hold of his arm. Sophia was pleased. It meant she knew. Frau Bruder also knew. She was the only one who appeared scared.

Sophia enquired after Frau Litmann. She asked Herr Kuhn, and Frau Schloss, even Frau Mueller. But she wasn't getting their attention. They seemed to be too embarrassed, doing their best to ignore her. Because she was deemed mad, Sophia assumed. It was entirely understandable. So she pulled out the pistol she had brought from the attic.

Frau Bitzel screamed. Frau Kuhn swung towards her husband causing her glasses to fall from her face. Suddenly, Sophia realized how small her eyes actually were, more like tiny buttons. She had now won everyone's attention.

Sophia informed them that she knew about the Litmanns. What they had done. How they had kept the secret of their presence, and then betrayed them. She passed round their photograph, but no one dared to look. Frau Bruder was weeping.

Sophia had never witnessed Frau Eckermann so subdued, almost humble. Her intimidating aura seemed to drain from her very being, as if unplugged from its generator. Sophia could almost feel sorry for her, a barren woman who had made a desperate grab at immortality. But she had committed a sin, which, for a good God-fearing Catholic, was the gravest of all, a mortal sin. She had killed a soul. Sophia pictured her tumbling and tumbling towards hell. And she saw her passing Rolf making his glorious ascent to a great night star.

Sophia next announced her Christmas gift. She produced a bag which she gave to Frau Bitzel, requiring her to affix to each person one of the small yellow crucifix pins of the Sisterhood of the Immaculate Virgin. Sophia addressed their bemusement by explaining that they must now all bear the sign of a murdered Jew.

Sophia then turned to Dieter. He appeared apprehensive which Sophia couldn't understand. This was all for him. She gestured him over. Frau Eckermann tightened her grip on his arm but he still came. That was the moment when everything went berserk. Frau Eckermann was shouting. Frau Schloss joined in. They were calling her names. That she was insane. Evil. A crazy bitch. That she was to be taken away and locked up.

Sophia thought how sad it was to see the fluttering of the

yellow crosses to the floor. What had happened to their faith? She couldn't believe their lack of humility. 'Shame on you!' Sophia screamed back at them. 'Shame-on-you!'

Frau Bruder collapsed to the floor, causing Herr Bruder and Frau Kuhn to rush to her. Herr Schloss stationed his formidable form in front of the door but it was Dieter himself who insisted he stand clear. Dangling the gun's menace, she escorted him up the stairs. Frau Eckermann attempted to follow, yelling out a harangue until Sophia pointed the weapon directly at her.

Sophia locked them in behind her apartment door. Dieter was motioned to the sofa. On the wall in front, next to the Snowdrops painting, hung Sophia's recently executed drawing of Dieter and, alongside, a drawing of baby Oliver she had made from his photograph.

Sophia assessed Dieter's expression, its heady mix of anxiety and disdain.

'You can get help,' Dieter began. He spoke in a voice of elaborate calm. 'No one is against you here. We like you.'

Sophia smiled. 'Do you know where you are?'

'Yes, I do!'

'This is the home of the Litmanns. They lived here until the war.'

'Why are you doing this? Why are you dressed up like that?'

'Just listen!' Sophia raised the gun. 'You're such a great talker. You think you know so much, don't you. But you don't listen. Dieter, you don't hear yourself. Listen to what's inside!'

Sophia moved across to a wall. She started to caress the dramatic blue/yellow wallpaper. 'Look at the wall, Dieter. Do you remember when you came back here with me and you first saw it, remember? Do you remember what you saw that so upset you? Think! You saw something!'

Dieter stared at her with a defiant blankness. They could now hear the screech of police sirens. His face abruptly lifted in an apparent acknowledgement. 'There was some sort of fire at Bonhoffs this morning. I heard it in the news. That didn't have anything to do with you, did it? Tell me it wasn't you. Oh my God!'

The sirens were in the Rheingasse, outside the Coralena. Sophia made Dieter position a strip of material across his eyes as a blindfold. She guided him up the attic stairs.

'If I did anything to upset you, I'm sorry. The relationship didn't feel right any more. I didn't want to hurt you!' Dieter's anxiety was now in the ascendant.

Sophia placed him on the mattress. She forced his face down onto it, making him inhale its smell. She then spoke softly in his ear. 'Think,' she whispered. 'Stop talking. Think about where you are.'

Adding to the churning wail of sirens outside, Sophia could now hear ferocious banging at her door. Dieter lay motionless on his side on the mattress. Her thoughts turned to the words – *RAGE, ALONE, LOST, BABY*, and how they had come from somewhere deep inside. She peered up at the skylight and watched the passing flurry of hundreds and hundreds, thousands of returning pure white souls.

'You're Oliver Litmann. You lived here. You know this place!'

Sophia swapped the gun for the toy clown, and tightly wound it. She was listening to loud thuds and the shriek of her front door cracking. She released the toy onto the floor and it thrust forward, whacking its cymbals in a blustering onslaught of noise.

Sophia then knelt beside Dieter, nestling his head to her chest, in her arms. She saw him now as such a pathetic figure. Just a lost little boy. This wasn't the way she had wanted it. She told him that.

'This is your only chance, Oliver! If you don't make it now, you never will. Please come back!' Sophia was now feeling so tired. It was all too overwhelming. 'It's safe now. I'll look after you, I promise!' She was shaking – crying. 'I believe in you Oliver Litmann. Please believe in me!'

Sophia slipped the blindfold from Dieter's face. He blinked, stunned by the surroundings. He stared at the manic clown thrashing across the floor. Sophia was sobbing above him, touching and playing with his hair. The apartment door could be heard crashing open. Heavy footsteps were running up the attic stairs. Dieter suddenly convulsed in a torrent of tears.

'It's okay, Oliver. It's me.' She started lifting the tears from his face with her fingers. 'I'm your mother. Erica Litmann. I'm back now. I'm never going to leave you again. You're my sweet sweet boy.'